THE
Montana
Women

FOUR BOOK SERIES

NANCY PIRRI

THE MONTANA WOMEN
Copyright © 2020 by Nancy Pirri

ISBN: 978-1-68046-601-0

Published by Satin Romance
An Imprint of Melange Books, LLC
White Bear Lake, MN 55110
www.satinromance.com

Names, characters, and incidents depicted in this book are products of the author's imagination or are used fictitiously. Any resemblance to actual events, locales, organizations, or persons, living or dead, is entirely coincidental and beyond the intent of the author or the publisher. No part of this book may be reproduced or transmitted in any form or by any means, electronic or mechanical, including photocopying, recording, or by any information storage and retrieval system, without permission in writing from the publisher except for the use of brief quotations in a book review or scholarly journal.

Published in the United States of America.

Cover Design by Caroline Andrus

KATIE AND THE MARSHAL

Bozeman, Montana's new marshal, James Freeman, has big plans to close down every brothel in town, including Katie's Palace. Katie O'Malley has the fight of her life on her hands—convincing James she's running a legitimate establishment—a saloon, diner, and boarding house.

James soon finds himself falling for Katie, but when an incident occurs, marring her reputation and forcing her to close down the Palace, James loses what trust he has placed in her.

Will Katie be able to save her business? And will she lose her heart in the process?

PROLOGUE

1865
Butte, Montana

"Jimmy boy, ain't nothin' you can do about yer mama's occupation. Ye just can't change things. It's her choice," the man said, a wide, lecherous grin on his lips. "Besides, ain't she keepin' vittles in yer stomach and clothes on yer back?"

Fourteen-year-old James Freeman glared at his mother's latest 'friend.' Beau Hanson sat in his mother's tiny parlor, cocky expression on his face, a wicked gleam in his eyes. Big and blonde, he was a lummox of a man. While Hanson had treated him and his mother fairly over the past month since he started 'courting' James' mother, he knew to keep his anger buried deep inside him and his mouth shut. The man must be able to read minds, or James hadn't done a good job keeping the scowl from his face, for the man had guessed his feelings.

For two years, James had suffered abject humiliation because of his mother's work. But then James knew she'd had no choice. Margarite Freeman had been desperate.

After his father died two years ago, their lives had changed. The family home had to be sold to pay off debts neither of them knew his father had incurred at the gambling tables. And his father's stake in a once thriving silver mine had resulted in little monetary value since it went dry within a few months of its discovery.

3

James had managed to secure farm labor work, but the pay was low and back-breaking. That lasted a month. Out of nowhere, Margarite informed him she'd found work and he could return to school once more.

His heart had pounded with joy at her words. James loved school and planned to make something of his life. Once he had his degree, he could care for his mother, and no longer would she be forced to accept men into their home.

From the first, she'd been evasive about the type of work she'd found, but it wasn't long before James heard kids at school calling her a 'slut.' After many bloodied noses, James found the courage to confront his mother about the allegations. As she'd always done, she gave him the truth. While he hated her words, he understood her desperation and was proud of how she cared for him.

James heard Margarite's light step from down the hallway, and he slunk lower in his chair. He watched her move gracefully into the parlor. She was a beautiful, caring woman, meant to have a wonderful life. He'd do everything in his power to protect and care for her—once he was able to earn a good living.

His gaze left her when he heard a chair scrape against the wooden floor. Hanson rose from his chair, his face changing from friendly to dark and…

James shuddered at the expression on the big man's face.

Hanson took two steps so he stood directly in front of Margarite. The man took her in his arms, grabbing her buttocks and kissing her fiercely, pressing her tight against his body.

James fisted his hands on the table in front of him in impotent fury before shutting his eyes tight against the awful scene. It took all of his willpower not to leap out of his chair and pounce on Beau's back. Only when the bastard finally released her did James breathe a relieved sigh. Margarite sent James a warning look and a small shake of her head before facing Hanson with a brilliant smile. Then she put her arm through his and sashayed from the house.

James' eyes got teary as he thought ahead to a lonely night of cursing and worrying about his mother, knowing she wouldn't return until the break of day.

Three years later, the future for him and his mother that he'd envisioned had ended precipitously when she died of syphilis.

Now, on a cold winter day as he stood before her grave, he smiled. He thought of her words when he'd confronted her about the men in her life. She'd replied, *"What, James, will you be my knight in shining armor come to rescue me? You can't, you know, it's my choice. Besides, you're a child. Perhaps one day, after you've grown..."*

No longer was he a child, but he'd been too late to save her.

I was too late to be your knight, Mother, sad to say.

But he vowed, in future, to charge to the rescue of any other woman who needed his help.

CHAPTER 1

1884
Bozeman, Montana

Saturday was the busiest morning of the week at the Sapphire Palace. Filled to capacity, the noise of conversation and laughter caused Katie O'Malley to feel a headache coming on. She appeared outwardly calm as she approached Marshal James Freeman's table in the dining room, though deep inside her temper raged. If she were a teakettle, she'd be steaming! She had no doubt her cheeks were about the same shade as her red calico day dress. Why couldn't she be a pretty blonde like her friend, Annie Callahan, instead of red-haired and freckled?

Annie passed by just then, carrying plates heaped high with the breakfast special. Dressed prettily in a robin's egg colored gown that set off her blonde hair and matched her cool blue eyes perfectly, Annie threw her a smile and said under her breath, "Be calm, Katie."

Katie sighed. Annie had to know about all she could do was try.

Once again last evening, the marshal had done his blasted duty by closing down Marie Hannigan's establishment across the street—a diner and brothel, the last establishment of its kind in Bozeman.

Katie thoroughly despised James Freeman's holier than thou attitude. Since he'd begun charging through on a swathe of questionable (in his opinion) business destruction, she'd vowed he would find no cause to

7

close down the Palace, fondly called Katie's Palace by most folks who frequented the combination saloon, dining room and boarding house.

The Palace had been her mother's dream. Katie's father died several years ago, in a mining accident, leaving his wife and daughter a modest fortune. Grace O'Malley had seen a need for a room and board place in Bozeman, and had opened up the Palace. With Katie's assistance, and a few other helpers, they ran the place efficiently together for the past six years. Luckily, Katie's mother was a no-nonsense woman with a clear mind for business. Katie had been in business three years, after acquiring the business from her mother, who'd found a second love and moved to Texas.

Balancing a platter filled high with buckwheat cakes, over easy eggs, half a pound of bacon and two pieces of toast with marmalade, she wondered if Freeman's conservative nature explained why he ordered the same breakfast every day. She felt tempted to fake a stumble and dump the entire contents on the good marshal's head. No, spending time in jail wasn't in her plans.

Just as she reached his side, he looked up and gave her one of those steady lawman looks that seemed to penetrate her body and soul. Searching, she decided waspishly. The man was always searching for some evildoer to toss into one of his jail cells. She smiled to herself at the image of the marshal sleeping in one of the cells each night. Being rather new to town, he'd yet to find or build a home of his own.

He sat back with his arms crossed over his brawny chest. Her hands shook as she set the plates of food in front of him. "Thank you, Miss O'Malley."

His deep baritone caused a shiver up her spine. His voice had been the first thing she'd noticed about him. Annie said his voice conjured up dreams of something about which she had no business fantasizing. On principle, Katie insisted she found his voice cold and crude. She didn't try to explain why it affected her so profoundly every time he spoke, if she truly hated him.

Katie gave him a brief nod, unable to meet his penetrating gaze any longer. Turning her back on him, she'd taken just two steps away when he spoke again. "More coffee would be appreciated when you've got the time."

Keeping her back ramrod straight and her hands on the tray, she closed her eyes and counted to twenty. She'd already poured him several cups of coffee while he waited for his breakfast. Now she turned to him with a vivid but false smile on her lips. "Coming right up, Marshal."

Her stride back to the kitchen was long and furious. She'd fix him up with coffee all right! She'd fetch the damn burr under her saddle his own personal pot.

Upon her return to the dining room to deliver breakfast to other customers, she wasn't the least bit surprised to see he'd cleaned up more than half his breakfast. He was a huge man with an equally huge appetite —some appetites she could imagine more vividly than others, to her shame. Not for the first time, she found herself noticing his muscular frame, sandy hair and attractive brown eyes.

More so than others, she knew there was more to a man than looks. Her last two beaus were utterly gorgeous. Too bad neither of them possessed much by way of manners where a lady was concerned. She was a woman, full-grown now—twenty-seven years old. Some in town thought her a spinster, but she just hadn't found the right man and refused to settle.

Bozeman remained a young town filled with youthful, wild men, some permanent and some passing through, but never would she accept outrageous behavior from her beaus or patrons. She expected any man entering her establishment to behave as a gentleman should, and that included removing his hat and leaving his gun with Brewster Johnson, the doorman she'd hired to keep the peace. Only the marshal was allowed to keep his gun, owing to his job.

Back in the kitchen, she grabbed the handle of a coffee pot. Blinding pain shot through the palm of her hand, and she gasped, dropped the pot back down on the burner, pulling her hand back. Annie dropped the plate of food she'd been dishing up on the counter to run to her. Grabbing her hand, she stuck it into lukewarm dishwater nearby.

"Katie? Whatever were you thinking?" she scolded.

Tears filled Katie's eyes. "That's the problem—I wasn't thinking. Darn it! That man has the ability to make me forget common sense."

Annie stood back with hands on curvaceous hips. "I gather you mean the marshal?"

Katie caught the wry tone in Annie's voice as her friend dried her hand gently with a cloth. Turning a sheepish look on Annie, she gave a curt nod. "When will he stop spying on me?"

"Likely not until he finds a reason to shut you down," Annie said with a nonchalant shrug. "The man seems to have a personal vendetta against brothels."

"But we all know I'm not running a brothel here!" Katie protested.

Annie paused before leaving the kitchen. "But he doesn't know that, does he?"

Katie watched Annie take up the plates and leave the kitchen. Scowling, she remembered how Brewster told her about the new man in town who'd refused to give up his weapon upon entering Katie's Palace. She confronted James Freeman herself then, and her cheeks burned with humiliation when he merely smiled as he pulled his badge from his pocket. At the time, she hadn't wondered why he hadn't been wearing the badge, but she knew the answer now. He was hoping to employ entrapment to shut her down.

He'd used his initial entry as a method of enforcing the law. Because he had been new to town, the brothel owners assumed he was simply a customer. Once he discovered the nature of a particular business, he would produce his tin star, make arrests, then close down the establishment.

Faster than fire across a dry plains field, he'd closed down four brothels since he'd arrived a month ago. This, of course, meant more business for Katie since the brothels had also served meals. She couldn't complain given the increase in her own business. She'd been able to hire on more servers and maids as well. She knew the marshal hadn't liked that, for often she'd seen his narrow-eyed gaze focused on workers she guessed he recognized from the disreputable establishments—some of them having spent time in his jailhouse. *Too bad!* She could hire whomever she liked.

She grabbed a dishcloth this time and wrapped it around the handle of the coffeepot to pick it up, then snatched up a metal trivet as well. Once she reached the marshal's side, she leaned over, placed the trivet down in the center of the table and poured him a fresh cup of coffee before setting the pot down.

"Remember to use the cloth to pick up the pot," she advised.

When he didn't reply, she sent a fleeting look at his face. His wide smile disarmed her.

"Thanks for the reminder. I probably would have forgotten."

"You're welcome," she said, tired of keeping him at bay. Her establishment was squeaky clean. When would he learn she would never allow prostitution to go on in her Palace?

"I gotta say you make the best coffee in town, Miss O'Malley."

Watching him raise the cup of coffee to his lips, she glared at him. The reason she made the best coffee in town could only be because now she was the *only* place in town open that served coffee.

"Call me Katie, or Miss Katie, if you prefer. Anything else?" she asked.

He nodded to the chair opposite him and she squirmed inside at his appraisal of her. "How about joining me for a cup of coffee? You look like you could use a break."

What game was he playing now? She shook her head and stepped back. "Sorry, I've customers to tend to. As you can see, we're doing a booming business."

"'Course you are. You're the only place open in town because you *appear* to be legitimate."

Her spine stiffened again, and her hands shook. She clenched them into fists at her sides as she glared down into his lazy-smile expression. "*Appear*, did you say?

"Appearances can be deceiving, can't they?" he intoned softly, setting his coffee down.

Katie gasped. "Then you are accusing me of running a..."

"I'm not accusing you of a thing."

"Then what did you mean?" she snapped.

"Just making sure you understand why you're still open while the others aren't. Now take a load off. I've some questions to ask you."

"About...?"

"Something of a...personal nature."

"Which I refuse to answer," she inserted.

He straightened in his chair, his lips quirked. "Not *that* personal. Call it a business proposition."

Business? He'd roused her curiosity now.

Katie had never been one to turn a business proposition away without careful consideration. But then she thought about her most recent employees and her eagerness to hear him out dissipated. No doubt he wanted to know her motives for hiring them. The marshal had given her no choice, of course. It was his fault she'd taken the ladies from the last two brothels he'd closed down under her wing, after serving jailtime. After all, she couldn't leave them destitute, and she needed the help. Then she thought of the vivacious Marie Hannigan, who'd been sentenced to six months jail time in Helena. How unfair life was for women in this man's world.

James leaned forward and cupped his hands around his coffee cup. He raised his dark eyes, looked her square in the eyes and murmured, "I need a place to stay. A place to hang my hat, other than a jail cell."

She sat there, utterly still, astounded by his words. Then she saw his face turn a dusky shade of red beneath his tan—saw how he looked back down at his cup again. Obviously, it embarrassed him to ask her for the favor of renting a room, but could she really blame him for wanting to live any other place besides his makeshift home in a cell at the jail?

She had never been in one of the cells herself, but had heard plenty of complaints from some of the traveling cowboys. After a night of hard drinking, which usually resulted in a brawl, the cowboys complained how the bed cots were too short and harder than the dry ground upon which they slept during cattle drives.

Currently, she had five rooms to let. Unless she managed to find one more boarder, she'd be short paying her employees at the end of the month. The marshal moving in would help. After a moment's thought, satisfaction fled in light of the headaches his close proximity would likely cause her.

"I thought I heard you were building yourself a place at the end of town," she said. "Didn't you buy up that old silver mine past Flaherty's Mercantile?"

"Sure did." His voice was curt. "Got a problem though."

"What would that be?" she asked.

"I haven't been able to find folks to help me build a house."

Katie resisted—by the skin of her teeth—the urge to laugh out loud. Raising her brow, she drawled, "Why, I can't imagine why none of the men folk in town would help you build a place, can you?"

His scowl nearly set her to rolling on the floor with laughter. For the most part, the men in Bozeman were God-fearing, good folk—the married ones, at least, good husbands. But a fair share of them liked a dalliance now and again. Mostly innocent little things like a night out drinking, especially after a harvest or cow-run. Sometimes the drinking got a bit out of hand, and that was where some of the ladies of less fortunate means plied their wares. Life wasn't easy in Montana, and Maggie had never faulted the brothel owners for trying to make a living.

But he'd changed all of that as he closed the brothels down one by one. The men in town were as gentlemanly as the hard life would allow. Releasing steam and relaxing in one of the brothels kept them quiet and tame, which helped keep the peace at home. Most wives tended toward pragmatic acceptance, turning a blind eye to their husbands' occasional trysts.

Katie had known for as long as she could remember that she wouldn't be so acquiescent as a wife. Perhaps it explained why she hadn't married yet, perhaps never would.

"Well?" he said gruffly. "You got an extra room or not?"

She gave him a long look, wanting to say no, but ended up agreeing with a sharp edge to her voice. "Sure do. Follow me, and I'll show you the vacant ones."

He joined her without delay. Katie nearly laughed at the relieved expression crossing his face as he scrambled from his seat. One of these days she'd ask him to give her a tour of the jailhouse.

"Woo-ho, Miz Katie! You going to show the marshal a…"

'Good time' was left unsaid, but insinuated.

Katie paused on the steps to the second floor and glared down at Duke Bright, one of her regulars and, unfortunately, a trouble-maker at times. He grinned ear to ear up at her from his position at the bar. She opened her mouth to give him 'what for' when James intervened.

"Apologize to Miss Katie, Bright." James's low voice boomed in the silence.

Duke Bright didn't live up to his last name, that was for sure, Katie decided when he hauled his hefty frame off the bar stool and faced the marshal, jaw jutting. It didn't help that he was drunk either. "Miz Katie knows I was just funning' with her," he said, his words slurring. "What's it to you?"

"I'm not telling you again," James warned, heading back down the steps. "Apologize."

Katie froze and watched the men square off. Then Bright did the most ridiculous thing; he pulled a gun—fast. But not fast enough.

Light flashed and a booming sound filled the Palace, followed by a high-pitched scream.

Katie gasped and looked down at Bright who lay in the fetal position, squeezing his wrist to staunch the blood flowing from his mangled hand and onto the wooden floor. Then she gazed at the marshal, bent over... She couldn't move, couldn't think, even as the room started spinning so she latched onto the railing and willed herself not to faint.

*T*he shooting silenced the crowd. "Get me something to staunch the blood!" James snarled, snatching up Bright's gun from the floor. "And call for Doc Adamson."

Annie Callahan ran into the dining room, her hands full of cloths from the kitchen. James started ripping the cotton into strips when he happened to look up. He saw Katie on the steps, noting the whiteness of her face, then her eyes rolled back. Cursing, he dropped Bright's hand, ignoring the man's loud, painful groan. In two strides, James arrived at the steps and caught Katie as she crumpled and swooned in his arms.

Damn! Shooting Bright, protecting himself from the blasted fool's trigger finger, happened so fast James hadn't had a chance to think the situation over. He would have been a dead man if he'd taken the time to think instead of following his gut-reaction, as lawmen have always done.

James looked down the steps, saw Bright trying to get up off the floor.

"Brewster!" James called. "Lock the doors, then come over here and keep an eye on Bright!" James met the injured man's furious expression. "You aren't going anywhere. You're under arrest."

"You shot me for no good reason!" Bright shouted.

Meeting several men's eyes, James knew he had their support. "I've got witnesses that will back me up you drew first."

Brewster, who'd been at his usual position at the door, met Annie's gaze. She looked at the marshal, then nodded at Brewster. James offered

Annie a gentle, thankful smile. From the moment he'd met Annie, he liked her, but not romantically. She was only eighteen but the sweetest woman he'd ever met. Yet, she didn't compare to Katie, a woman full-grown. He'd fleetingly entertained the notion of courting Annie, but then just as quickly set the idea aside in accordance with the vows he'd made to himself. Besides, he was thirty-three years old, likely a good ten to twelve years older than Katie. What would a pretty young thing like her want with an old codger like him?

James made his way up the stairs and marveled at Katie's lightness in his arms. Meat on her bones, that was what she needed he decided as he placed her gently on the bed in the first room at the top of the steps, on the right.

He grabbed a neatly folded quilt from the rack in the corner, started to cover her up but paused. It was hotter than Hades this August day. Eyeing her long-sleeved, buttoned-up-to-the-neck dress he decided she'd die of the heat with the quilt atop her. Dropping the quilt over the rack again, he turned to Katie, gingerly sat down beside her on the bed and chafed one small hand. He noticed the other hand at her side, palm up and blistered. He frowned.

"Come on, wake up," he coaxed, wondering about the vivid red burn marks. Then he thought about her work in the Palace and decided it likely wasn't the first time she'd been burned in the kitchen.

Her hands felt cold—lifeless. Shock, he decided. He'd shocked the poor woman into a dead faint. James had always lumped brothel owners into one category. Tough as nails they were. This one, however, was far from tough. Would a hard-as-nails brothel owner faint at the first sign of a gunfight? He didn't think so, but Katie had, which left him in a dilemma, having second thoughts about how he thought she'd been running a brothel.

Truth be told, it was just one reason he wanted to take up residence at Katie's place, to keep a close eye on things. He hoped he was wrong in thinking the place might not be legal. There was something comforting about Katie's Palace, and he'd hate to have to close it down. Besides, he couldn't endure another night in a jail cell on a lumpy cot and looked forward to sleeping under Katie's roof.

Soon color started returning to her cheeks, and that's when he noticed the smattering of freckles across her small nose for the first time. With her red hair, it was no surprise. He found himself wondering again about her age. She wasn't eighteen, he knew, but still, she appeared young, healthy…pretty. Too pretty for his own peace of mind.

He looked down when Katie moaned, then Annie ran into the room.

James rose from the bed and stood beside it, arms crossed.

Katie opened her eyes and looked up at James as she frowned and swiped a swathe of hair off her face.

"No need to worry, ma'am. You're fine."

"What happened?"

"You fainted, Katie," Annie said worriedly.

"Oh." Katie looked up at James in confusion. "You didn't get shot?"

Raising his brow, James said, "Not me. Bright tried though." Scowling, he added, "Thought Brewster had everyone check their weapons at the door before entering the Palace?"

She sighed. "He doesn't physically check people, though I can see he'll have to in the future. I hadn't realized Bright possessed such a nasty streak."

"He was drunk, and drunken men do impulsive, stupid things."

Katie frowned. "Hmm, no one's ever shot a gun inside my place—until you walked through the doors. So you weren't hit?" At the shake of his head, she added, "I'm beginning to think you're going to be trouble, marshal, living under my roof."

James took umbrage with her words and stiffened his spine. "If you've changed your mind, ma'am…"

"No, no. Just an observation's all I'm making."

She started to sit up but sank back when Annie pressed down on her shoulders. "You need to rest a bit more, Katie."

"No." Katie sat up and smiled at Annie. "I'm fine. Besides, the marshal here is in the process of picking out a room. He'll be living here until his house is built."

Annie's brows shot up. "Is that a fact?" She smiled at James and reached out her hand. "Well then, welcome, marshal. We'll take good care of you here."

James took Annie's hand gently in his and squeezed, then released it. "Thank you, Miss Annie." A slow grin crossed his lips. "I think I'm going to like it here."

Dryly, Katie said, "I imagine any place would be better than a jail cell."

"True." Sweeping his hand toward the door, he added, "If you're well enough, Miss O'Malley, I await the tour."

"I'd better get back to the kitchen," Annie said.

James doffed his hat with a nod. "Thank you, Miss Annie."

~

*K*atie figured he'd choose her most spacious room. It was also located at the opposite end of the hall from hers. Ironically, he chose one of the smaller rooms, directly across from hers.

As long as Annie had been with them, Katie had felt comfortable with James, but she'd left them upon beginning the tour. Not wanting him so close to her room, she suggested "Wouldn't you be more comfortable in the larger room I showed you at the other end of the hallway?"

He shook his head and guided her back down the steps with a hand at her waist. "Nope. The location's wrong."

As she stepped off the last step, she faced him and gave him a quizzical look. "Why?"

"Too far away for an escape route other than the main staircase. I'd be like a sitting duck in that room."

"I see. Um, are you expecting trouble?"

"Always, Miss Katie. Call it the nature of my job."

"Have you ever thought about pursuing some other sort of work?"

"No."

His flat, firm tone made Katie curious. He wanted to end the conversation with no further discussion.

"You're welcome to move in any time then."

He nodded. "I'll be by with my stuff in the morning. Thank you, Miss Katie."

"Just Katie is fine."

His smile widened. "Katie, it is. And I'm James."

She looked into his gentle eyes that crinkled in the corners from his smile. Glancing down, she saw he'd stuck out his hand—something a man would do to another man—sealing the deal. She started to take it but paused and pulled the hand back, remembering the burns.

He didn't say a word as he slowly moved his hand back, but she couldn't miss the disappointment in his eyes. Before she could defend herself not taking his hand, he touched the brim of his hat. "'Evenin', ma'am," he said curtly, turning on his heel and leaving the Palace.

Katie watched him, her gaze drifting appreciatively over his broad back and narrow legs as his long legs carried him across the lobby and out the door. His slight swagger brought a smile to her lips. Her feelings were mixed though. In a way, having the law right under her roof might be a good thing. She'd fibbed to him earlier, about no shooting at the Palace, thinking a year ago how she'd had her fair share of trouble with cowboys passing through town during the last cattle drive.

The Palace was empty now, the lunch crowd having left, yet she knew, as she headed for the kitchen, within four hours, the place would be full for supper.

～

*T*he marshal didn't wait for morning, but arrived in the midst of the busy supper hour with minimal possessions. A few suitcases and a blanket and saddle over one wide shoulder was all. He tossed her a nod while he headed up the stairs. With two heaping high plates of fried chicken, she paused at the foot of the steps, watching him easily take the stairs with his load.

She settled the dinners in front of two new-to-town cowboys with a smile and turned to leave when a tug on her apron made her glance over her shoulder. One of the men had caught her apron string and held it gripped in his hand.

Katie sighed. *Here we go again. Just like last year.* And she knew more men would be arriving in the next several days. "Did I forget something?" she innocently asked. Then her eyes caught Marshal Freeman's from the top of the stairs, his eyes narrowed.

The cowboy released the string and sank back in his chair. "When we're finished eating, maybe you can fill us in on what's going on in town."

"And where we can find some feminine company, ma'am," the other cowboy inserted.

"Well," Katie said slowly, turning to face them with her hands propped on her hips, "maybe the marshal here can help you out with your requests."

The second, younger cowboy blanched. "Did you say marshal?"

Katie nodded. "Yes. Our law enforcer lives right here at the Palace. I'm certain he'll be here for supper any moment. You can ask him then."

The men fell silent, the younger one blushed to the roots of his tousled blonde hair, the first one scowling at Katie as she turned away and headed for the kitchen again.

"Miss Katie!"

Katie looked to her left and found old Timothy Patterson, one of the town's blacksmiths calling for her.

"Yes, Timothy?"

"Any chance I could get a refill?"

Katie noticed his empty plate, then tried not to focus on the man's substantial paunch." She knew his wife would not be happy with his eating a second helping, but that wasn't Katie's problem.

"Sure, thing, Timothy. Be right back."

Oh, that was too easy. Katie headed for the kitchen again. Having the marshal's protection would be comforting, she admitted. Her step was light and lively when she shoved through the kitchen's swinging doors.

Annie looked up from her position at the stove where she stood frying chicken pieces in cast-iron skillets on every burner.

"Glad to see a smile on your face," Annie said, grinning back at Katie. "Want to let me in on the fun?"

Katie chuckled. "I was hesitant about Marshal Freeman staying here, but now I'm glad of it."

Annie sighed. "He's a handsome man but somewhat glum, don't you think?"

"I'd be glum if I had his job," Katie said. She filled a plate with chicken, mashed potatoes and gravy. And the worry he must experience in his daily work, she decided, thinking about the incident with Duke Bright. Lord, but she'd never fainted in her life until then—when she'd thought James had been shot. Thoughts of being married to him sent chills up her spine. As his wife, she would worry every day about his safety. Whatever was she thinking? Marriage to the man would be impossible!

Upon her return to the dining room, she frowned thoughtfully. Now why in the world had she defended that man when he'd made so much trouble from the moment he'd stepped foot in town?

She had just placed the plate of food in front of Timothy when she caught sight of James. Her jaw gaped as she stared at him, dressed in a black jacket, pants, crisp white shirt and string tie. Never had she seen him attired in anything but his law enforcement uniform consisting of a denim shirt and pants, buckskin vest and a Stetson on his head. Why, if Katie didn't know better, he appeared ready to go-a-courtin'.

The room full of people fell silent. Every patron had noticed the marshal's change of attire. Every one of them as stunned, it appeared, as Katie.

He sank into a chair at the back of the dining hall, his elbows on the table. Overlooking the street, the table was positioned next to the window.

Protecting his back again, Katie decided, heading toward him to take his order.

Pausing at his table with a smile, she asked, "What would you like, Marshal?"

CHAPTER 3

hat would he like? As he looked his fill of Katie, still dressed in a pretty flower-sprigged day dress, apron covering it, he sighed. What he'd like to do is settle her into the chair across from him and enjoy a night of sweet, feminine company with her. She'd make some man a fine wife. Unfortunately, *he* was not that man. He had long ago decided, due to his career, he would never marry. He refused to jeopardize the safety of a wife and children, so he'd go it alone for the rest of his life.

Not that he was any saint. He was a man with needs, but he made sure, with his occasional trips to Helena, that the women with whom he dallied knew from the start his shortcomings, including his inability to commit.

He had no doubts Katie would fulfill every one of his needs if he allowed her into his life. Then he thought, chagrinned, why would she want anything to do with him when there were far more handsome—far more charming men than him that would possibly make her a marriage offer? Men who had a chance of living a hell of a lot longer than him, besides, he decided, thinking of his hazardous occupation.

"Marshal?"

He shook his head to clear it and murmured, "Call me James, Miss Katie. I'd prefer it."

She frowned. "Oh, do you think that would be proper, though, you being the law and all?"

"Who cares about proper? I want you to call me by my name, not my title. Besides, I'll be living in the same house with you. Marshal just seems plain silly to me."

If folks didn't know right away he was the law, he could lay low and watch for trouble from any newcomers passing into town. The element of surprise would be in his favor.

"All right, James," she softly replied. "Now what would you like for supper?"

"How about the beef stew?"

"Excellent choice. Annie makes the best stew around these parts. Biscuits, too?"

He was so busy staring at her lips he missed every word she said.

James cleared his throat when he noticed her staring at him with a quizzical expression. "Excuse me?"

"Biscuits?"

"Oh, yeah, biscuits, fine."

"Be back in a minute."

She turned away, but he stopped her when he said, "One more thing, Miss Katie."

She whirled around to face him. "What would that be?"

"Coffee would be mighty good."

She grinned. "Of course."

James let her go then, watching her hips swing as she sashayed toward the kitchen. Sweet woman, he mused, wondering why he'd ever doubted her and her business. She and her Palace seemed to be genuine and exactly like she said. A boarding house, restaurant and saloon—no brothel.

While eating his supper, thoughts of Katie filled his mind. If Bozeman turned out to be as safe, sleepy and quiet as it appeared to be, maybe he could take a wife. But only one woman would fill that need inside him. Katie. He hadn't known her long, but he knew he wanted her —only her.

~

*B*y week's end, Katie wanted to pull her hair out at the roots. She was also ready to evict her new tenant. While she needed the money, James Freeman's presence was another matter. His persona, while dressed in his lawman gear, appeared terse, cool and suspicious.

Terse and cool she could deal with, but suspicious—no. It meant he didn't trust her. She liked him so much better when he dressed in his black suit, his manner toward her gentlemanly and friendly. She had no idea why he kept changing clothes, instead of always wearing his lawman's clothing, as the previous lawmen of Bozeman had done. The man was an enigma, and he'd been tricking her—lulling her into trusting him when what he really wanted to do, she suspected, was close down the Palace.

A week had passed since he'd moved in, and now, on this balmy Friday evening, Katie found herself peering over the swinging doors to the kitchen, watching James from his typical position at the back of the dining hall. He'd settled his Stetson low on his forehead, his intent gaze focused on two men she didn't recognize sitting at the bar, chatting with Marion and Ethel. The women were former owners of a small brothel down on Cook Street. She'd hired them to wait tables but found them more often jawing with the customers rather than serving them. The women were a bit older than her, heavy in the hips and breasts, which appeared to greatly interest the two men at the moment.

Katie had given the women free room and board and small pay for their work. Katie knew she offered them a second chance in life, and a nice deal living and working at the Palace. Even though they weren't earning their keep, what could she do? She couldn't leave them out on the street—homeless.

She sighed. James was dressed in his black suit—civilian clothes—and hadn't pinned on his tin star. He was setting a trap. She could feel it inside her. Her gaze darted back to the women. She saw the lewd looks on the men's faces, and the heated desire in her employees' eyes. *Please, don't do anything foolish, ladies!*

Annie called to her then. "Katie! Table five's been waiting ten minutes for their food! It'll be ice-cold by the time you deliver it," she scolded.

"Sorry," Katie murmured. Snatching up the two plates of fried fish, she headed out of the kitchen. Quickly, she made her way to table five, setting the plates down carefully in front of two cowboys, strangers in town. "Sorry about the wait," she muttered.

The men said not a word but gave a curt nod and dug into the food.

Glancing at James again, Katie saw him still at his table, leaning forward with his hands folded in front of him. His hat he'd settled further back on his head and, with his head turned to one side, it appeared he was trying to listen in on the animated conversation at the bar. Katie wondered how long he planned on staying. He'd already been sitting in the same spot for two hours. Deciding her employees' behavior was over the line, Katie made to intervene into the foursome's conversation at the bar when Annie called to her again.

She grabbed two more plates of fish, which happened to be the night's special, when she heard loud laughter and the pounding of feet up the stairs. She hurried from the kitchen and found James still in the same position, saw him glance down at the watch he'd pulled from his pocket. He looked up, pierced her with a long, hard look before looking at the stairs. Katie glanced at the bar and saw the two men and women had left. James had been waiting for something to happen—and it had. The two men were not boarders at the Palace but cattlemen who'd arrived in town this morning.

Katie moved to the stairs, stopped, and stared up at the top, listening. All was quiet—which was not a good sign. She looked at James again, saw him staring directly at her. As he slowly rose from his seat, he kept his gaze on her. Then he ambled to her side and stopped, looking down at her. For once she wished she wasn't so much shorter than him.

"Any reason why I should be suspicious of the foursome who just traipsed upstairs, Miss O'Malley?"

Katie's skin prickled at his calm question, hearing and not liking the accusation in his tone. "No. You know that, aside from the rooms I let, there's a card parlor upstairs."

"Then you won't mind if I follow them?"

She shrugged nonchalantly, though her heart beat a rapid, nervous staccato. "Do what you like," she snapped. "I've nothing to hide."

His expression and voice softened somewhat. "I hope not," he said. "Move aside then."

"I'll come with you." She plucked up her skirts and turned but she froze when she felt his hand at her waist. She looked at him then over her shoulder and saw the cold look on his face.

"Stay put," he ordered.

She stopped with one foot on the first step and glared at him. "This is my place, Marshal. I've a right to check on my guests."

"You mean you have the right to warn your guests, don't you?"

Katie felt the chill in the air from his frosty words. She took umbrage at his comment and said, "There's no need for me to warn them of anything! I'm certain they aren't doing anything illegal."

"If that's the case, you'll stay down here until I'm through upstairs."

He sent another warning her way. Helplessly, she stayed riveted on the step until he reached the hallway upstairs then disappeared from sight.

Katie counted to ten before rushing up the stairs after him, praying Marion and Ethel were behaving themselves. Just before reaching the landing, she heard angry female shrieks and bellowing male voices.

She saw James standing outside an open door in the middle of the hallway a moment before disappearing inside. Katie groaned, knowing it was Ethel and Marion's room. She tore down the hallway, came to a screeching halt at the sight within. The women reclined on their beds, shirtwaists and camisoles removed, corsets unlaced, breasts bared. The two cowboys had removed their vests, unbuckled their belts and dropped their pants. Katie grimaced at the sight of the denim pooled around their ankles, buttocks on display while they each bent over a woman.

*I*f the sight hadn't been so pitiful, Katie would have thought it laughable. She stared at the horrified looks on the young men's faces. They scrambled from the beds, bent and tugged up their britches.

"Get out," James ordered. He stepped into the room, allowing them space to leave.

Leaving behind their vests, the men tore out of the room, nearly knocking Katie over in their rush to leave.

James glared over his shoulder at Katie. "Didn't I tell you to stay downstairs?"

"You did, but I've never allowed a man to order me about and don't plan on starting now." She groaned inside when she saw money on each bedside table, knowing how damning the evidence appeared. She *was* in trouble!

He sighed. "You've got problems," he said. "I'm afraid you've been lying to me about the legitimacy of the Palace, which is a damned shame."

Katie ignored him. Later she'd consider how he'd condemned her and her place. For now, she looked at Marion and Ethel who sat up in their beds, the bedding pulled high over their bosoms. "Explain yourselves, ladies."

Marion said, "Charlie passes by every year to visit me when he's through with his cattle run."

Sullenly, Ethel added, "Same with Sam, Miss Katie."

Disappointment set in. The two women had been in her employ almost a year, and never before had they broken Katie's rules for working and living at the Palace. "Didn't I tell you I don't run a brothel? That the Palace is legitimate?"

"Yes, ma'am," they said in unison.

"Then I'm afraid you are both through working for me."

"They'll have to be," James said. "They're going to jail until the circuit judge comes by to hear their case. Sorry, Miss Katie, but I'm afraid you'll be jailed, too."

"What!" Katie exploded. "What did *I* do?"

"The infraction happened in your business. Ultimately, it's your responsibility to keep your place legitimate. I'm closing down Katie's Palace."

Katie couldn't believe he doubted her integrity, and that hurt. Closing down her business? No! Her mother had worked hard to establish herself in Bozeman, and Katie planned on keeping the business, no matter how tough she suspected it would be. What pained her most was that she'd grown to like James Freeman, had entertained the idea of his possibly courting her. He was a fine, upstanding man—who gave no one the benefit of the doubt. To him the law was the law, no matter who you were. No more ideas of courting entered her mind. She wouldn't cross the street with him now.

"But…but…why, that's the most ridiculous thing I ever heard!"

"Ridiculous or not, that's the law."

"And you just love enforcing it, don't you?" she snapped.

He sighed. "It's my job. Come along now, the three of you."

∼

*A*ll of Bozeman was in an uproar over Katie being jailed. Within a day, townsfolk already felt the loss of Katie's Palace. There were no other eating establishments in town, and the unmarried men were in a quandary as to how to feed themselves.

Luckily, there were several smart lawyers in town who came a-calling on Miss Katie to represent her. She chose Richard T. Jackson, a seasoned veteran of the criminal justice system, who crisply quoted the law to James. The solicitor informed James that, upon receiving two-hundred dollars bail, he had to release Miss Katie, then he produced the cash.

James had no choice but to release her.

"No leaving town, Miss O'Malley. Judge Hopkins won't be here for another two weeks," he reminded her.

Lordy, but she was a beauty, he mused, watching her storm past him. He hadn't wanted to jail her, but he'd based his whole life on being honest and law-abiding—and protecting women, even if it meant jailing them. He expected no less from everyone in Bozeman. Already he regretted closing down Katie's Palace, but she'd given him no choice.

"Where would I go?" she snapped. He cringed when she slammed the door.

James was beginning to see the error of his ways when he once again took up a bed in the jailhouse—in the cell next to the one that housed Ethel and Marion. The women hollered the roof down for hours, refusing to sleep in the cell next to him. When he realized he wouldn't get any sleep that night, he left the women, locked up the jailhouse and slept on the ground with his horse's saddle and bedroll under the starry night. Midway through the night, a summer storm passed through. By the time he found shelter under the eaves of the jailhouse, his clothes were soaked through to the skin.

Quietly, he entered the jailhouse, took the hardwood chair from behind his desk and went out the door again. He dropped it on the wooden planking, then settled down under the eaves for the rest of the night. He woke the following morning to a warm, clear-sky day. Groaning with stiffness, he raised himself up from his slouched position on his chair, opened his eyes and found himself staring into a pair of pretty gray eyes.

"My, my," Katie drawled. "Did you have a comfortable night's rest, Marshal?"

"What do you think?" he groused. He rose to his feet, his bones aching, his clothes still damp, his boots wet, too. *Damn! My good boots! How in the hell did I forget to remove them last night?*

She just smirked at him, and he sighed.

"What's that?" he asked, eyeing the picnic basket over her arm.

"Breakfast for Ethel and Marion."

"Sorry. Visiting hours aren't until noon."

"I see. What will you do about serving them breakfast then?"

He blinked and thought what he usually did; order breakfast from

Katie's Palace. He hadn't found the need to do this very often since it was rare for anyone to be incarcerated in Bozeman.

"Uh, hadn't thought that far ahead yet." Gruffly, he added, "Seeing as you've already got it made up and all, you can just leave it here and I'll give it to them when they wake up." He dug inside his pocket and pulled out a dollar. "Here ya go."

"We're already awake!" Ethel shouted.

Instead of taking the money, she stepped back. "Since the ladies will be here for a while longer, I'll bill you at the end of their stay."

He looked at the barred window. Sure enough, he found the women staring out between the bars, eyes riveted on the picnic basket.

"Oh, Miss Katie. How thoughtful of you to think about us in this awful place, and after us disappointing you and all. It's horrible! Hot and stuffy and just plain…awful!" Ethel wailed.

"What did you expect?" James said. "Modern conveniences in jail?"

Ethel ignored his reply and shouted, "We're starving!"

"Come on then," James said. He turned, unlocked the door, and motioned Katie in ahead of him. Closing the door behind them, he leaned against it and watched her open the basket and take out the most heavenly smelling food. Moving closer, he saw her remove a towel, revealing a platter heaped high with scrambled eggs, onions, and green peppers. Below that platter was another with fried potatoes on one half of the plate and crisp fried bacon on the other. His stomach lurched, hunger calling to him when he smelled golden brown biscuits and churned butter.

"If you'll serve up the food on these plates," she said, looking up at him and producing three white dishes, "there's plenty for you, too. I'll be back in a minute."

She headed for the door but paused when he said, "Where you off to?"

"Coffee. I couldn't carry the pot and the basket."

"I'll go back and get it while you dish up the food," he said gruffly.

"All right," she said, turning back to the basket.

He watched her a moment, his gaze lingering on her calico-gowned figure. She was such a sweet thing. Was it possible he'd made a mistake about her? She seemed too innocent to run an illegal business. But then he yanked down his still damp vest and left the jailhouse. He returned within moments with the pot of coffee and four white cups and set them down on his desk.

James saw she'd served the women and had dished up a plate for him. He motioned to the chair beside his desk. "Join us, Miss O'Malley."

She shook her head. "No thank you. I'm meeting with my solicitor this morning."

"I see," he said, unable to keep the stiffness out of his voice. "So you can plan strategy, I assume?"

"You are bound and determined to think the worst of me, aren't you?" She jammed her hands on her hips. "Have you always been such a bad judge of character?"

James felt his face grow warm at her question. Had he been a bad judge? No. He'd never made a mistake in judgment, though he had his doubts a few times about Katie.

"Thanks for the breakfast," was all he said. He tucked into his food, cringing when he heard the door slam. He suddenly lost his appetite.

Katie was furious as she strode back to her establishment. How dare the man entertain such evil thoughts about her! She'd never broken the law and was, in fact, a victim of circumstances. Then her anger turned to Ethel and Marion, who hadn't been able to control themselves. The others in her employ had been so happy to have a second chance when Katie offered them jobs, they'd followed all the rules. Quite a few of the women had gone on to marry and live respectable lives.

Then she thought about James—and his personal vendetta in cleaning up Bozeman, expecting and demanding respectability from everyone in town. Maybe someday she'd find out his true reasons for his high expectations of all living creatures. Still, it hurt that he had put her in the same category as criminals. He'd soon learn how wrong he was about her.

~

*A*s expected, two weeks later Judge Hopkins arrived. Upon hearing the evidence and listening to the entire town's testimony on Katie's unblemished character and honesty, the judge dropped the charges James had filed against her. Ethel and Marion were initially charged with prostitution until, much to the surprise of the marshal, the two cowboys declared their love for the women and asked to marry them. Judge Hopkins was happy to perform the marriages and planned on doing so the following day before leaving town for his next destination. Before the judge left the Presbyterian Church, the only place large enough to hold court, James confronted him.

Stepping in front of the dark-haired man with greying temples, as he left the church, James said, "A word if you will, Judge Hopkins."

"Of course, Marshal Freeman. What seems to be the problem?"

"Was there a reason you made me look like a fool today?"

The judge offered James a sympathetic smile. "Miss O'Malley was innocent, and you know it. You simply didn't have the proof. She had numerous good people of excellent character step up with believable character recommendations about her. She was a victim of an unfortunate incident." Looking around, the judge lowered his voice and added, "This personal vendetta has to end, James. Since you've shut down every other place in town, Katie's Palace is the only one left where people can go for room and board."

"I closed those places with good reason," James snapped.

"And good evidence," the judge countered, "but not this time. So let's leave it at that."

As James watched the judge climb up onto the buckboard seat, flick the reins and leave, he wondered how he could have been so wrong. Why had he accused Katie?

He knew the answer; all he could think about was his mother's desperate life—and how she'd died of the dreaded syphilis. God, he wouldn't want that for Katie, and the only way he could protect her that he knew of—and other women in town—was to close down houses of ill repute.

But, now it seemed he'd made a mistake, and the Palace was legitimate. He hated himself for not having believed Katie when she told him she'd known nothing about her employees' liaisons with the men. He hoped she'd accept his apology.

He waited outside for Katie while she finished up business with her solicitor. The man came out of the church first, gave a curt nod at him and went on his way. Katie came out shortly afterwards, pausing with a surprised look at him before averting her gaze.

"I thought you'd left," she said.

The fact that she wouldn't meet his eyes made him feel even worse. "It appears I owe you an apology," he murmured, jamming a finger inside his shirt collar.

"It does. Whenever you're ready, Marshal, go ahead."

"I just did."

"Did what?"

"Say I'm sorry."

She scowled at him, meeting his eyes for the first time. "Pardon me, but you said you owe me an apology, which isn't the same as apologizing."

He felt heat seep into his cheeks and admitted, "You're right, of course. Accept my sincere apologies for not believing you, Miss O'Malley."

She nodded. "I accept because I believe you are sincere. But let me give you some advice that may help you in the future. It would serve you better in life if you had some faith in humanity and weren't always so suspicious of people."

His jaw tightened. "Old habits die hard. In my defense, it pays to be suspicious in my line of my work."

"Then you need to learn to be a better judge of character. I've said this from the moment you arrived in town. You appear to have a personal vendetta against people—women in particular—whom you believe aren't living their lives to your standards."

"Now who's not giving someone the benefit of the doubt?" he said, though he knew she was right. But he wasn't the type to spill his guts to folks. Never had he told a soul about his mother and how, in the end, she'd died a horrible death.

She shrugged. "And now you know how others feel, don't you?"

Thrusting out his jaw, he jammed his hands on his hips and looked over her head, unable to meet the censure in her eyes. Finally, he glanced at her once more and saw sympathy and concern on her face. *Damn! I don't want her pity.*

"Again, I apologize. I'll leave you and the Palace alone from now on. That's a promise. Unless you call on me for help, I won't darken your door again."

Turning on his heel, he took a few steps when he heard her call to him. "James!"

He stopped and turned to her. She bit her lower lip, looking at him in a way that caused his heart to leap.

"You're welcome to have your room back, if you want it."

Sleeping in a cell again was not to his liking. His feelings for Katie grew even more at the thought that she was not a grudge-holder.

"I appreciate it, ma'am." With a curt nod, he added, "I'll move back in tonight, after supper."

He strode away, headed for the jail, all the while thinking about sweet Katie, angelic Katie, Katie of the utmost patience and fairness. The woman was a blessed saint!

Which means she's too good for the likes of me.

Chagrined, he vowed to never again doubt her word.

CHAPTER 5

*K*atie watched James leave, his stride long, shoulders straight. He tipped his hat to her once he mounted his horse, then pulled the animal around and headed down Main Street toward the jailhouse.

Making her way down the boardwalk to the Palace, Katie thought deep and hard about her feelings for James. She'd been hurt when he believed her to be a less than virtuous woman. She wondered what caused him to assume that, to behave the way he had. Then she thought about how he'd looked with pity upon Ethel and Marion when he'd arrested them—not the same look he'd given her. Beneath his cool, lawman's veneer she had a feeling he knew all along she was not a fallen woman, that she'd known nothing of Ethel and Marion's antics upstairs with the cowboys. But she also wondered then why he'd been so quick to blame her.

Demons lurked deep inside the man and, while she wanted to pry the truth out of him, she knew the best thing to do was leave him alone.

She hurried back to the Palace to start cooking supper. By the time she arrived, the throng of men waiting at the front of her business separated, allowing her to unlock the doors, cheering her arrival and the opening of the Palace. Once inside, every seat was occupied. Thankfully, another cook, Mabel Larson, arrived in time to take over the cooking Katie had started.

Annie arrived with two of her other employees to help Mabel while Katie took orders.

Half an hour later, Katie and Annie busily ran plates of food to customers. On the way back to the kitchen from her last run, Katie saw James enter. Folks quieted, and Katie felt the knife-edge of their animosity toward him. Some of them glared at James while others chose not to acknowledge him. Katie decided to offer the olive branch in front of the customers. Though misguided in his efforts, James had been trying to do his job.

She moved toward him with a smile, happy he'd returned, for more than one reason. Other than the fact she was more than a bit attracted to the man, she needed his patronage and his room and board money.

"Welcome, James," she said loud and clear, pausing in front of him. "I believe you know your way to your room. We're serving supper now, so come down and eat once you've settled in."

"Thanks, Miss O'Malley. I could use some vittles. Haven't eaten all day," he murmured.

Katie watched him head up the stairs, appreciative of the view again. After he disappeared from sight, she still stared up the stairs. Then she heard laughter. Looking around, she saw several men grinning at her knowingly. Heat rushed through her cheeks as she tore into the kitchen.

She was too embarrassed to serve food and stayed in the kitchen helping Mabel prepare the food. She couldn't face those men now, knowing that they'd seen her looking at James with more than a hint of appreciation on her face.

Within an hour, James appeared and settled into his typical place at the back of the dining room, facing the doors. Annie took his order since Katie was still hiding out in the kitchen.

"The marshal wants steak and potatoes, Katie," Annie said, hustling in. Her cheeks were flushed from rushing about taking orders and clearing tables.

Katie felt guilty that she'd been hiding instead of helping. "I'll serve him. Annie, take a load off your feet for a bit. Better yet, it's slowing down. Why don't you head for home?"

Annie's drawn, tired expression lightened. "Are you sure?"

"Yes," Katie said with a nod. "And thanks so much."

"You're welcome." Annie untied her apron and hung it on a hook. She turned, bussed Katie's cheek, and whispered in her ear. "Go easy on him. I can tell from the way he looks, he feels real bad about closing you down."

"I know."

Annie smiled. "He likes you."

"Don't be silly," Katie said, yet pleased to hear the words. Annie had always been a highly perceptive woman. She seemed to know how people thought, what they felt, just by observing them. Often times she'd hear whispered comments from people in town—that Annie was a witch because of her abilities. Katie didn't think so. The woman simply had an uncanny gift.

At twelve-thirty, Katie locked up the Palace, though midnight was the normal closing time. It had taken her some time to encourage the last of the card players to leave.

James had gone upstairs to his room hours ago. His work hours were early to bed, early to rise, so he was usually in bed no later than nine. If he'd stayed downstairs the men would have left immediately when she announced she was closing with the marshal standing by. But then she thought of the past few years of managing without him and decided she could handle it on her own, until Brewster returned from taking care of his ill wife. All it took was a casual reminder that the marshal was now housed upstairs in one of her boarding rooms for the men to toss down their cards with a grumble and leave. But she needed that extra hour of drinking money from the men in order to pay salaries at the end of the month.

She'd turned the spigot on the last table lantern, extinguishing the light, when she heard James calling down the stairs to her.

"Everything all right down there, Katie?"

"Yes," she said. "I'm on my way up."

"Good. Just checking," he said.

Before she reached the top landing, she saw James looking down on her. He'd removed his vest and stood in his shirt and jeans only, though she noted the gun on his hip. Had he heard what was happening downstairs?

He stepped back when she took the last step up to the second floor landing. "Thought I heard some problem downstairs."

She shrugged. "Nothing I couldn't handle. It seems the last six men were involved in a poker game they didn't want to end, but I convinced them it was time to leave."

James scowled. "You shouldn't have to sweet talk them to leave. Once you ask them to, that's all you should have to do. Why didn't you call me?"

"Because I depend on those men returning. You'd scare them away and I'd lose their business." Which was the truth, she knew. The marshal had intimidated plenty of people in town since his arrival.

"I'd be tactful."

"Uh-huh. Yes, I've seen that side of you." She smiled. "I've been handling this place and its patrons on my own since inheriting it from my mother. I can manage." Her smile widened. "It's sweet of you to worry about me though. I appreciate it."

"I was worried. I think you need to close down at ten instead of midnight. Why stay open so late anyway? All that does is encourage problems. And where's Brewster? Isn't he the one who usually handles the late night folks?"

"Normally, yes, but his wife has been very ill so he's taking some time off to care for her."

"As to the late hours, where else would these men go for entertainment?"

"Home to their wives and families where they belong," he snapped.

"Many of these men have no homes to go home to, and you know it. They drive cattle from town to town and sleep on their bedrolls outside. Besides, I need their patronage in order to stay afloat."

"So, it's the money then?"

"Mostly, yes."

"I'll pay you double what I pay you now for room and board if it means you can close by ten."

Katie narrowed her eyes. "No, and I don't appreciate you ordering me about. These men depend on my doors staying open until midnight, and that's that, Marshal."

James jammed his hands on his hips. "So, do you think your husband will allow this to continue?"

"You know I'm not married."

"But once you do marry, do you think your husband will allow this?"

"Since I'm not married, it doesn't matter."

"But what if you were married?"

"Why do you care, James?"

Thrusting out his jaw, he said, "Because I'm thinking no wife of mine would be staying up all hours of the night taking care of other men. Besides, it's not safe. You need someone to look after you."

Katie bristled at his dictatorial tone, yet, deep down inside, his words made her think he must care for her or he wouldn't be angry. It was possible he was aiming toward proposing marriage to her but was nervous and hadn't figured out a way to ask. Lordy, if she didn't have to worry about society's rules, she'd broach the idea of marriage to him herself. Instead, she would have to bide her time and wait for him to get the courage to ask. Still, even if he did care and they were married, she didn't like his tone.

"Well, I'm not your wife so I'm not your worry. Good night, James."

❧

*L*ying in bed that night, sleep eluded Katie. She couldn't put the memory of James's words from her mind. Though she had no perceptive abilities like Annie, she had a feeling James had been thinking about marrying. Her! She'd escaped before he could say anything more. Alone, she could think over their exchanged words, think about the heated look in his eyes as he gazed down at her.

He didn't like the idea of her staying open so late at night and handling her patrons by herself. She smiled. Maybe the man was falling in love with her.

Katie sighed, thinking it unlikely, but the thought was comforting, in a way, even his dictatorial behavior made her feel, well, wanted. Her eyes grew heavy as she examined her feelings about the man. He was several years older than her, but not that many, and his age certainly didn't detract from his appeal. She sighed, thinking she could learn to love the marshal, if she allowed herself. And hadn't she always wanted children, a family? She thought about that with a smile as she drifted off to sleep.

❧

*A*cross the hallway, James didn't find sleep easily. He fought with himself through the night hours, drifting off to sleep then waking to consider his lonely life, about how marriage between him and Katie could be possible.

Bozeman was a quiet town with law-abiding citizens. It was only when the cowboys came through town on their way to the next destination that ruckus happened.

No, he couldn't abide Katie being up late into the night tending other men.

Too many shades of my mother. Even if I know Katie isn't doing anything wrong.

There was only one way to handle the situation. No matter how many times he went around it, he came back to the same solution.

And, once he'd made his plans, only then did his mind allow sleep.

~

*T*he following morning, Katie arose and opened her doors for breakfast at five a.m. It was an ungodly hour, but so much of her revenues came from the cowboys who arrived in town looking for a big, hot meal to begin their herding work for the day. Then they'd move onto the next town, gathering cattle along the way.

James came down at six and settled into his usual seat. She gave him a nod, but didn't officially take his order for she knew he always ordered the same breakfast along with a pot of coffee.

She'd just settled his food on the table before him, the huge empty tray balanced on one hand, when he took her free hand, raised it to his lips and kissed it.

"Thank you, Katie."

Katie tugged her hand away, her face flushed with heat. "You're welcome, Marshal."

"Thought I told you James, not my title."

"Sorry. After last night, I wasn't sure you wanted me to."

"I do. Nothing has changed since last night."

"Including how you feel about my business hours?"

"Absolutely. It's not safe to be open all hours of the night."

She sighed. "Well, I'm not going to argue with you. You are entitled to your opinion, though none of this should really matter to you."

"I care about you, Katie," he said haltingly.

She gulped. "You do?"

He nodded. "We need to talk tonight."

"Yes, I believe we do."

"Later then," he said.

Rising from his chair, James stunned her with a kiss on her cheek. Then he sat down and began eating.

Katie backed away, her hand brushing the skin on her cheek. She bumped into the empty table behind her. James looked up and met her eyes. He gave her a knowing grin before focusing on his meal again.

In the kitchen, Katie swiped a hank of hair back off her forehead, glanced down at her dark blue calico dress, happy she'd worn her best one today. She was on edge the rest of the day and evening at the thought of having a discussion with him once she'd closed for the night. For once she wanted to close her doors at ten and regretted keeping them open until midnight.

A little before midnight, three cowboys she didn't know strolled into the Palace. She met them at the door. "Gentlemen, we're closing for the evening. We'll open again at five in the morning. You're welcome to stop by for breakfast."

One gruff, elderly cowboy said, "Heard there was a hot poker game happening here, ma'am."

"It ended an hour ago."

A dark-haired, handsome, younger man stepped past her. "Well then, we'll just have to have ourselves our own game." He headed for a poker table in the corner and threw over his shoulder, "And a bottle of whiskey would be mighty fine, too."

"But—"

All of sudden, the other two men brushed past her and seated themselves at the table. The younger one picked up the cards and proceeded to shuffle them.

Katie had followed them to the table and now stood beside it with her hands on her hips. "I said I'm closed."

"Hear that, Stan?" the elder cowboy said, his tone amused. "The lady says she's closed."

"Then how come the doors weren't locked?" Stan said.

"You came in just as I planned to do exactly that," Katie snapped.

The two older men just stared at her. Stan said, "We'll be leaving when we're good and ready."

Katie heard the cold anger in his voice but dug in her heels. "You're good and ready now."

Stan snarled, "We ain't leavin'. Now fetch us that whiskey, woman."

Prickles of fear rushed up Katie's spine at his angry tone.

"All right," she said. "One game only and one drink, then you're leaving."

"Fine," Stan said.

Half an hour passed. The men played and drank. And drank. The entire bottle of whiskey disappeared, and Stan asked for a second one.

"No."

Katie rose from her seat behind the bar and made her way to the front door, opened it and raised one eyebrow.

The three men looked at her, then slowly laid down their cards. The older cowboys left, their walk lurching due to inebriation. Stan followed slowly. When he reached Katie's side, he paused to give her a lewd grin. "Come on, sweet thing. I hear tell this Palace is a brothel, too, ain't it? How about you and me making a night of it upstairs?" He hauled her into his arms and kissed her. His slobbering lips slid across her mouth, pressing hard. She tasted blood in her mouth.

She managed to jerk out of his arms and yell, "James! Help me!"

CHAPTER 6

*J*ames lurched upright in bed, waking from a deep sleep. He sat there and slid his fingers through his hair, listening, alert for any signs of danger. All was quiet.

He lay back down and frowned. Hearing Katie call for help must have been a nightmare. He hadn't slept well last night, once he'd decided to ask Katie to marry him. And he sure as hell hadn't meant to fall deeply asleep before she closed up for the night.

He sat up again as the feeling came over him that something just wasn't right. That was when he heard her screams. "Help, please! James!"

That was no nightmare! He flung himself out of bed and down the stairs, hiking up his long john pants the inch they'd crept down along the way. His blood boiled when he found Katie sprawled on her back over the bar with a cowboy hunched over her, oddly silent and unmoving. The cowboy palmed her breasts, one in each hand. *Touching my future wife!*

His fury mounted when he saw the man had flung her skirts up so they covered her face. Her white stockings, once held up by her garters, were down around her ankles, her tiny black shoestrings untied.

James charged across the room just as the cowboy tore Katie's bloomers down, exposing her sweet curves. He reached the man and yanked him off Katie, downing him with an upper cut to the jaw and a left to the gut. The creep was young, though, and was out only seconds before springing up again. James faced him with a scowl. Anger rippled through him when he saw the gun in the man's hand. *Damn!* In his rush to reach Katie, James realized he'd left his gun in his room.

"Katie," he called softly without turning toward her, his gaze necessarily fixed on the gun, "slide down to the floor behind the bar and stay down."

He didn't hear a sound behind him, nor did she acknowledge him.

My God, she couldn't be dead! He hadn't heard any gunshots, but then there were other ways a man could kill a small woman like Katie.

Cool, stay cool.

He faced his adversary.

"What are you, her boyfriend or something?" the cowboy said, his voice slurred with drunkenness.

"Yes," James said. "I'm also the law in Bozeman. Leave while you have the chance."

The man's laugh made James even more furious.

"Well, look at you," the man snarled. "A lawman without a gun and nearly naked?" His laughter grew hysterical. "I was just showin' the little lady a good time, that's all. Problem was she didn't wanna have a good time right now. Wanted me to leave. I had to get rough with her." He frowned and swayed on his feet as James gauged his state of inebriation.

"What did you do to her?" James demanded.

"Cuffed her upside the head, that's all." The man backed along the length of the bar, heading for the back way out, James figured. The bastard had hit her—hit Katie—upside the head, hence why she wasn't moving.

James raised his fists and strode toward the drunken cowboy. "Drop the gun and fight fair—like a man should."

"Hell, no! You take me for a fool?" Stan stopped at the end of the bar and aimed the gun at James. "If I don't shoot you, you'll arrest me. I ain't got nothing to lose."

~

Katie had been feigning unconsciousness, giving herself time to think with a cool head. Through her narrow-slit eyes, she saw James with his back to her and the cowboy at the opposite end of the bar. She eased her skirts back down as unobtrusively as she could, turned over and slid down to the floor behind the bar. Wriggling her bloomers up, she pulled herself to her knees and found herself facing the bartender's special on the shelf—a loaded Colt .45.

She picked it up, praying she had a steady hand and dead-on aim. Rising slowly, she faced the cowboy, heard him say, "Drop your drawers, lawman. I want to see why the ladies in every town I pass through are in love with the town lawman."

"Drop, James!" Katie shouted.

Without hesitation, he did, and the blast from a gun filled the room. Katie held the gun so tightly, she barely felt the kick-back. The cowboy fell flat on his back, howling.

❧

*J*ames rose to a crouching position, moved to the cowboy and saw blood spurting from his thigh. Quickly, he removed a bandana from the cowboy's pocket, folded it in a long strip, wound it around the thigh above the injury and yanked it as tight as he could.

The man's scream gave him pure satisfaction—the least he owed Katie for his outlaw behavior. The bandana should hold and staunch the blood flow, James decided, until the doctor arrived.

Knowing the cowboy wouldn't be going anywhere, James relaxed, then swiveling around and, rising, he strode to her side. He removed the smoking gun from Katie's hand, set it down on the bar and took her in his arms.

The sound of pounding feet on the steps let James know the other boarders had heard the gunshot. Two cowboys James knew tore down the steps in their long johns. "Go for the doc," James said as Katie huddled against his chest, her face buried there.

With quick nods, they took in the scene, then headed upstairs. Returning within moments dressed, they left the Palace.

"He's dead, isn't he?" Katie whispered, her voice trembling.

James eased her away slightly, and his heart lurched at the agony on her face. Tears slid down her cheeks. "No, but I'd say he's not going to be walking around any time soon. Damn, woman, who taught you how to shoot?"

She sniffed. "My mama, but this is the first time I've shot at anything, or anyone, that was alive."

James admired her in his gaze. "I wish I could meet your mama."

Looking up at him through her tears, she said, "She lives in Texas and comes to visit once a year. If you're still here when she comes, you'll meet her, I'm sure."

The doctor arrived with a curt nod at James, the two cowboys right behind him. James addressed his friends. "Stay with the doc. If there's any trouble, you'll find me out back on the porch."

With his arm around Katie's back, he walked with her down the hall that led to the kitchen, then out the back door. "We need to have a talk, darlin'."

She nodded. On the porch, he brought her close to him again. He cradled his hands around her face and said, "You scared the living hell out of me, lying on the bar so motionless."

"Playing 'possum', you mean?"

"I saw the blood…"

"Yes, he did slap me, but not all that hard. I knew if I had any chance of surviving, I needed to pretend he'd done greater damage."

He nodded, taking a deep breath. "You need a man to protect you, Katie."

She jerked her chin from his hands. "I beg your pardon! I believe *I* saved *your* hide this night, didn't I, Marshal?"

That gave him pause. Then, leaning close to her so that his lips were mere inches from hers, he said softly, "You sure did, sweetheart." He pressed his mouth against hers for a moment, then backed away. Her eyes were opened wide. "I should have been the one to save you. But, with you saving me, things have changed."

～

Katie ogled him in shock. "Pardon me?"

"I want you to be my wife, Katie. And I planned on continuing to use the excuse that you needed my protection. Which you obviously do not."

He turned away and took two steps. In profile, Katie saw the look of dejection on his face.

"But I do!"

He whipped around, his brow raised. "You do…?"

"Need your protection, I mean."

He shook his head at her. "Now, Katie, don't go all soft and feeling sorry for me..."

"I need your friendship, James. Rather, I want it, and your love."

"Same here, sweetheart," he said softly, drawing near.

She stepped toward him with tears in her eyes and waited for him to make the next move.

"I—I have a question to ask you, of a personal nature," he said, clearing his throat.

She smiled gently. "About...?"

"A personal proposition. Marry me, sweet Katie." He wound an arm around her waist, pulling her against his lanky frame. He murmured, watching her face carefully, "You look surprised."

Katie grasped his strong forearms and grinned. "I am surprised, very much so."

"Surprised that I love you?"

She shook her head and laughed. "No, surprised that your manly pride allowed you to accept my proposal."

"Wait a minute. *I* proposed to *you*, little lady."

"But only after I confessed my love for you first." She frowned. "As a matter of fact, you haven't said a word about love."

Gathering her close again, he said, "Each night, as I laid on my bed listening to you close up the Palace, I knew I was falling in love with you. Knew I needed you to be my wife. And I'll tell you now, I never thought to find love and marriage in my life. I couldn't deny my own heart when I met you."

He moved back and gazed into her eyes. Katie saw a gentleness mixed with long suppressed desire in his eyes. "Why didn't you think you'd ever marry?" she asked.

James lowered his head until his lips nuzzled the side of her neck. She melted into his arms. In between kisses, she heard him say, "Because of my work, I'd always thought I'd worry about some criminal going after my wife in retribution against me. I decided if I wanted you to be my wife, if I ever wanted to have happiness in my life, I'd need to suppress those fears. Once we're married I'll tell you more. I'll tell you about my mother, and the hard life she lived. The one I wanted to save her from but couldn't. But we won't talk about it now. We've time."

She traced his lips with her fingers, understanding that men had a hard time speaking of sad things in life. Once he became more comfortable with her as his wife, Katie felt sure he'd open up to her. "Did you decide all this tonight, James?"

He laughed. "No, I've been thinking about it ever since the judge found you innocent of any wrong-doing. I've loved you since the moment I came to town and set eyes on you. What cinched my feelings was when you invited me back to the Palace after I arrested you wrongly, offering me back my room. Your acceptance and forgiveness humbled me, Katie."

"Forgiving you was easy, because of my own love for you," she said softly.

He tightened his hold on her, slid a hand behind her head, angling it to accept his kiss. Lordy, but the man knew how to kiss! Katie groaned and wound her arms around his neck. He kissed her long and hard, soft and gentle, taking her breath away. And, when he released her, she wanted him to take her in his arms again.

Shaking a bit, she stepped back with tears filling her eyes. They slid down her cheeks when he got down on one knee and looked up at her with an intensity she'd never seen in the eyes of any man. "Will you marry me, Katie my love?"

She couldn't deny her heart. "Yes!" she choked out. "And will you marry me, Marshal Freeman?"

"I think I will at that, Miss Katie, just as soon as the judge is back in town."

THE END

ANNIE AND THE OUTLAW

Recently released from prison for a crime he didn't commit, Cane Smith returns to Bozeman to claim the son he's never met, only to discover the boy's mother is dead and the boy has been adopted by a rancher and is being raised by his twenty-year-old daughter, Annie.

When Annie refuses to part with the boy, Cane makes her an offer: Miss Annie will have to marry him if she wants to keep the boy in her life. Annie will do anything to keep her little boy with her—but can she live with the hard, rough Cane Smith?

PROLOGUE

Christmas Day, 1887
Huntsville, Texas Prison

Cane Smith had a son.
A son.

The letter from Mae Franklin, dated a year ago, had found its way to him. During the six and a half years he'd spent in prison, he'd never received a single letter until now. There was a note tucked inside the envelope with Mae's from Judge Simon Hopkins, the man who'd sentenced him to prison. Mae had written the letter but had never sent it. In Bozeman, Montana, U.S. Marshal James Freeman, had found the letter addressed to Cane after Mae had been found dead in her home. She hadn't included an address but Freeman had recognized Cane's name from his trial and passed the note on to the judge.

Cane learned that a boy being raised in Bozeman by the Callahan family resembled Cane. The boy's mother, Giselle Hanks, had been a prostitute. She'd spent nights in the arms of many men, including Cane. On her deathbed, Giselle confessed to her friend Mae how she was certain Cane was her baby's father. Mae had asked her how she knew for certain, after being with so many men. Giselle's last murmured words convinced Mae. Only with Cane had she left herself unprotected, for she loved him and believed he loved her.

Tears welled in his eyes at the same time hope filled his heart. He had a son, a reason to live when he'd wanted to die. After spending almost seven Christmases in prison, he had a purpose in finding a way out of this hellhole. He folded the letter and stuffed it into his shirt pocket. He lay back on his lumpy cot and imagined being a father—imagined what his life would be like with a son.

His happiness fled quickly at the thought of his life up to this point. How would he take care of the boy, even if he were released? He'd been a wandering cowboy for years before going to jail. He was twenty-eight years old and had accomplished nothing good in his life. Nothing except for fathering a child.

Cane thought back to the day he'd been sentenced to twenty years in prison—for a train robbery he hadn't committed. Without proof, he never had a hope in hell of clearing himself. The few folks on the train who'd witnessed the robbery had accused him.

Was there a chance of turning it around now? He had to find a way. Sitting up with renewed determination, he decided he'd find a way out of prison and claim the boy. He came to his feet. "Hey! Jailer!"

The only reply he received was from the inmate in the cell to his right. "You prick! You woke me up."

Old Warren Strom was no threat. Truth be told, he was Cane's only friend in this godforsaken place. "Sorry, Strom, I need to see a guard."

"What for?"

"I need to write a letter and don't have any paper or pencil."

A hand holding a scrap of paper, a yellowed envelope and a broken stub of a pencil appeared out of the bars at the front. Cane reached over and grabbed them. "Thanks. I owe you."

Strom muttered gruffly, "Now shut the hell up and let a man get some sleep."

Settling down on his bunk again, Cane wrote back to the judge. When he finished, his heart felt weighed down in grief as he thought about sweet Giselle who'd died, strangled by some drunken cowboy passing through Bozeman shortly after the birth of their son. The poor woman hadn't had any chance in life, having been born of a prostitute, the only home she'd known a brothel.

He'd been no better than any other man who'd swaggered through her boudoir door. After living on the plains for weeks at a time, spending a night with a prostitute was one of the few joys in life a cowboy had to look forward to when he came to town. A few visits to Giselle, and he knew he'd fallen in love.

The last time he'd seen her he promised he'd return once he saved enough money. Then he'd marry her and take her away with him. He thought of her tear-filled eyes and the longing in them as she'd nodded. It was only after he left town that he realized she hadn't believed him for an instant. He guessed she'd received similar offers from other cowboys who hadn't kept their promises. He'd meant to keep his and would have if he hadn't gone to jail. Sadness filled him then as he thought of Giselle dying before he could show her he meant his declaration of love.

Cane hadn't been able to save the woman he loved, but, by God, he would find a way out of prison and find his son.

He thought about Judge Hopkins, the man who'd deliberated over his trial. He'd come to know the judge a bit the few times he'd come to Bozeman before being accused of the train robbery. Had sat and drank a beer with him and played a few hands of cards. From that little interaction, he knew the judge was a good, honest man. Before Cane went to prison, after his trial, the judge had taken him aside and said he believed in his innocence. Unfortunately, the jury hadn't. Then the judge had told him to keep his ears and eyes open while in prison.

Prisoners came and went—none of them shedding any new information—until a month ago, when two new prisoners had arrived. Prisoners were allowed out of their cells only a few hours a day. Cane was watchful, planting himself near these men to hear more talk whenever he could. The longer he listened to them, and the more he watched them, he began to recognize them. They'd been two of several cowboys working a cattle run with him before he was arrested. One of the men bore a striking resemblance to Cane.

In the letter he'd just written, Cane asked Judge Hopkins to open his case once more, based on what he'd heard. Meanwhile, he would keep his ears open for more information. He'd befriend the two men, hoping they'd take him into their confidence.

CHAPTER 1

October 1888
Bozeman, Montana

*A*nnie Callahan sat patiently, waiting for her seven-year-old-brother, Mark, to leave the schoolhouse, even though she had chores to do at the ranch. Waiting for Mark was never a waste of time. Besides, these precious moments gave her the opportunity to mentally organize all of the tasks she needed to complete in preparation for the holidays.

She'd already started sewing chambray and woolen shirts for the ranch hands, a tradition that had been passed on to her from her mother, and a task she thoroughly enjoyed. She still had several more shirts to sew for the men, plus the new pants and shirts for her brother. She smiled. Unlike the ranch workers, Mark wasn't as excited about getting new shirts. His Christmas wish list included a gun, slingshot, a bow and arrow, and a tomahawk. The thought of Mark handling a weapon made her shudder.

Suddenly, like lightning on a stormy night, a premonition struck Annie from where she sat outside the schoolhouse in her wagon. She saw herself sitting on the ground. A man's shadowy form stood over her. She fought to remain conscious; fought to ascertain the man's identity.

No!

She didn't want to know him!

Pull yourself out of it, Annie!

Forcing away the presence, the man disappeared and sanity returned. Breathing easier, she blinked several times. Looking around at the calm, peaceful schoolyard, she breathed a sigh of relief. She was still sitting on the bench in her wagon, her horse's reins gripped tightly in her hands.

She tugged her shawl close around her shoulders to stave off the cold, wishing Miss O'Gara would release the class. The temperature had been tolerable during the day but, with the lowering of the sun, the air had grown chilly.

Suddenly, searing pain pierced her skull. She slammed her eyelids shut and collapsed against the back of her seat as the premonition returned, full force this time.

A man with a muscular build stood over her as she clutched Mark in her arms. Her eyes widened in horror when he bent closer. She saw nothing but his shadowy form, unable to make out his features. He reached for her brother, big hands stretched out, fingers clawed. Screams tore from her throat. Her mind screamed, Run! *But she couldn't. Her feet seemed to be locked in place. The man wrestled Mark away from her and fled, her brother's screams piercing the air. Sobbing inconsolably, she remained helpless as the child's shouts dimmed.*

Annie's breathing calmed as the premonition faded away. Nevertheless, she kept her eyes closed. No, Mark was safe. He was here, in school.

She had no desire to look into the future, no desire to feel any pride or satisfaction in the "gift" God had given her. Why He'd chosen her, she had no idea. Due to skepticism in town from some, fear and suspicion from others, she'd learned to keep the premonitions to herself. She guessed if hunting witches were in fashion, she'd be gone from this earth by now.

A door creaked, and Annie looked up to find the door wide open. Then the schoolchildren poured from the building. Still, Mark didn't appear, but she knew the teacher was helping with his arithmetic for a few minutes after school.

She looked around again and saw a man walking toward her. Seeing him pause as he watched the children scattering in all directions, she shivered.

With the sun low in the sky behind him, she saw only his silhouette. Apprehension settled in. Could it be the man she'd just seen in the vision? The man's hair was dark as the night, framed by a black Stetson. The closer he came, the more she saw of him. She noted that the color of his hair was identical to Mark's.

"Miss Annie Callahan?"

"Yes." At his low, raspy tone, she froze in her seat. "Are you here for a student? I'm afraid they've all left for the day."

Removing his hat, he strode toward her, then stopped beside her wagon. "I'm here for my son."

"As I said, they've all gone home. I'm just waiting for my brother."

His son, he'd said. She knew everyone in Bozeman, but not this man. Her heart stalled at the handsome, square-jawed face. His dark eyes were hard and searching. His finely chiseled lips made her wonder for an unbidden moment what their touch would feel like. She also caught the weariness etched in his face, and the thick, dark hair that bristled along his jaw and on his chin. He appeared as though he'd been away from civilization for a while. A shave and haircut were certainly in order.

She swept him another look from head to toe. Never had she seen such a tall man save for her neighbor, Jed Porter. Lately Jed had gotten pushy about trying to court her, forcing her to be firmer in declining his suit.

The man drew even closer, and she stiffened once more in her seat.

She stood up despite the awkwardness in the wagon. "Who are you?" Because no evil thoughts entered her mind, no premonitions concerning him filled her heart and soul, just those few shivers, she guessed this man wasn't violent and would do her no harm. But then she hadn't seen the features—only the shadowy bulk—of the man in the premonition she'd had...

"My name is Cane Smith, and I've come for my son."

She frowned. "What's his name, sir?"

"Your family named him Mark."

~

Cane Smith grimaced when he saw her face drained of all color. "Miss Callahan? Maybe you should have a seat."

"Yes," she whispered.

She just stood there, showing no signs of heeding his advice. Reaching up, he gently took her elbow and pulled her back down on the bench seat. Breathing in deep, he enjoyed the sweet honey scent of this pretty, fair-haired young woman.

Eight months of befriending the bastards he believed committed the crime he'd been accused of had finally afforded Cane the proof he needed. In front of several prisoners and a few guards, the braggarts confessed they had indeed robbed that train. The prisoners and guards had promised Cane they'd stick up for him when he went to court with the new evidence. In late August, Cane had his day in court and, after all testimony was given, was finally released. He made it a point to find Judge Hopkins once he arrived in Bozeman to thank him, and to claim his son.

Heaven help the man or woman who stood in his way—even this Callahan family who'd taken the boy in.

Upon his arrival in Bozeman, he'd inquired in town about the Callahan family. Katie Freeman, proprietor of Katie's Palace, informed him that the Callahan family lived several miles outside of town on a spread called the Moonstruck Ranch. She also informed him Annie worked at Katie's Palace and had just gone to pick up her brother at the schoolhouse on the outskirts of town. Cane left Bozeman on foot, since he had no carriage or horse, to meet Miss Annie Callahan and his son.

He settled his hat on his head, watching her gather her composure. When she rose, he assisted her down from the wagon. She stood before him, the sweetest confection of womanhood he'd ever seen, with tears in her eyes.

He couldn't see much of her since she had averted her gaze. After a moment, she visibly squared her shoulders, tossed back her head and glared up at him. "Mark may be your son by birth, but my father and I have raised him since infancy. He's a Callahan now."

Cane felt his face turn hot as he straightened to his full height. First irritation, then anger, flared through him but it quickly subsided. If he'd learned anything in prison, it had been the virtue of patience, which would serve him well for the rest of his life. Long gone were the angry, impetuous days of young manhood.

"He's a Smith, and he'll soon learn the fact of the matter. And there's nothing you can do to stop me from telling him."

She jammed her index finger into his chest. He stumbled back a step out of sheer surprise.

"No, you can't claim him! You aren't the one who fed him, clothed him and changed his diapers. You aren't the one who stayed up all night caring for him when he was ill and burning up with fever," she choked out.

She reacted much as a mama bear would when her cub was threatened. He liked that; liked how she had so much love for his son. It meant that she and her father had cared for him well. Cane ached for her...just for a moment.

It was time to make the woman understand he wasn't backing down, though he had to admit he admired her lack of fear of him.

He took a step forward, and she backed up a step but still kept her chin tilted up at him. *Stubborn woman!* He saw unshed tears sparkling in her eyes and groaned inside. Tears were the worst weapon she could use on a man, especially this one.

Cane tried reasoning with her. "By no choice of my own did I not claim him earlier. I want to experience everything I can now. It's my right. He's mine." Cane had been born illegitimate himself and never knew his father. He wouldn't allow that to happen to Mark.

"No!" she wailed. "My father adopted Mark. He won't let him go without a fight."

"I understand. If I were your father, I'd do the same. If you don't mind, Miss Callahan, I'd like to speak to him now, as soon as Mark comes out."

Cane wound his hands around her tiny waist and lifted her easily onto the seat of her wagon. Off balance, she plunked down hard on the seat and grimaced. She gasped but held her tongue. Sitting in the driver seat, her eyes focused straight ahead, tears tracking down her cheeks.

"He might fight me, but, when all is said and done, Mark will be mine. I came all the way from Texas to claim my son."

Cane understood men better than women. He'd spent most of his life with them and quite frankly knew little about the fairer sex—with the exception of prostitutes who'd serviced him when he needed a woman. He'd spent months crossing the country without fair company, except for the occasional town he passed through. And, when the opportunity arose to spend a night in a willing woman's arms, Cane, like most cowboys, took it.

He guessed, in the end, Tom Callahan would give Mark up. He would understand that the boy belonged with his true father.

"I need to get home," she whispered.

"I'm riding with you, so scoot on over."

She scanned the area, then looked at him. "How did you get here?"

"I walked."

"From the stagecoach depot?"

He nodded.

"Why, that's three miles!"

"A mere Sunday stroll," he said dryly. "I told you that I'm claiming my son. Nothing can keep me from him. Now move on over."

She obliged him.

Good. The woman was sensible and smart. He smiled to himself. She was far from the quiet type. The element of surprise had changed what he guessed was usually a confident, bossy woman. But he'd also heard the softness in her voice, especially when she spoke about Mark.

He wasn't fond of the name Mark, but hell, the boy was nearly eight now. Mark he'd remain.

The school door swung open, and a child's voice shouted, "Annie!"

He centered his attention on a boy running toward them.

Mark! Cane recognized himself in the boy who had to be his son tearing down the walkway with black hair flying and dark brown eyes filled with joy. Then he noticed how Mark's gaze was riveted on Annie. Turning toward the woman next to him, Cane's heart wrenched at the aching love he saw on her face. For a fleeting moment, he had doubts about taking the child away from her and the only life he'd known since birth.

He hardened his heart. He deserved some happiness, some love in life, damn it all. He would find it with his son.

He hungrily watched Mark while the boy ran to Annie's side of the wagon. She helped him scramble up onto the seat, then hugged him. Cane watched her take him into her arms, saw her breathe in deep to catch his little boy scent. Once again, Cane's heart ached to hold the boy, but he couldn't. He would have to take things slowly.

"You learning your arithmetic?" She tousled the mop of dark hair.

Mark nodded then pulled out of her arms and jammed his hands against the sides of his head. "No scrubbing my head! It's not bath time."

She laughed.

Cane was caught, mesmerized by how she looked even younger and prettier, as she grinned at his son.

The boy slanted his gaze away from Annie, turning serious when he faced Cane. His son stared at him for the longest time, his gaze riveted on him. After a while, he said, "You have black hair like me."

~

*A*nnie's heart started racing at Mark's words, and she saw the curious look in his eyes. It'd only been in recent months that he'd questioned why his father and sister had blonde hair while his own was black. Until he grew older, Annie and her father had decided they'd wait to tell him about his parentage, though they had informed him in the past year that they'd adopted him. She'd easily managed to divert his attention in the past but guessed it wouldn't be easy for much longer. Especially if Cane Smith had his way.

"Yes, it is. Almost the same exact color." Cane held out his hand. "I'm Cane Smith, a friend of your sister's. I'll bet you're Mark, aren't you?"

"Yep." Mark pumped Cane's hand, squeezing it as tight as he could. "Mark Callahan."

Cane's smile widened while he shook the boy's hand. Annie couldn't help but notice that Mark was a "chip off the old block." Releasing Cane's hand, Mark looked at Annie again.

"Can we go home? I'm hungry!"

"Of course! Mr. Smith is driving us home tonight. He'll be having supper with us. How does that sound?"

"Great!" Mark shouted.

"Then let's be on our way," she said.

Mark settled between the two of them on the wooden seat and Cane snapped the reins to get the horse moving.

"What do you think Mrs. Williams made us for supper?" Mark asked.

"Mrs. Williams is under the weather today, so I'm cooking supper, honey."

Mark's eyes widened. "You are?" At her nod, he yelled, "Yippee! I like your cooking a lot better."

"Mark! Mrs. Williams is a wonderful cook."

"But not like you, Annie." The boy turned a brilliant smile on Cane. "Annie makes the best fried chicken, and taters and cornbread."

"Sounds mighty good," Cane said.

To Annie's mind, the man looked about ready to salivate. She wondered when he'd eaten last. She glanced at Mark. "How did you know I was making chicken?"

"Saw Pa kill a chicken this morning."

"You watched?"

"Yup, sure did. You shoulda seen Pa wring his neck, then chop its—"

"Enough. I believe you. Father knows I don't want you watching such violence."

"It's not violence," Cane interrupted.

Her eyes widened. "Excuse me?"

"Nope. It's a natural life cycle for an animal that we use for sustenance. Mark needs to learn these things. Your Pa's right to show him."

She frowned. "That may be, but not yet. Mark's only seven years old."

"Old enough." Cane looked at Mark. "While your sis is cooking, we can talk and get to know each other."

Giving Cane a coy look, Mark asked, "You play checkers?"

Cane nodded. "Sure do."

"Woo-hoo!" Mark whooped with delight.

Annie smiled at Mark's exuberance and glanced at Cane. He wore the biggest smile. The stone-faced, taciturn man's expression softened as he gazed at Mark. She found it hard to believe him capable of having a soft bone in his body—for anything or anyone.

The wagon rumbled through town. They were just passing Katie's Palace when Annie saw her friend Katie Freeman step outside with a broom, her two-year-old daughter, Melanie, on her heels with a smaller broom in hand.

Mark hollered, "Hi, Mrs. Freeman! Hi, Melanie!"

Katie waved and called out, "How you doing, Mark? Annie?"

"Stop a moment, please," Annie said.

Cane stopped the horse in front of Katie.

Katie leaned on her broom. "Any chance you can serve on Saturday, Annie?"

"Serve, not cook?"

"Doc says since I'll be having this baby any day, I need to put up my feet more often." She grinned. "Tough to do running this place though. After I have the baby, I know I'll need even more help. Judge Hoskins knows of a woman who needs employment so I'll be meeting with her soon. For now, it would help if you served and I cooked. Think you can help me out on Sundays, too?"

"I'll tell Father that you need me the extra hours. Are you and James prepared for the new baby?"

Just then, Katie's husband, James Freeman, ambled outside. Pausing beside Katie, he took the broom from her hands and set it against the building. He scolded her, "Didn't doc say you need bed rest, not work?"

Katie rolled her eyes. "Yes, but I'm going stir crazy!"

He hugged her as close as he could with her expanded stomach. "I know, but it won't be for much longer." He glanced up then. "Hey, Annie. How are you?"

"Just fine, thank you." Annie looked between the two of them; saw the mock scowl on James's face and the frown on Katie's brow. "You two are more than ready for that baby to be born, aren't you?"

"Baby!" Melanie exclaimed, excitement in her eyes.

James lifted Melanie in his arms, laughed and rubbed noses with her.

Annie laughed, marveling at the likeness between Katie and Melanie. Almost nine months to the day after James and Katie married, they had Melanie. It took another few years of praying for another child before Katie was pregnant again. Annie looked at James and saw his curiosity as he stared at Cane.

Where are my manners?

"Oh, uh, Katie, James? This is Cane Smith, newly arrived from Texas."

James stepped forward and reached across Annie. "We've met before, briefly," James said.

Cane took James's hand. "Thanks for passing on the letter to the judge. I appreciate it."

"No problem." James stepped back from the wagon and looked at Annie, then Cane. "How long you going to be in Bozeman?"

"I'm staying permanently. Looking for some land to raise cattle and horses."

"When you get a chance, take a look at the Ames place south of here twenty miles or so. It just went up for a sale. It's a prime piece of property, so I don't expect it to be unsold for long."

Cane nodded. "Thanks for the tip."

"We need to get home," Annie said. She smiled at Katie. "See you Saturday."

"I really do appreciate your help, Annie." Katie's gaze slid to Cane. "So how long have the two of you known each other?"

James warned, "Honey…"

Annie laughed. "I should have mentioned that we just met. Cane has business with Father."

"I see," Katie said.

Annie met Katie's curious eyes and tried communicating through her own. *I'll tell you later.* "We have to get home for supper."

"I'll see you Saturday then."

Cane tipped his hat to Katie and a nod to James before slapping the horse's rump with the leads. The sun had nearly set by the time they reached the Moonstruck Ranch. Mark scrambled down from the wagon and tore into the house. "Pa! Pa! We're home, and Annie's cooking us supper!"

Annie went to leave the wagon and found Cane standing with his arms raised to help her down. She bit her lower lip with indecision. He made the decision for her when he wound his hands around her waist and easily plucked her from her seat. "I don't bite," he said softly.

She raised her brow. "Oh! That's good to hear."

Cane chuckled. Annie's face heated up in embarrassment.

On the ride home, she'd thought about the premonition at the schoolhouse. Could this be the man threatening to take Mark from her?

CHAPTER 2

$\mathcal{C}$ ane liked the fact she was cautious around him. Caution had been his friend on more than one occasion. He took Annie's arm, ready to release her if she showed any signs of reluctance. When she didn't, he was surprised. He frowned then and thought most everyone who crossed his path, before and after his imprisonment, was wary around him.

She held up her skirt as she climbed the steps ahead of him. Cane gulped when he saw her slim, delicate ankles. Lordy, but she was a beauty, and such a lady. Reaching around her, he opened the door to the big ranch house, and she swept in ahead of him.

He stood uneasily in the hallway with his hat in his hand. The interior of the house held a gracious yet rustic quality, same as the exterior. Highly polished wood floors smelled of wax. To the right was a large, square dining room with a beautifully crafted table and chairs covered in fabric-tufted cushions. A chandelier dripping with small crystals shone with a warm sparkle. He saw several open doors to his left and guessed these led to other rooms such as a parlor, library and, of course, the kitchen.

"Wait here while I find my father," Annie said and rushed down the hallway.

Suddenly he felt self-conscious in his dusty dungarees and sweat-stained chambray shirt. He touched his bristly jaw-line and grimaced. He should have gotten a place in town where he could shave and clean up before he went hunting for his son. Too late now.

He saw the second door down the hall open. A short, muscular man with blonde hair and graying temples, dressed in shirtsleeves strode toward him. Annie followed. Cane braced himself, ready to battle the man until he caught a twinkle in the older man's eyes despite his serious expression. Cane liked Annie's father immediately.

"Annie doesn't often bring company home." The man offered his hand, and Cane shook it. "I'm Tom Callahan."

"Cane Smith. Annie probably told you we need to talk."

Callahan nodded.

While the man didn't make it obvious, Cane caught the older man's swift, assessing gaze and straightened up, silently waiting for the older man's condemnation.

"Come into my library."

Cane followed Callahan, Annie at his side. Outside the library door, he stopped short and took his daughter's hand. "Go see to supper, honey."

"But—"

"I'll let you know all that we talked about later."

Cane saw the gentle but firm look on Callahan's face. Cane expected fireworks to start any moment. Cane had seen his share of headstrong women in his life and he expected this spitfire to protest. Annie's face clouded with indecision, then she gave a curt nod. Surprised, he watched her turn on her heel to leave them.

"Mr. Smith?"

Cane felt heat rush into his cheeks when he found Callahan waiting, watching him. Cane lurched into a library, filled floor to ceiling with books on three walls of the room. Astonished, Cane could only stare at the volumes, his eyes and mind eager to delve into them one at a time.

Behind him, Callahan said, "Please, sit down. So, you claim to be Mark's natural father. What proof do you have?" Callahan took a seat behind a desk.

Cane set his hat down on a corner of the desk and sank into a seat across from Callahan, digging inside his shirt pocket. He pulled out the letter encased in its envelope and handed it over. He watched the older man peruse the address on the envelope before removing the letter. He unfolded it and read it. Within moments, he looked at Cane and heaved a deep sigh.

"It appears what you say is true." Chagrined, he added, "Truthfully, from the moment I laid eyes on you, I knew Mark was your blood kin. You know it'll be difficult to pull him away from Annie, don't you?"

Cane nodded. "She seems real attached to the boy."

"Correct observation. I am, too, of course. Why were you in prison, son?"

"Train robbery."

"I'm assuming you didn't do it since you're a free man now. Or are you?"

Cane didn't expect the question and hesitated in replying for a moment. "It was a case of mistaken identity. When I finally had the evidence to clear myself, I wrote to Judge Hopkins, who re-opened the case and freed me."

"After all these years," Callahan said. "Wish you'd gotten out sooner. We've had Mark with us since a few days after his birth. Needless to say, he's part of our family."

"I know. I'm sorry." Cane's eyes felt gritty. "I've no home and not much to offer Mark, but I am his father. And I promise I'll do everything I can to make a good home for him."

"But will you be able to love him?" Callahan softly inquired.

"I already do."

Callahan studied Cane. "I believe you. So how do you plan on making a home for him?"

"I like Bozeman. I'm thinking of settling here. I heard there was land for sale. Have you heard of any good acreage?"

"For sure there are several parcels. I'll get hold of a newspaper so you can check them out. I noticed you came here with Annie and gather you've no horse or wagon?"

"No. I'll buy a horse in town tomorrow."

"I've horses for sale you may want to take a look at."

"I'll do that. Now maybe you can give me some advice as to how to get Mark from your daughter's clutches."

Callahan laughed. "I'll talk to her, but you know she's got a real stubborn streak."

"Hmm, she didn't give you any grief about not sitting in on this meeting."

"Yes, I've got to admit her compliance surprised me."

"How so?"

"It means one of two things. She's getting' her eggs in order and making plans to fight us, or she's in agreement with us."

"I've a feeling it's the first one."

"You may be right." Callahan rose from his chair. "This may be easier than it seems. We recently informed Mark that we'd adopted him as an infant."

"That's good," Cane said.

"Don't discount the fact though that it'll still be difficult pulling Mark away from the only family and home he's ever known. I suggest we do this in stages."

Cane frowned. "Now how would we do that? We tell him or we don't, and the second is not an option."

Callahan nodded. "I understand, but it would behoove all of us to take this slow and easy. We don't want to frighten him. He'll be confused enough once we do tell him."

Cane stood as well. "Sounds reasonable, and, since I do plan on staying in the vicinity, I don't think that should be a problem."

"Good." Callahan walked with Cane to the door. "Once Mark gets used to seeing you around, once he grows comfortable around you, we'll tell him. It'll be hard for him, though, no matter what and when."

"Yes, I suspect it will, but he'll adjust."

"Eventually," Callahan replied.

"What exactly do you propose at that point?"

Callahan swung open the door. "Allow me to think about it overnight. We'll meet up again in the morning."

"Then I'd better head back to town. I haven't found a room yet."

"Nonsense! You're our guest. Stay as long as you like—even until you get your own spread. We've plenty of room here." A broad smile covered Callahan's face. "It's nearly time for supper, Mr. Smith." He took a deep breath, then released it. "Do you smell that chicken? And baking powder biscuits?"

"Call me Cane. And, yes, I do. Better than anything I've smelled in years."

Callahan led the way to the kitchen. "Yes, my Annie's one of the best cooks around. Not only does she take care of the house and cook, she works at Katie's Palace, in town, cooking meals."

"Yes, I met the owners, James and Katie Freeman today."

"Good," the older man nodded. "Yessir, Annie will make some man a wonderful wife someday."

"I'm sure she will, sir," Cane muttered, pulling at his collar uncomfortably as he followed Callahan down the hallway.

Eating supper like a civilized human being, sitting at a table, made Cane squirm inside. He'd spent years in a jail cell, eating scraps off a tin plate with his fingers. Prisoners weren't allowed eating utensils for fear of "picking" their way out of jail, or injuring or killing a guard.

Cane passed through the dining room and paused in the kitchen doorway. His gaze fell on Mark who squirmed in his chair, tapping his fork impatiently on the table. Cane smiled. He recalled being seven—nearly eight—and being so hungry he'd done the same thing...until his mother scolded him to sit still like a gentleman.

Then he looked at Annie who stood at the stove, forking pieces of cooked chicken from a cast iron skillet onto a platter. They were golden brown and steaming hot. Suddenly, Cane's stomach rumbled so loudly all eyes settled on him.

"Sorry," he muttered as he stood awkwardly in the doorway. "Been awhile since I last ate."

"Then take a chair," Callahan said. "Hope you don't mind the informality of eating in the kitchen. Unless we have company, there's no point hauling the food into the dining room."

"But, Pa, Mr. Smith *is* company!" Mark said.

"Uh, that's true," Callahan said. "If you prefer..."

Cane replied, "The kitchen's fine with me."

"Guess I'm inclined to include you as family, Cane," Callahan said.

"Me, too!" Mark grinned at Cane.

Cane glanced up and caught the frown on Annie's face as she moved to the table with a platter in hand. Apparently, *she* wasn't ready to think of him as family.

Cane pulled out a chair beside Mark and sank into it. Callahan sat at the head of the table.

Silence ensued when Annie placed the chicken in the center of the table. She reached for the chair opposite Cane and Mark. Cane scrambled from his seat and tore around the table, bumping into Annie in order to hold her chair for her. Grateful for the gentle smile she gave him, he didn't feel like quite the bumbling idiot when she sat down and he eased her close to the table.

In his own seat once more, he started to reach for his fork but quickly pulled his hand back upon seeing the others bow their heads.

"Heavenly Father, we thank You for the excellent food, provided by Your generosity, and for the guest at our table tonight. Amen," Callahan prayed.

They ate supper, and it was only after Cane had taken his fourth piece of chicken that he realized the silence. Looking up, chicken leg in mid-air, he met Annie's wide-eyed expression. He glanced at Mark, who was happily gnawing on a chicken leg, meeting Cane's eyes with a gleaming, satisfied look in them.

He lowered the chicken leg to his plate. Picking up the linen napkin on his lap, he swiped at his mouth and sat in silence, feeling self-conscious. He'd made a pig of himself, but he hadn't eaten much since going to prison, and he sure hadn't eaten any better since his release. He'd been on a mission to find his son and had eaten little in the last week. Now that he'd accomplished that deed, he'd given in to his hunger.

"Hey, Mr. Smith, didn't I tell ya Annie can cook real good?" Mark said proudly.

"You sure did, son."

Cane, Annie and Callahan looked at each other before bursting into laughter.

"What's so funny?" Mark asked, confused.

"We're happy to have Mr. Smith share a meal with us. I'd say that's something to be happy about, wouldn't you?" Callahan replied.

"Sure is, and he's got black hair like me, too. How about that, Pa?"

The adults' humor dissipated at the innocent remark. Cane swore inside. Damn, telling Mark that he was his natural father wouldn't be easy for any of them.

The meal ended, and Cane and Mark went off to the library to play checkers.

~

*H*er father finished his coffee. "Cane's willing to take things slow, honey."

Tears filled her eyes. "That's one good thing."

"Do you know the man just got out of prison, after serving seven years?"

Annie gasped. "Oh, my heavens! Is he…I mean…is he danger…?"

"He'd been unjustly accused of a train robbery. Judge Hopkins re-opened the case recently upon new evidence that cleared Cane of all charges. He's a good man, Annie, and you know it."

She nodded. "I know he is. I feel it in my heart. How awful that he's lost so much of his life though."

"Yes, and he means to atone for those lost years by making a life for him and Mark. He's planning on staying in the Bozeman area, and starting up his own ranch."

"Oh! That's wonderful."

Callahan eyed his daughter. "You know, Annie, I think I've hit upon a solution to this problem."

She frowned as she rose. "What would that be?"

"You could marry him."

"Father! You can't be serious."

"But I am. As I said, I've a good feeling about him."

"I think you're right. My instincts tell me he's good and he's suffered too much in life, but I can't marry him. We barely know each other. Not to mention the fact he hasn't asked me, and likely won't."

And until I discover the identity of the man from my last vision, I can't think of Cane Smith as anything but my enemy.

"Just thought this would remedy the situation is all."

"Once he learns about my queerness, I don't think he'll want me for a wife."

He grinned. "You never know, honey. It might be the very thing that attracts him."

She scoffed, "You dreamer you."

He left the kitchen, and she turned back to her work. The few men who'd come a-courtin' ended their interest real fast once they heard the talk in town about her gift of "sight." People were spooked about her abilities, even those who'd known her all her life, with the exception of a few people. Her father, of course, and Katie and James Freeman. She couldn't change who she was, what she was. Maybe someday, some man would appreciate her gift and not think was crazy.

As she cleared the table, her mind raced at the idea of marrying Cane. She *could* marry him. It would solve all of their problems. Mark would have parents and a familiar home, too, and they wouldn't have to move away. They would live in the Bozeman area, close to her father.

She thought about the handsome, cool Cane Smith and shook her head. How could she be considering this? She could never marry him. The man was a tortured soul. More than once, she'd seen the sadness in his dark eyes. She didn't trust him, and wouldn't—until her premonition came to fruition one way or another.

Maybe the vision was meant as simply a forewarning that Cane was coming to claim his son, and nothing more. She shook her head.

No.

The premonition held nothing but evil. She decided Cane wasn't the man in the vision. She didn't know him well but, like her father, knew instinctively he was a good man.

As she lay in her bed that night, she was stunned when the premonition played in her mind again. She'd never had the same vision more than once. What could this mean? More importantly, who was the man who yanked Mark from her arms?

~

The following morning, Annie was the first to rise. She started breakfast, knowing soon her father, Mr. Smith, and Mark would be up and about. Her father would supervise the work on the ranch as he did every day. Annie was scheduled to work at The Palace. Mark would accompany her, as usual. He played well with Melanie while the adults worked.

She wasn't prepared for Cane to saunter into the kitchen first, clean-shaven, hair still wet and combed back from his forehead. He wore a pair of clean dungarees and a chambray shirt. She noticed how broad he was across the chest, how long and powerful his frame.

He cleared his throat. "'Mornin'," he said.

"Good morning," she replied before turning back to the flapjacks. Why was her voice so unsteady? Darn the man for being so handsome.

You need a beau, Annie Callahan, that's the problem.

"There's bacon, toast and beef hash on the table if you'd like to start while I finish cooking the cakes. Coffee's there, too."

"Anything I can do to help?"

Annie shot him a glance and saw he was serious.

Bless the man.

She couldn't recall if her father had ever offered to help with household chores. The Lord said woman was helpmate to man. She smiled, thinking of Cane's offer in reverse. Mr. Cane Smith was looking more and more attractive.

As she watched him reach up to the shelf for a coffee cup, she said, "You're our guest, Mr. Smith, so just sit down and eat."

She heard a chair scrape across the floor. All the while, as she poured the batter and flipped the cakes, she felt his gaze on her—his intense gaze. For once she was glad of her gifts. An unexpected chill raced through her then and she frowned. Nervous as a polecat in a room full of rocking chairs, she finished cooking.

Annie forked several pancakes onto Cane's plate. He moved so quickly to allow her elbow room, he nearly tipped his chair back. She jammed her free hand down on the back of it and tipped him forward until all four legs settled on the floor.

"Thank you, ma'am," he muttered.

The loud, sharp sound of shoe-clad feet running down the old rickety stairway that led into the kitchen made Katie scowl. Mark opened the door at the bottom and ran to the table, sinking into his seat. "Smells good, Annie!"

"Haven't I told you not to use those stairs?"

"Sorry, but I'm hungry and they're closer."

"Next time you won't get any breakfast if you use them. They're dangerous. Understand?"

"Yes, ma'am. When we gonna fix those stairs?" he grumbled.

She sighed. "Hopefully sometime this winter."

Moving to her own chair, her thoughts returned to Cane. She wondered why he was so flustered around her. She was unused to men being self-conscious with her. Usually, it was the other way around.

She didn't ponder the idea long when Mark piped up, "Flapjacks! Yippee! My favorite."

Annie gave him a mock scowl. "Did you wash up first before you came to the table?"

"I sure did, and Pa will tell you so," Mark said self-righteously.

"He did," her father said as he entered the kitchen. He nodded at Cane. "Hope you slept okay, Mr. Smith."

"Call me Cane, please."

"Cane, then."

"I slept better than I have in seven years."

~

Silence ensued as Callahan and Annie stared at Cane. He didn't want their pity, but he saw it in their eyes. His jaw tightened instinctively.

"Uh, Mr. Smith?"

Cane looked at his son. "Yes, Mark?"

"You better get yourself a new bed if you haven't been sleeping so good."

Cane raised his brow. "You may be right."

Mark tilted his head to the side and stared at him for a long while. Eventually, he said, "How come you always call me 'son' like Pa does?"

Have I been calling him that? He cleared his throat. "No reason," he replied. Taking a sip of coffee, he glanced at Annie who sat across from him, her eyes filled with tears.

Damn!

He didn't want to make her cry.

Cane ate quickly, rose and moved to the sink where he washed his plate and coffee cup in the soapy water, then rinsed it in a second pan of clear, hot water. Leaving the dishes on the sideboard to dry, he looked at Annie. "Excuse me. I'll hitch up your wagon, ma'am."

"Thank you."

Callahan said, "After Mark and Annie leave for the day, can you meet me in the library?"

Cane nodded, then strode outside, breathing in deeply of Montana's fresh air. If anyone asked him what he missed most in life, it would be years of lost liberty.

He hitched up the horse and wagon, and then took a seat on a wooden rocking chair on the porch. The chair creaked as he started rocking. Cane frowned, deciding he better stop before he broke it. When he pushed himself to his feet, Annie came outside.

"Sit. Rock. You won't break it. It's always squeaked," she informed him.

Cane raised his brow, thinking the woman was a mind reader! "I could fix that squeak for you, ma'am."

"Don't you dare. We like the chair, squeak and all. Father is waiting for you in the library."

He watched her head for the wagon, then followed her. Once he caught up with her, he placed his hands around her waist and eased her up onto the seat. She scowled down at him, picking up the leads. "Would you please stop sneaking up on me like that?" she scolded.

"Sorry." His lips quirked up into a half smile. "Just wanted to help."

She narrowed her eyes on him and he looked away, afraid he'd burst out in laughter. The situation wasn't all that funny, but he hadn't felt this carefree—free—in years.

"I don't mind the help, but let me know somehow you'll be helping," she said.

"Will do," he murmured. It seemed he could do little right around this woman but he admitted to himself he enjoyed her skittishness around him. It meant she felt something...for him. Then he thought, *Nah!*

She sighed. "Sorry. I'm just crabby because I believe I should be part of this discussion, but it seems I won't be."

Cane nodded, understanding her shortness now.

Mark tore out of the house. Scrambling up onto the seat beside Annie, he said, "Bye, Mr. Smith!"

Annie snapped the reins, encouraging the horse on its way. "Good day to you, Mr. Smith," she called.

He watched her expertly handle the horse and wagon until it disappeared from sight. Annie Callahan was too independent, he decided, scowling. No woman of his would go off in a wagon by herself. Plenty of danger lurked on the roads.

Inside the library, he sat with another cup of coffee. Together, he and Callahan planned how to break the news of Mark's parentage to him.

"I say we just sit him down and tell him," Cane said.

By the look on Callahan's face, he knew the man would argue the point.

"We can't just blurt out the fact you're Mark's father without some preparation."

"Then what do you suggest? I've lost time in life and need to get on with it. I can't move ahead and make plans for my life until Mark's told."

"You say you plan on staying here, right?"

Cane nodded. "Soon as I can find myself a spread."

"Money is no object?"

Suspiciously, Cane murmured, "Pardon me for saying so, sir, but that's my business."

Damn the man for making him feel inferior. He'd managed to save quite a sum of money from his cattle-driving days, with plans then to return for Giselle, Mark's mother. Upon his arrest, the money had been taken from him by Texas law enforcers, who believed it to be evidence—money that'd been stolen in the train robbery. When Cane was released from prison, they'd returned his money to him, with interest.

"You're right. I apologize," Callahan said. "How about this arrangement? Stay and work for me for a while so Mark can see you every day. During that time, he'll get used to you and the two of you can bond naturally. Instead of Annie taking Mark with her to The Palace when she works, you can take him along with you on ranch jobs here. Oh, and I pay my hands well."

Cane had to admit it was a reasonable plan. Steady money coming in was even better.

Callahan added, "I won't charge you boarding fees while you work for me either."

"How long?" Cane asked.

"For as long as it takes Mark to form an attachment to you."

"We have no idea how long that will be."

Callahan sighed as he leaned back in his chair. "We've never talked with Mark about his past. He's never asked, though, as I mentioned earlier, we did tell him he'd been adopted. We'll begin telling him now, in bits and pieces."

"All right."

"You know, you deciding to stay around here will help ease the changes the boy will be facing."

"I don't think I'd want Mark to live completely without the people who've raised him. The people who love him."

"Actually, I was thinking about my daughter's attachment to Mark, and not the other way around." Callahan frowned. "It'll be difficult for her."

"Uh, pardon my rudeness in saying this," Cane said, "but how come she hasn't married yet?"

Callahan narrowed his eyes on Cane. "You're new to town and haven't heard anything about my daughter, have you?"

"Nope, haven't really spoken with anyone but the judge, you and her, and Mr. and Mrs. Freeman, when I first arrived in town."

"Annie has a rather unusual gift."

The tactful way the man spoke immediately made Cane wary. "What do you mean?"

"She can see things others can't, future events, in particular."

One of the books passed onto Cane in jail had been the story of a man who had second sight—the ability to see things in his mind others couldn't, especially things in the future that hadn't occurred yet. He'd been skeptical. "I don't believe in all that crap."

"Most people don't. I didn't myself when Annie was just a girl— thought she was pretending. She was eight years old, very young at the time when I first noticed how different she was."

"Even if she does have this unusual ability, you can't deny the fact your daughter's a beautiful woman and should have found someone to marry by now."

"She is that, for certain. I'd love for her to marry and give me grand-children, but no one's asked her yet. Maybe someday someone will. Jed Porter, a rancher nearby, has made overtures of late. She isn't all that old. Just twenty-two."

Cane thought twenty-two was plenty old enough to marry. Heck, he knew women who'd married at fourteen. "Well then, claiming Mark may help your daughter see that she should get married and start her own family. I suspect Mark fills that void in her life right now."

"You're right about that." Callahan rose and stretched out his hand. "Are we in agreement then that we'll ease Mark and Annie into these changes?"

Cane stood and took the older man's hand. "Agreed. It's October now, so I'd like to have Mark with me by Christmas, in our own place."

"Then you'd better start looking at some property while you're staying here. I suspect you'll want to find a place with a house on it since you won't have time to build one."

"That's right."

Callahan opened a desk drawer and pulled out a folded newspaper. "Here's the *Bozeman Herald*. It comes out three times a week. Folks list their properties for sale. Go ahead and check out some of these places."

"Thanks, Callahan."

"Thank *you*, Cane, for giving our family the time we need to adjust."

Cane left the library, detouring to the kitchen to refill his coffee. Sinking into the creaky rocking chair on the porch, he quickly scanned the property ads. He circled those that interested him, tucked the newspaper between spokes of the porch railing, and thought about Annie.

Second sight. Even after reading a book about the reality of this phenomenon, I can't get myself to believe it.

He leaned back in the chair and closed his eyes. Strange, unexpected things happened in life all the time. Whether he believed in her abilities or not, it didn't matter to him. But then, if she did have this particular gift of seeing things in the future, it might come in handy sometime.

CHAPTER 3

$\mathcal{W}$ ith the loan of a horse from Callahan, Cane spent the day looking at two ranches. The properties, separated by other ranches, were too small in acreage for raising cows and horses.

Then he rode the ten miles back to Bozeman to check out what folks in town had to offer by way of horseflesh. After looking at several for sale, he decided the horse he'd ridden in was better than any he'd seen and decided to make Callahan an offer. He returned to the Moonstruck Ranch, arriving just as Mark and Annie drove their wagon into the drive.

Mark jumped down and ran into the house. Raising his arms to assist Annie, Cane lowered them when she just stood there, one hand braced on the back of the seat.

"You too independent to accept a man's help?"

Damn. I didn't mean to sound so self-defensive. Seven years in prison will do that to man.

She stared at him a long moment before she let go of the seat and leaned forward, reaching for his shoulders. His hands spanned her waist, and he eased her down to the ground. She *was* too independent for her own good. Surely, she had to see that herself.

She smiled and shrugged her shoulders. "Perhaps."

"If I were your pa, I sure wouldn't allow you to drive that wagon all by yourself the way you do. It's not safe for you or Mark."

"I've been driving myself all my life. Nothing has ever happened to me."

"There's always a first time. It's not just your safety I'm thinking of, but Mark's. I want someone to drive you."

She laughed mirthlessly. "Who, for instance?"

Cane scowled. "Your pa's got plenty of ranch hands. He could spare one of them the short trips to and from town."

"All right. Since you've no employment or ranch to run, Mr. Smith, *you* may drive us."

He nodded. "Now you're being sensible."

She gaped at him.

He smiled. She'd expected him to refuse.

Pivoting on her heel, she huffed into the house.

Cane looked after her with a smile. While he'd been out looking at properties, every time he pictured Mark in his life, he pictured Annie, too, as if the two were a packaged deal. Home, family and work all appealed to him. If he married Annie, the boy would have parents and a loving grandfather, too. Marrying Annie would be the right thing to do for Mark.

That wasn't the only reason, of course. He could take care of her, protect her. In time, they would grow to love each other. He had better hurry, too, if the neighboring rancher had his sights on Annie. First, he'd talk to her father and get his blessing and... But what if Callahan didn't give it? What man in his right mind *would* want his daughter to marry a man who'd done time?

Damn, I was innocent! Maybe I'm the only person in the world to believe it, but I'm as good as the next decent man. Somehow, I have to lay to rest any doubts Callahan and his lovely daughter have about me. How can I prove myself?

Inside the house, he found Annie cooking again.

"Cook still sick?" he asked.

"Mrs. Williams is still ill, and now her mother, as well. She quit permanently to care for her." She eyed him up and down when he rolled up his sleeves and washed his hands. She still stared at him when he glanced back at her. Cane felt something then—a pleasant awareness of her beside him as she cooked up slabs of ham. Potatoes and a pot of greens boiled on the stove. Biscuits turned golden brown in the oven.

He found her grinning as he dried his hands on his thighs. Looking down at his wrinkled, stained shirt, self-consciousness set in.

"What's so funny?" he said.

"You've two missing buttons. Do you know where they are?"

He shook his head. "Long gone, I suspect. These are the clothes they gave me when I left prison. Hand-me-downs. And call me Cane."

She nodded. "I've extras, Cane. After supper, give me your shirt and I'll sew them on."

"Just hand over needle and thread, ma'am, and I can do it."

One silken brow lifted. "Annie, please. You can?" At his nod, she added, "I don't mind."

He smiled. "Sounds good. My mother used to do it."

"Where is your mother?"

"She met a Canadian who'd come down to work as a cowboy back home in Texas. When he'd made the money he needed to buy his own spread, he set himself to buy a place back home. He and my mom married, then she left with him."

"And your father?"

"Never knew him."

"Oh, sorry."

Tom Callahan arrived home with two of his hands, their neighbor, Jed Porter, and the circuit judge, Simon Hopkins. Callahan was lucky his daughter had cooked enough food since Cane knew, by the surprised look on her face, she hadn't been expecting company.

Cane sat down next to the judge, then shook his hand, knowing they'd already had this conversation when Cane got into Bozeman. "I can't thank you enough for all of your help, Judge Hopkins."

"If there was ever a man who didn't belong in prison, it was you," said Hopkins. "I've always been a fair judge of people, and I had a gut feeling you were innocent. Sorry that it took so long to prove it though."

"What's all this about?" Porter asked his eyes narrowed on Cane.

Hopkins explained Cane's predicament, including being sent to jail for a crime he didn't commit. Afterwards, Jed sent unsettling looks at Cane. Cane stared the man down, silently daring him to make some snide comment. He knew of men like Porter—privileged, tough, unfair and unkind to humanity in general.

During dinner, Cane decided Porter was showing too much interest in Annie. If the cowboy said one wrong word to her, he'd toss him out on his ear.

She wasn't a flirtatious woman, but she was a beauty with long, wheat colored hair bundled up at the back of her neck and pretty blue eyes. She was petite—he'd noticed when he'd helped her up and down out of the wagon—and her laughter was contagious. He found himself grinning whenever she laughed.

"So, what brings you here, Jed?" Annie asked.

He gave her a devilish grin that made Cane see red. "Just bought a few horses from your pa and he invited me to stay. Glad I did."

Mark finished eating and fidgeted in his chair. Cane took pity on him. "How about some checkers, Mark?"

"You bet!" Mark's face lit up brighter than a full moon on a clear, starry night.

"Excuse us?" Cane said. At Annie's nod, he looked at Mark. "Come on, son."

Cane tried concentrating on the game but found his attention drifting toward Annie's laughter in the kitchen. With the library door open, he heard nearly every word of conversation. Then he heard Porter murmur, "Come set out on the porch with me, sweet Annie."

Once again, he heard her girlish laughter and grimaced.

"You got a stomachache, Mr. Smith?"

Cane met Mark's inquisitive expression. "No. Why?"

"Your eyes are all squinty, and you got a frown on your face. You look like you got a stomachache."

"I don't. I'm just thinking about something that doesn't agree with me."

Like Annie sitting out on the porch with Porter. Sounds too much like courtin' to me. I should be the one on the porch with her.

Tonight, after the company left, he decided he'd speak with Callahan. If he got a blessing, he'd propose to Miss Annie—hopefully by tomorrow. What would her answer be?

Cane looked across the table at his son. Maybe she'd accept his proposal before any other man's because he was Mark's father.

❧

"Jed, I said no for the second time." Annie scowled up into the frustrated face of her neighbor and would-be suitor.

"Why won't you marry me, Annie? What did I ever do wrong?"

"Nothing." She sighed. "Nothing at all. Simply put, I appreciate our friendship, but marriage? No, it wouldn't be right. I've no romantic inclinations toward you, Jed. Now don't ask me again."

They sat in chairs on the front porch, having a discussion Annie did not want to have.

Her stomach somersaulted in dread when, as the sun set, she caught Jed's face in profile. Everything about him was familiar to her, but something else stirred inside her. She'd seen that profile in anger before, his set jaw. At the same time, he looked at her again, she realized it.

The premonition! Jed is the man in my vision. No! It can't be. He'd never harm me or Mark. He's always been a perfect gentleman. He's helped us in so many ways over the years.

She scampered up from her chair. "Good night, Jed." She swiftly entered the house, ignoring his protests.

Detouring into the library, she found both Cane and Mark bent over the checkerboard concentrating. She sat down on the divan. From a wicker basket beside her, she picked up a wool sock to mend.

Smiling, she watched the two, thinking how they'd assumed the same hunched over position, elbows on their knees as they studied the checkerboard.

"Mind if I join you?" she softly asked.

~

*C*ane looked up. "Not at all." He glanced at Mark. "Hang on a minute, pardner." Rising to his feet he slowly unbuttoned his shirt, his eyes focused on Annie.

Interesting. She looked shocked, which made him hesitate, but only for a second. Her eyes were half closed and focused on his chest. He saw her sniff, her nostrils flaring a bit, as if catching his scent. It took him a second to remember what that look meant—it had been so long. Arousal —gut wrenching, body drenching, hot between the legs arousal—was the look on her face.

"What are you doing, Cane?" she whispered, dropping the sock to the floor.

Mark looked at Cane. "Looks like he's getting ready to turn in, don't it? Cane, you promised to finish the game," he protested.

"I will, while your sister sews the missing buttons on my shirt."

Cane shrugged out of the slightly tight shirt and held it out to her.

She snatched it from him and dug around in the sewing basket on the floor. He sank into his seat to finish the game with Mark, conscious of her eyes on his bare back. Damn! It felt good to know she was attracted to him.

He made his move on the checkerboard, then looked at Annie again, watched her swiftly thread a needle with blue thread that was a fair match to his shirt. She picked up a white button from a small basket and sewed it on, chattering, "Father went to bed early with a headache. He gets them occasionally…"

She picked up the second button and quickly sewed that on the shirt, too. She bit the thread between her teeth and tossed Cane his shirt. "There. All done."

"Sis? Somethin' wrong?" Mark asked.

Her head shot up. "What do you mean?" Her gaze left Mark and moved to Cane who had donned his shirt, still sitting in his chair, his back to her.

"Uh, maybe you need to have your eyes looked at by Doc. You sewed 'em on crooked, Annie."

Cane swiveled around to face her, a slow smile forming on his lips.

Annie glanced down at her work and sighed.

"That's okay," Cane said. "As long as there are buttons sewed on, I don't care if they don't line up so well with the buttonholes."

He watched her face turn an interesting shade of pink before she bent to pick up the sock she'd dropped earlier. He swiveled around to continue the game. Then he thought about Jed Porter. Casually, he said, "Something happen out on the porch?"

It took her almost a minute to reply he noticed.

"Why do you think anything happened?"

"You seemed fidgety when you first came in from the porch. I heard it in your voice. And you were talking real fast."

"Jed Porter proposed to me."

Cane froze. *Hell, did she accept? Am I too damned late to ask her myself?*

Cane released his breath. "I passed by his ranch today. It's quite a place. He appears to be doing real well for himself."

"Jed never dirties his hands with ranch work. His hired hands do it. He inherited the ranch from his father, who did all of the initial backbreaking work."

He looked over his shoulder at her. "So did you accept his proposal?"

"Of course not!" She scowled at him. "We grew up together. It would be like marrying kin."

One up for me.

"Uh, Cane, it's your turn," Mark said.

He shook his head and continued playing checkers with his son. After a while, Mark's head dropped to his chin.

"Mark?" Cane said softly, not wanting to startle the boy.

Mark started anyway and rubbed his eyes.

"Time for bed, Mark," Annie said. She dropped the sock into the basket beside her and rose to her feet. "I'll help you get ready."

"I will, too," Cane said.

Mark gave Cane a curious, sleepy look. "You gonna tuck me in?"

"If you want me to, I will."

"Annie always reads to me first."

Cane nodded. "I can do that."

Mark gave Annie a kiss good night. Cane saw sadness—and resignation in her eyes. It'd begun. She seemed to accept that it was time for him to be Mark's father—for Mark to become a Smith and not a Callahan.

Mark took Cane's hand and they went upstairs. Cane could hardly breathe, so sweet and innocent was his son's gesture. The boy trusted him. Cane's eyes smarted.

He read from *Tom Sawyer*, until Mark fell asleep. Then Cane made his way down the stairs and back to the library, intent on asking her to be his wife, now, instead of waiting to talk to her father. Now, before he lost his courage.

He found her sitting on a window ledge seat, staring out into the night. He went to her, and she rose from the seat as though expecting a confrontation. Then she astonished him when she threw herself against his chest and he took her into his arms.

Holding her against him, he heard her sobs. She cried against his shirtfront until it was wet and clammy. Eventually, she said, "I can't let him go, Cane. I just can't."

Cane took her shoulders and stepped back from her.

Now or never.

With a trembling finger, he traced a tear down the porcelain slope of one cheek and slowly said, "Maybe you won't have to, Annie."

∼

*S*he raised her brows in amazement. Had he changed his mind about claiming Mark? Searching the gentle expression in his eyes, she looked up at him in confusion, her legs feeling numb, and then she sank to her seat. "I don't understand," she whispered.

"I meant what I said. You won't have to give up Mark...if you marry me."

Hope and joy soared through Annie. My heavens, she felt giddy at the thought of marrying Cane. Astonished at the idea of his asking for her hand in marriage, she paused, then frowned. But *had* he asked her?

No, he hadn't proposed, not really. Not in the way she believed a man should propose to a woman. She bit her lip, deep in thought, then straightened her shoulders, deciding it was a proposal, albeit not a traditional one, but still a proposal. "Why are you asking me to be your wife?"

"You want Mark in your life, don't you?"

"Of course I do. More than anything, but marriage is a drastic step. We're all but strangers, Cane."

He bent down and pressed firm lips against hers. They lulled her, made her want him more than she'd ever wanted a man before. She sighed against his lips, then turned her head, breaking the kiss.

"We'll grow to know each other, love each other." Taking her hands, he pulled her to her feet and slid his hands around her waist.

Though she found she enjoyed his masculine size and warmth, Annie pressed her hands against his chest to make contact with his gaze.

"You're right. Over time, we'll learn to care for each other. But at first I'd need time to..." She couldn't meet his eyes, embarrassed yet thrilled at the thought of sharing the same bed with him.

"You can have all the time you need to get used to me. Hopefully, it won't take you too long to decide you like me enough to make ours a true marriage. Say yes, Annie," he encouraged her. "Then we can get your father's blessing."

"Wait. I need to tell you about me, something important."

"You mean the visions? Your father already did."

Astonished, she widened her eyes. My God, he'd asked her to marry him, even knowing about her unusual gift. "Well...well...how do you feel about that? About me?"

"Nothing to be ashamed of."

"A gift, yes, if you can call it that. It took me years to get used to it.

I've had a recent premonition, one that's alarming to say the least, and it's occurred three times. This has never happened to me so often before—the same vision."

He pressed down on her shoulders until she sank to the window seat once more. Sitting beside her, he again took her hands in his. "Tell me what you saw."

She sobbed and tears filled her eyes. "A man trying to take Mark from me."

"When did you have this vision?"

She sniffled. "Moments before you walked up to my wagon at the schoolhouse."

"What you saw was me claiming Mark."

Annie shook her head. "No. It wasn't you. It was another man. I believe it was Jed. He tore Mark from my arms. I can still hear Mark's screams."

"Then what happened?"

"The premonition stopped. I've no idea what happens after that."

Cane stroked her cheek, helping her trembling abate slightly. "Don't worry. I'm here to protect both of you. No one will dare take Mark from us."

She smiled at him and nodded.

"I'm asking again, Annie. Will you marry me?"

Tears filled her eyes even as she whispered, "Yes."

He raised his brow. "You mean it?"

"This is a sensible solution to this dilemma, not to mention the fact that it'll be so much easier for Mark."

"Is that your only reason for saying yes?"

"Isn't it the only reason you asked me?"

She looked into his eyes and caught a glimmer of disappointment. She had to be truthful with him. While she was attracted to him, she didn't love him. She believed that love would come to them over time, as they grew to know each other.

He dragged his fingers through his hair. "I was hoping for... Never mind. When do you want to get married?"

amn! So much for romance. So she doesn't love me. What did I expect? We've known each other only two days, yet I half convinced myself I was already falling in love with her. But then, a lot has happened in these two days.

"I think we owe it to Mark to get to know each other better before we marry. Perhaps in a few months we can say our vows."

"Sounds sensible," Cane said.

"When will you talk to Father about us?"

"As soon as I can." Cane turned on his heel and headed toward the door.

"Where are you going?"

He came to a halt and quirked an eyebrow at her. "Turning in for the night. I've got a big day ahead of me and several properties to look at. I'm rising before the sun. Good night."

"Yes, good night, Cane," she said faintly.

After he left, she took up her darning again, joy bubbling up inside her. He'd asked her to marry him. Mark would be secure, and she'd still have the boy who was like a son to her in her life.

She hadn't missed the disappointment on Cane's face and guessed he'd expected her to declare her love for him. He hadn't declared his love for her either. She greatly admired Cane's strength and determination to make something of his life. His love for Mark was genuine. Though convinced she would grow to love him, she harbored doubts about him falling in love with her. His purpose in life had been to gain the custody and love of his son. He would achieve that goal with their marriage. Was that his only reason for proposing?

It would be enough, she decided, though she hated the idea. She finished darning the sock and tossed it into a basket. She thought about Cane's dark hair and eyes, his swarthy complexion and strong body when he'd pulled her against him.

Love made no difference to a man who'd lived without love for most of his life, a man with the single-minded purpose he'd had in coming here. Love mattered to Annie, enough to make her determined to be such a good wife to Cane, he would have no choice but to fall madly in love with her. She would show him the difference love could make in his hard life.

*A*fter a few days of living with the Callahans, Cane's desire to marry Annie and take her to his bed had grown faster than a brush fire. It was all he could think about—holding her sweet body in his arms, taking down her wheat-colored strands of hair, planting his lips against hers. He was going insane with wanting her! Yet he knew he had to wait. He'd give her the time she needed to get used to him. He'd promised.

He'd had no luck finding property on which to build a ranch and a home for Annie and Mark. It had to be the right property. With the approaching winter, he knew he was running out of time, too. He was weary and somewhat discouraged as he rode into town, cold and hungry. For the past hour, he'd been looking forward to enjoying a meal. There was Annie's wagon outside Katie's Palace. *Darn it! Didn't I tell the woman I didn't want her driving by herself?*

His stomach rumbled when he smelled beefsteaks. He swung off his horse, tied him up and ambled into The Palace. Removing his gloves, he welcomed the heat as he stood in the entryway and looked around. With a quick sweep, he decided there was no vacant table. Then his gaze honed in on Annie. She was setting a table at the opposite end of the restaurant. She turned, smiled, and motioned him back.

He pulled off his Stetson. She looked pretty in a russet-colored dress embellished with ivory lace. He was nothing but a hard cowboy who'd seen and experienced too much pain and violence in life, yet her femininity intrigued and enticed him—softened him.

He strode to the table she'd just cleaned up. She pulled a chair out for him and waited for him to take it. As he sat, he said, "You sure are a sight for these tired eyes."

"Ah, your words are poetry to my ears, Cane."

Narrowing his gaze on her, he saw her sweet smile but knew her reply was anything but flippant. "Poetry, huh? That's the first time anyone has ever accused me of that. I read, but I'm no poet."

"All right, how about this then? You're just being nice to me so I'll keep sewing buttons on your shirt when you lose them."

"Yup, that's the size of it." He grinned at her. The woman knew how to put a man at ease. His chest expanded when she grinned back and tilted her head.

"You know, if you want I could sew you some new shirts."

Cane gulped down the lump forming in his throat. Outside of his mother, no woman had ever offered to do something so nice for him. He didn't know what to say to her offer. He just sat there like a dunderheaded fool, staring at her.

"No, thanks," he eventually managed to say, looking away. "I can't afford to spend a dime on clothing until I purchase my property and figure out how much I'll have left over for cattle and horses and gear."

"I've bolts of chambray and woolens at the ranch. You won't be the first man for whom I've made a shirt. Every hand on our ranch has had at least one made by me."

"Why?" he asked, even as jealousy tore through him at the thought of her hands measuring another man's body.

"I enjoy sewing, for one, and most of the men have never had anything done for them—certainly not a homemade shirt. I appreciate their work for us at the ranch, and one way I show my thanks is to make shirts for Christmas. Some of our hands have been with us since I was a girl. They're family to me." She clapped her hands and laughed. "Oh, you should see how we decorate the house for the holidays. The baking and cooking in preparation! And, on Christmas morning, the hands who have no other family open gifts with us and share a festive meal."

He nodded. "Then I look forward to you making me a shirt for Christmas, Miss Annie." *And sharing our first Christmas together, even if it's not as man and wife for I can't marry her without a home for her and Mark.*

She gave him a shy smile. "I...I have to get back to work. Would you like the special? It's beefsteak."

"Much appreciated, and coffee," he said. "Oh, and one more thing."

"What's that?"

"I'll be back in a couple hours to escort you home."

She frowned. "I don't have Mark with me, Cane. It's not necessary."

"Maybe not to you, but it is to me."

"Hey, Annie, our food's sitting up on the kitchen shelf getting cold!"

Cane looked beyond Annie to see Jed Porter glaring at him. "Go on. We'll talk later," he said.

Annie nodded and left him. He stared out the window, deciding there'd be plenty of time to ponder on how pretty Annie was once they were married. It wasn't long before he looked toward the kitchen and followed her activity as she delivered plates of food to one table then another. When she paused with her hands full at Jed's table, Cane's world turned red. Jed sat with two other men and, with a smirk on his lips, slid an arm around Annie's waist after she set his food down.

Cane scowled. Then he grinned when she whipped a wooden spoon from her apron pocket and smacked Jed's hand. Jed retaliated, wound his hand around her neck and yanked her down to meet his lips.

Cane rose from his chair with a vivid curse and tore down the aisle. Stopping beside Jed, Cane grasped the man's wrist and pulled his hand from around Annie's neck. "Let go of her," he growled.

Jed stumbled to his feet, knocking his chair over in the process, fists raised. "Who in the hell do you think you are?"

Cane maneuvered Annie behind him, conscious of the silence in the room, knowing now they had an audience. He took advantage of the quiet and said, "The man who will be marrying Miss Annie, that's who."

Jed glared at Annie. "Is that true?"

Annie nodded. "Yes."

"And don't propose to her again, either," Cane warned. He started to turn Annie away with him but paused, focusing on Jed again. "And one thing more, don't you ever lay a hand on her again. Understand?"

Jed didn't reply, just glared mulishly at Cane.

James Freeman entered The Palace. He eased up to them. "There a problem here?" he asked.

"Oh, James, why..."

"Not anymore," Cane inserted. "Porter here was just leaving. Weren't you?"

Jed sent smoldering looks at Cane and Annie, then curtly nodded. "Come on, boys."

Cane's gaze followed Jed and his men until they left the saloon, then he looked at Annie.

"I'm marrying Cane," Annie said. "Jed's not too happy about it."

"Is that right?" James replied with a grin.

Annie nodded.

The swinging kitchen doors opened as James said, "Bet you haven't told Katie yet, have you?"

"Told me what?" Katie asked, joining them.

"The two of them are getting married," James said. He wound an arm around Katie's expanding waist. "Ain't that something?"

"Oh, Annie! When were you going to tell me?" Katie said accusingly.

"It pretty much just happened, ma'am," Cane said. "We're getting married sometime around Christmas."

Annie's eyes went round. "We are?"

"Yes," Cane said decidedly. "By the way, I never did get my cup of coffee or my supper."

Katie laughed. "Sit down, Mr. Smith. Coming right up."

James stared at Cane a moment, then he stuck out his hand. "Hope you realize you're getting a real treasure with Annie."

"I do," Cane said and shook the marshal's hand.

Cane returned to his seat, glad folks were involved once again in their own table conversations.

Annie rushed up. "Here's your coffee, Cane. Supper should be up any moment."

"Thanks. No rush," he replied. "You okay?"

She nodded but wouldn't meet his eyes.

"Are you mad at me for making the announcement like I did?"

"No." She hesitated, biting her lip a moment before replying. "No one's ever stood up for me like you did. Thank you for that." She leaned down and planted a quick kiss on his cheek, surprising him.

He reached for her. "Annie, I..."

"I'll be back in a minute." She rushed to the kitchen. Within moments, she delivered his food, and he forced himself to eat slowly even though hunger gnawed at his belly.

Cane finished his meal, left money on the table, including a generous tip for Annie. Jamming his Stetson on his head, he paused at the door and caught Annie's eyes as she left the kitchen with a tray loaded with plates of food.

"I'll be back, like I said, to fetch you."

She nodded and delivered the food on the platters.

Uneasiness settled over him. He'd ride home on his horse, return in two hours, then escort her home in her wagon. As he mounted his horse, he smiled. *Home. I like the sound of that, especially coming from Annie.*

∾

*A*nnie was exhausted when she left The Palace at half past nine. As she neared the double doors, she heard the rain before she smelled it. Beside her, Katie said, "I can't thank you enough for coming in. I owe you. Again."

"You don't owe me a thing," Annie replied. She laid her hand on the big swell of Katie's belly. "Moving a lot, isn't he?"

Katie placed her hand over her friend's. "It might be a girl, you know, but you always say 'he.'"

"I think this baby is a boy."

Katie gasped. "Tell me, did you *see* something?"

Annie shivered, grateful that she hadn't had any more premonitions since Cane's arrival. "No, sorry, I've seen nothing about your baby, Katie. Consider that a good thing."

Katie nodded. "I'll soon know. Every time he moves, I have to rush to the…well, you know."

They laughed. Stepping outside, a light mist fell around them. Annie pulled her coat close around her. "Wouldn't you know it? I took the wagon that leaks today."

"I can always send you home in one of mine," Katie said. "Besides, it'll be nearly dark by the time you get home. I don't like the idea of you traveling on your own."

"I got here on my own and I can return the same way," Annie said firmly. Besides, Cane would be on the way soon, if he was true to his word.

"The roads aren't safe at night," Katie protested.

"They're not safe during the day, either." Annie smiled. "Don't worry about me. It's only fifteen minutes to home." She paused for an instant before blurting what she knew she'd have to, sooner or later, "I guess I should tell you this. Cane Smith is Mark's true father."

Katie gasped, "Oh my! So is that why you're marrying him?"

"At first I thought it was the reason. You have to admit it's the practical thing to do. It'll be easier for Mark, too, adjusting to Cane as his father."

"But you don't know the man!" Katie protested.

"True, but I've good instincts, you can't deny. I've a feeling our marriage will be good, Katie. I feel things for Cane I've never felt for any man." Heat seeped into her cheeks. "Stirrings, I guess you'd say."

Katie nodded. "I know all about stirrings," she said, patting her stomach. "But, like I said, you don't know him. Maybe we should have James check up on him. What if he's some criminal?"

"As a matter of fact, he spent seven years in prison for a crime he didn't commit. He was released when the law found the real criminal."

"How horrible for him. But...do you want me to ask James to check out his past? Just to be on the safe side?"

"No. I believe every word he told me. Besides, Father spoke with Judge Hopkins, who verified Cane's facts."

"I suppose there's no chance you happen to love him, do you?"

"How could I? We just met."

"Yes, but don't forget those stirrings," Katie said with a laugh. "I'm happy for you."

"Thanks, Katie. I have the feeling you'll be having that baby very soon. You send someone to let us know about the baby right away. Okay?"

"I will," Katie promised.

~

$\mathcal{I}$t was half past nine and rain pounded the ground. It was time to go get Annie. As Cane rode, he was soaked to the skin within moments. Without the moon's light, he had difficulty staying on the road. He wondered how Annie managed traveling home evenings after working. But then she'd grown up here, and knowing her horse, he likely knew the way even if she didn't guide him.

He saw lights shining from Katie's Palace up ahead. He slowed down as he drew nearer and saw the shadowy shape of a wagon stopped in the road. Squinting through the rain, he saw a riderless horse beside a wagon and a hitched horse. Chills prickled up his spine. Could it be Annie?

Damn! Didn't I tell her to wait for me? Now it seemed her wagon had broken down. It also appeared someone had stopped to help her.

A woman's scream rent the night and he recognized it as Annie's. "Hee yah!" Cane hollered, whipping his horse into a gallop. He saw Annie, her arms flailing, legs kicking as she screamed at the man who was manhandling her as he sat on the seat beside her. Even though he saw only the shape of a big man, Cane's mind blared, *Jed!* He leaned over his horse's neck and thundered toward them. Once he reached the wagon, he flung himself into it, snatching Jed up by the collar and whirling him away from Annie.

"You can't have her!" Jed yelled over the rain. "She's mine!"

His fist darted out and clipped Cane's chin. Cane staggered but regained his balance. Like a bull on the rampage, he butted his head into Jed's stomach, satisfied at the sound of the man's groan. Straightening, he pulled back his right arm and slammed his fist into Jed's face. Blood spurted from his nose. Jed gave a maddening roar and hauled back his own fist, but Cane hit him again and the brute tumbled out of the wagon.

Cane saw Jed lying sprawled in the mud, saw him twitch. Cane warned, "Stay put, if you know what's good for you." Then he took Annie in his arms, and she sobbed against his chest. "Are you okay?" he asked. At her nod, his voice hardened. "Didn't I tell you to stay put until I came for you?"

She looked up at him. "I grew up in Bozeman and had no reason to believe anything bad could happen to me. Heavens, I'd had no forewarning, no premonition, of Jed setting upon me like he did." But then she remembered her visions. Surely, Jed couldn't do this horrible thing.

She sighed. "It seems you were absolutely right about my safety."

"Finally, you see the sense of things."

She lifted her chin. "I've always been safe in Bozeman. This is my home, Cane. Though I have to admit I owe you thanks for arriving in so timely a fashion."

"Yes, if I hadn't arrived, who knows how far Porter would have gone?"

"Oh, I know exactly what he would have done. He...told me!" she said in a shaky murmur.

"What did he say?"

"He meant to ruin me so I'd have to marry him."

"The bastard!" Cane glared down at Jed, who still lay on the ground, groaning.

Suddenly, the marshal rode up, and Cane and Annie told him what had happened.

"You'll be spending the night in a jail cell, Porter," James muttered, hauling Jed to his feet. "You're lucky Miss Annie will let it go at that."

Time to head for home, Cane decided. He whistled, and his horse trotted over to him.

"You know, of course, Jed attacking me is all your fault, don't you?"

He had just grabbed his horse's reins when he whipped his head around to stare at her. "What!"

"If you had let me take care of things with him at The Palace, he wouldn't have come after me like he did."

Cane looped his horse's reins over one arm, then picked up the reins from the harnessed horse and snapped them against his flanks, setting him into a trot toward home.

"I think you're wrong on that, sweetheart. I think Porter had reached the end of his rope—even before he found out you were marrying me. Even if he hadn't discovered you accepted my proposal, he would have attacked you sooner or later, with the intentions of ruining you, hoping you'd have to marry him to save your reputation."

"Perhaps you have a point."

"You agreed to be my wife." Gentling his tone, he added, "You have to learn to trust my judgment, Annie."

He waited for her blast of fury, but was stunned when she said, "I do trust you, Cane."

"Good. I protect what's mine, and you belong to me. You can't deny it unless you plan on backing out of marrying me. Is that what you want?"

"No," she said softly.

He nodded. "Good. I'm glad we see eye to eye on this."

Annie sighed. "Perhaps, with time, you'll learn to trust our community and respect my desire for freedom to come and go as I please. As your wife, I'll obey you, but I don't want to be a prisoner."

She had to be joking. A beauty such as her couldn't be allowed to travel on her own without an escort, no matter that Bozeman was her

ANNIE AND THE OUTLAW

hometown and she felt safe and knew everyone. Hopefully, with tonight's attack, she'd learned her lesson.

It was slow going through the mud, but soon they reached the drive leading to the house. He drove into the yard and stopped at the barn. A stable boy ran outside and unhitched the horse while Cane hustled Annie inside.

~

"*W*hen I left this morning, I hadn't expected rain." She shed her coat and wrinkled her nose at the smell of wet wool. Cane took it and hung it up beside his own on pegs to dry.

"I imagine Father has retired already, hasn't he?"

Cane nodded.

"Darn! We need to talk to him about…our plans."

"We will tomorrow. Join me for a libation?"

"I'd love that, but I think we both need to change our clothes."

"Agreed," he said with a grin.

Cane was already at the foot of the stairs, waiting for her, after they'd gone to their rooms to change into dry clothing. He took her elbow and escorted her into the library.

As she sat on the divan before a crackling fire, she listened to Cane making their drinks. Soon, he sat beside her and handed her a cup. With her first taste, she knew he'd poured them hot coffee with a liberal dash of whiskey in it. Taking small sips, she relaxed and leaned back but startled when she felt something behind her neck.

"Sorry," he murmured.

She saw him lifting his arm, and she said, "Don't move. Your warmth is appreciated."

Heat suffused her cheeks when she saw the smile on his lips. Looking higher, she saw the passionate look in his eyes. He slid his arm over the back again and pressed close to her. She sighed, loving the feel of him against her. Before long, she couldn't keep her eyes open as exhaustion overcame her.

~

ane grabbed her cup before she dropped it and set it down beside his on the table. He couldn't resist kissing her forehead, inhaling her lavender scent. His lips moved to the cheek near him. Her lips beckoned him, and he brushed his gently against the full curves of her own.

Dynamite exploded inside him, and he felt his body harden, readying for her—his woman. She woke slowly, turning her head toward him to kiss him back. Then she wound her arms around his neck and pulled him down further, returning his exploratory kiss.

When he felt ready to take her then and there, he came to his senses and eased her arms from around his neck. "Annie, we have to stop."

He smiled when she sighed in disappointment.

"I suppose you're right. Perhaps we should get married sooner."

His smile widened. "You won't find me objecting."

She nodded. "We'd better speak with Father first. He's always wanted me to get married in church, in a white dress, with flowers and a reception. I don't think we can plan something that elaborate so soon, but we'll see."

"The sooner the better," he said. His voice sounded raspy to him, and he couldn't resist kissing her again. She turned into his embrace. Cane couldn't help pulling her even harder against him, then his hand wandered higher, cupping one breast. He thought of the irony of telling her they had to stop when he couldn't, not when she was so willing in his arms.

"Ah!" she whispered when he raised her up from her seat and settled her on his lap, facing him. He palmed one of her breasts while the other stroked her lower back and bottom. Damn all the clothes women wore, he mused, wanting to strip her naked now, this moment, while the fire blazed high, his wanton desire for her just as hot.

"God, I want you," he murmured against her cheek. "Do you have any idea how long it's been since I've made love to a woman?"

Her laughter surprised him, and he looked down at her, his lips quirked. "That's funny?" he asked. At her nod, he added, "Not from where I'm sitting."

"For you it's been seven years." He noticed how her smile left then and tears filled her eyes. "For me it's been a lifetime."

He groaned. "Don't say that or I won't be able to stop."

"I don't want you to stop. Besides, what difference does it make? We are getting married, remember?"

He set her down beside him, then rose. Pacing in front of the fireplace, he said, "Yes, but I won't dishonor you, and I respect your father and how he's taken me in. We'll wait until our wedding night, and no complaints," he warned.

She pouted. "Have you always been so dictatorial?"

Had he? He thought a minute then grinned. "No. Never. Maybe this arrangement—this marriage between us—means more to me than I thought." He pulled her to her feet. "To bed with you now, sweetheart."

"All right. But I'd much rather stay here with you."

At the foot of the steps, he pulled her against him and kissed her until she went limp in his arms. "And I'd much rather you stayed here with me, too. See you in the morning."

Cane watched her ascend the stairs, her hips swinging. At the landing, she paused and smiled down at him, then blew him a kiss. "Good night, Cane."

Temptress! Scowling, he put one foot on the first step, ready to go after her when she swiftly disappeared down the hallway.

~

"*N*o! No! Stop! You can't!"

Through Annie's closed bedroom door, Cane said calmly, "Annie, Annie, wake up. You're having a bad dream."

He heard her moaning, then a scream rent the air. Cane stood at the door, ready to open it when her father came charging from his room. Callahan opened the door and rushed inside. Cane saw Annie lying on her bed. Her eyes were tightly shut, and she was shaking her head wildly from side to side. Slowly, he moved into her room, his eyes steady on her.

"Annie, honey? Wake up," her father ordered as he bent over her and shook her shoulders.

Slowly, she quieted, then opened her eyes. Seeing her father, she sat up and threw herself into his arms.

"Another premonition?" her father asked as he held her.

Annie nodded. "It was awful. It was the same one, that man trying to take Mark away from me."

Cane's jaw tightened at her words, and he said, "As long as I'm living, no one will take Mark away from us. Go to sleep. You're safe. I won't let anything happen to either of you."

She looked up at him with sad but trusting eyes and nodded. "Good night. I'm sorry I woke everyone." She turned her back on them and closed her eyes.

In the hallway, Callahan said, "Come. Have a drink with me in the library."

"Good idea. I need to speak with you about something."

After they'd settled down with glasses of Irish whiskey, Cane tried to decide how to tell Callahan that he'd asked Annie to marry him and she'd agreed. True, he should have asked the old man's permission first, but getting Annie's agreement had seemed more urgent.

Finally, Cane came out with it. "I've asked Annie to marry me."

Callahan smiled and nodded. "Glad you're seeing things my way."

"I should have declared my intentions to you first, but—"

"Asking a father's permission was common in my day, but it seems to have slipped out of fashion. Thanks, though, for telling me, after the fact. I've always wanted to have a traditional wedding for her. She is my only child, after all, but I will understand if expediency is necessary for the two of you."

"It's true, for Mark's sake, we'd like to be married soon. I've yet to find a home for us though. Sure, there are plenty of properties, but they're all too small for my plans."

Sitting forward, Callahan said, "For a wedding gift, I'd like to give you and Annie sixteen-hundred acres of my property to the west."

"You don't have to do that," Cane protested, shocked.

Callahan shrugged. "I've wondered what would happen to the ranch once I've passed on, since I've no son. Truth be told, it was one of the reasons that made sense for me to adopt Mark. Naturally, Annie would get it, but I can't think of a better man to run this place than you, Cane, as my daughter's husband. Then you'll pass it onto Mark."

Cane gulped down the growing lump in his throat and nodded, staring down at the floor. "It's a mighty generous wedding gift, and we appreciate it."

Callahan nodded. "Someday it'll all be yours, Annie's and Mark's."

"Just how much land is there?"

Callahan just smiled. "We'd better get some shut-eye. We'll be up riding most of tomorrow. You'll get some idea of the acreage at that time."

"I'm up for it." Reaching out, Cane took Callahan's hand. "Thanks for giving me your blessing, and your daughter. I never believed I could get so lucky. Luck has not been my friend," he said dryly.

Callahan slapped his back in a friendly gesture, then left the library.

Cane sank down on the divan and stared into the fire. Closing his eyes, he thought back to when he'd been in prison and received the letter that would eventually change his destiny. Thank God, he'd never given up hope, for hope was what had helped him survive the remainder of his incarceration, while both he and the judge tried to prove his innocence. Now hope would give him a future.

CHAPTER 5

*C*ane spent the next four days riding the range with Annie's father, amazed by the acres and acres of land comprised of small lakes, streams, mountains and plains. The Moonstruck Ranch was like paradise to him, and it would soon be his home. Excitement flared deep inside him at the thought of building a house, of having Annie and Mark in his life permanently. And perhaps other children...

On Saturday morning, he found sticks to make fishing poles and string, then rode to The Katie's Palace to fetch Mark. Soon the streams and ponds would be frozen and fishing wouldn't be possible. He was intent on having a talk with the boy about marrying Annie. He'd discussed the plan last night with her and she'd agreed, as long as Cane didn't blurt out the fact that he was Mark's father. She wanted to be the one to decide when the time was right and now was too soon. She insisted they'd tell Mark *together*. Cane had reluctantly agreed.

As he rode, he started thinking of Christmas, somehow wanting to make this one special for Mark and Annie, and for himself. It'd been so long since he actually celebrated the holiday, he wasn't sure how or what to do, with the exception of purchasing gifts. He'd already decided on a fine pocketknife for Mark that he'd seen in the mercantile, even though he suspected Annie might not like the idea. Then there was Annie. He had no idea what to buy her for a present, except for one thing—a wedding ring.

As soon as he stopped outside The Palace, Mark came running out the front door.

"You taking me home instead of Annie?"

Leaning on his saddle's pommel, Cane said, "Thought we'd go over to that pond near your house to do some fishing, before winter really sets in and it freezes over."

"Yes!"

"Go get your coat then."

Cane watched Mark run inside. His heart raced when Annie appeared in the doorway and smiled. Damn, she looked so pretty dressed in a modest blue gown that enhanced her fair complexion and matched her eyes. "You two have a good time."

"We sure will, Annie!" Mark said exuberantly as he squeezed past her.

Cane extended his hand to help him up on the horse in front of him. He tipped his hat to Annie. "See you at supper."

"Yes," she said, gave a little wave and went back inside.

As they rode down the street, Cane enjoyed the smell of little boy heat and dirt, feeling a stirring of love inside for this little man, sorry he'd missed so much of his life. He had plans to make up for the lost time.

For the rest of the day, the two of them fished, laughed, and talked. Finally, when Cane felt Mark was comfortable with him, he broached the marriage idea to him.

"What would you think if I married Annie?"

Mark frowned. "And take her away from Pa and me?" He shook his head. "I wouldn't like it."

"No," Cane quickly said, "I wouldn't be taking her away from you. Annie and I have decided we want to get married, and you'll come visit or even stay with us whenever you want."

"I can't leave Pa." Mark scowled. "But I don't want Annie to move away either. His eyes lit up then. "I know! You can live at our house," he offered.

Cane nodded. "For a while, while we build a house, we would. Your pa has given Annie and me some of his land on which to build our own home."

"Why can't you live with me, Pa and Annie? Our house is big!"

"It is, Mark, but it wouldn't be my home, and I need my own place real bad."

Mark thought about it and finally nodded. "Okay." Mark gave Cane a sad look. "I'm gonna miss seeing Annie every day."

"Count on seeing her every day, Mark. Things will still be the same."

Mark shrugged, then turned his attention back to his fishing pole. "Oh! I gotta bite! Look!"

Cane was thoughtful as he helped Mark pull in his fish. He'd promised Annie he wouldn't break the truth to the boy without her, but felt compelled now to do so. He opened his mouth, ready to ease into it, when he clamped it shut. A promise was a promise, and he wouldn't break it to Annie. He'd bide his time, until she felt Mark was ready to hear the news.

Mark whooped with joy when he saw his small fish. "Can we keep him?"

Cane grinned. "You know, son, he's a might small. I think he needs to go back into that pond. We'll try and catch a bigger one."

Disappointed, Mark said, "Okay, but he looks plenty big to me. I want to show Pa."

"We'll fish a bit more and see if we can catch one you can keep."

When it was long past time to leave the fishing hole, darkness had descended and the temperature had dropped. Unfortunately, Mark hadn't caught another fish.

"Time to go home," Cane said as he rose to his feet and brushed off his jeans.

Mark pouted as he scrambled up. "But I didn't get a fish!"

"You'll have a chance to try again soon."

"I don't wanna go home."

"Annie's probably home cooking supper."

"So can we come back tomorrow?"

"We'll see."

Mark's pout remained. "We *have* to."

Cane kept his patience, though he was somewhat surprised to see this petulant side of Mark. "I promised we'd fish again, and we will, though it might not be tomorrow."

Mark picked up his pole and trudged over to Cane's horse. Though Mark was quiet at the start of the trip home, Cane had him making plans for more fishing. He realized Mark had little concept of what tomorrow, or the day after tomorrow meant, yet, but he promised they'd go fishing

104

sooner rather than later, while the weather held out, and the pond remained without ice.

≈

*A*nnie was cooking supper when they arrived home. She looked up when they entered the kitchen and smiled. "So, how was the fishing?"

"Not so good," Mark said his lower lip protruding.

Annie met Cane's eyes with a questioning look. "So, you didn't catch anything?"

"Cane wouldn't let me keep my fish."

"He was a small fry, that's why you couldn't keep him. I explained to you we'll go fishing again. Soon. I'm pretty sure you'll catch a bigger fish to keep next time."

"But I wanted that fish!"

"Mark," Annie began, but was interrupted when the boy stamped his foot and scowled at Cane.

Cane leaned down to Mark. "I made you a promise we'll go fishing again, but not if you can't accept my terms. You stop that fussing right now," he ordered.

Annie slid up to Mark and pulled him against her. She tucked her hand beneath his chin and saw the tears in his eyes. "What's this? Didn't you have a good time?"

"Yes," he said reluctantly. "Pa always lets me keep fish I catch, even the little ones."

"Well, I think you owe Cane an apology," she said. "He took time to take you fishing when he certainly didn't have to, and likely had other things to do.

Mark looked shyly up at Cane. "Sorry."

"That's okay, son."

Mark looked at Annie. "I'm hungry."

Annie smiled, flitted her gaze to Cane, whose expression looked sad. "We'll be ready in a couple minutes. Go upstairs and wash up now."

Mark trudged off. As he passed Cane, Cane reached out to touch his hair, but Mark shied away from him.

Cane sighed as he watched Mark leave the kitchen, then looked at Annie. "Guess I didn't make points today with him, did I?"

Annie came around the table and took his hand. "He does seem rather out of sorts. I'm surprised that you throwing back his fish set him off like that. Father's done the same thing several times. I'm thinking it's something else that's really upset him. Did you tell him we were getting married?"

"I did, but that's all." Cane frowned. "It didn't seem to really bother him, though he thought the best idea was for all of us to live here together."

"How did you reply to him?"

"I told him we'll be living here temporarily, until we build our own house. I explained how he could visit between the two houses." He raked his fingers through his hair. "You don't know how hard it was for me to keep his parentage a secret."

"I can imagine," she murmured. "Thanks for not telling him yet. Spend as much time as you can with him over the next few weeks and then we can tell him." She squeezed his hand.

Winding an arm around her waist, he murmured into her hair, "I want to tell him soon. And I want us to get married soon—real soon."

She tried pulling out of his embrace, but he wouldn't allow it. "Cane!" she said frantically, "Mark and Father will be here any minute."

"Set the date and I'll release you, sweetheart."

She nodded. "How about right before Christmas? That would give me time to make plans."

She heard Mark's running steps heading for the kitchen, and she pressed her hands against Cane's chest.

He let her go. "I guess I can wait that long. You know, of course, we'll have to live here until spring. With winter setting in, that's the soonest we can build a house."

"I know. It'll be harder for you than me, I'm afraid. This is the only home I've known."

"You and your father have been nothing but hospitable. It won't be a hardship living here until we build our house. You let me know what you'd like for our house—anything you want," he promised.

"Thank you," she said softly.

Cane prayed the next several weeks would pass quicker than a train at full speed.

*D*ecember arrived, and Bozeman and its inhabitants began preparing for Christmas, Cane noticed. Bozeman had also had its first snowfall a week ago, but most of it had melted since temperatures had climbed to spring-like numbers. The warmer weather encouraged the men in town to get the decorations up before the next cold spell, which would set in and last for several months.

Though Annie was in the midst of planning their wedding, she'd roped Cane into helping the marshal and others decorate the town. It had started snowing just as James and Cane finished their work. They headed inside Katie's Palace, welcoming a hot cup of coffee. Cane came to a dead stop when he saw Annie sitting in a chair, rocking the new Freeman addition. Luke James Freeman, born a week ago at a healthy nine pounds, was sobbing pitifully.

Cane saw Annie duck her head and hold the baby close, but he didn't stop fussing. She stopped rocking and jiggled the baby until the baby's father arrived.

"Thanks, Annie." James took his son in his arms. "I'll go fetch Katie. It appears Luke needs a bedtime snack."

He left, and Cane took his place beside Annie. "You ready to go home soon? By the way, where's Mark?"

"I'm ready, and Mark's at home with Father, helping pick out the Christmas tree—the biggest ever, he wants."

"Let's go home and see how he's doing." He took her arm.

Some men came stomping in then, and he turned to find Jed Porter and several of his hands. Porter sneered at Cane. It took all of Cane's fortitude to keep his hands from forming into fists and plastering the bastard's face. Again. Porter had been gossiping worse than any old woman in town about Annie lately. Cane had heard, from James, that Porter had accused Annie of being a witch. His hands formed into fists, and he took a step toward Porter but stopped when a hand grabbed his arm. Looking down, he saw Annie's worried expression.

She whispered, "He's nothing but a pest. He's just mad I accepted your proposal, not his."

Katie and James returned, their daughter Melanie with them, the baby in Katie's arms.

"Thanks so much for your help, Annie," Katie said.

"Yes, thank you," James said, holding onto Melanie. "Both of you."

"Any time," Cane murmured, settling Annie's arm through his.

Anne smiled. "You're welcome. See you all later."

As they made their way out of town, Annie kissed his cheek. Cane looked back and saw Jed Porter standing outside The Palace, scowling, his face beet red. Cane turned back to Annie with a satisfied expression.

Cane hoped the bastard would choke on his regret.

CHAPTER 6

December, 1888

One week before Cane and Annie's wedding, Montana was struck by a snowstorm. Ten inches of snow fell across the territory, blowing and drifting in the howling winds, closing down all businesses in town.

Tom Callahan had purchased several hundred head of Texas Long-horns from the abundance driven by cowboys from Texas to Montana that fall. Tom and Cane had set out mid-morning to call in the ranch hands and gather up as many of the herds as they could, hoping to save them from the blizzard.

Now Annie stood at the library windows, listening to the howling wind, watching the swirling snow. A horse appeared, then another, and she breathed a sigh of relief. More horses, stumbling along, fighting against the howling winds and driving snow, came into sight. Thank heavens they'd arrived home before dark.

"Mark! They're back!" she called.

"Yippee!" Mark shouted as he met up with her in the hallway. She followed Mark to the door. Mark yanked open the door and stepped back as a snow-covered mountain of a man plodded through the entrance.

"Cane?" Annie said, barely able to make out his features. He was covered in snow, ice pellets were frozen on his Stetson, a shadow of beard on his face. Her father stood beside Cane, looking years older than before he'd left the house. She'd insisted they wear long woolen scarves over their heads before putting on their hats. All she could think was how the scarves probably helped in saving them from freezing to death.

Shocked, Annie nevertheless took charge, grabbing both men's arms to guide them into the library. Her father sank to the divan and closed his eyes. "No. Stay awake, Father," Annie ordered. When he didn't respond but kept his eyes shut, she snapped, "Wake up!" She slapped him hard on one cheek, and he opened his eyes.

Glaring at her, he muttered, "What in the hell are you trying to do, woman? Kill me?"

None too gently, Annie pulled at his coat with Cane's assistance. "I won't have to kill you. You'll be doing it to yourself if you don't keep your eyes open. We need to get you warm before you can even think about sleeping."

Annie looked at Cane, who looked just as cold and tired. "Cane, let me help you undress." At his wolfish grin, she added, "Your coat only, you devil."

She eased his arms out of his coat sleeves. The woolen coat was soaking wet and stuck to his body. Annie peeled it from him until he stood in his damp shirt and soaking dungarees.

He sighed. "Need a hot bath, but first one for your father. I'll just sit by the fire once we take care of the ranch hands."

"Didn't they head on home?" Annie asked.

Cane shook his head. "Most of them live at The Palace. The weather's too bad to go to town now. They took up our offer to stay here in the barn."

"But we've no heat out there!" Annie protested. "How many came?"

Bundled in her winter-wear, Annie went to the barn with Cane. "Come inside the house, everyone," she called.

Hours later, after the last hand and her father had settled down for the night, Annie fell into a chair before the fire in the library. She and Cane sat and drank hot rum until they were sleepy-eyed. Cane stood up and swept his hair back from his forehead.

Annie stirred and sat up straight in her chair. "Sorry, I didn't mean to fall asleep on you like that."

He ambled over to where she sat and sank down on his haunches. She stilled when he reached up, took her face between his hands and kissed her. He murmured then against her lips, "You're exhausted. It's past our bedtime."

When he went to release her face, she clamped her hands over his. "I gave up both of our rooms tonight to others. This room is the only vacant one in the house. I want you to stay with me here for the night."

Cane groaned and closed his eyes. "You know we shouldn't. Not until we're married," he insisted.

She choked on her words. "I almost lost you and my father. What if something were to happen to one of us during the night? Then I'd never know how it feels to be well loved by you. Never know how it feels to make love with you." Annie swiped a tear from her eye. "If something happened and I lost you, I'd never marry, Cane. There's no one else I want."

Frowning, he sank back on his heels. She leaned toward him, hands stretched out. He grasped them and said, "Have you had another premonition? Didn't I tell you to let me know if you did so we can—"

"No. No premonitions, Cane. I just don't want to wait any longer."

"Damn, neither do I," he said, pulling her to her feet. He locked the door. Then, taking her in his arms, he kissed her, even as he undressed her hurriedly. She eagerly waited for him to take her again in his arms, but he didn't. He just looked at her standing before him, clad only in her bloomers, chemise and stockings. She saw the raw desire on his face as he gazed upon her. He reached out and untied the ribbons on her chemise.

Cane's flaring nostrils and the hot-eyed look made her shiver. He moved slowly, increasing her anticipation.

My God! Make love to me!

As if he could read her mind, he picked her up in his arms and laid her down on the divan. He positioned her with her head on one of the arms. He removed her chemise and her bloomers, and she blushed to the roots of her hair.

"Beautiful," he whispered with reverence.

He splayed her legs apart until the sole of one of her feet was on the floor while the other remained bent on the divan seat. Then, standing there, he simply looked at her in pure passion.

Suddenly, she had misgivings and opened her mouth to stop him, but Cane leaned down and took her lips. She felt him beside her then. He was on his knees, at her side.

"I never did thank you for accepting my proposal, Annie." He looked up and she saw the love in his eyes. "But I'm thanking you now. Unfortunately, I haven't had a chance to get you a ring yet, but…"

"It doesn't matter, Cane. It doesn't. Now make love to me."

Annie lay there on the divan like a wanton as she watched Cane undress. Her eyes settled on every part of him, unable to believe his masculine splendor, for he indeed was more beautiful than any man should ever be.

He settled down upon her. He kissed her in places she never dreamed possible, carrying and culminating her arousal to unbearable heights, and she burned for more.

Finally, she begged, "Now, Cane, please! End this torment."

Smoothly, he eased inside her. She felt only a momentary pain before she raised her legs and wound them around his waist, urging him deeper.

Cane gasped. "Oh, sweet Annie, you are something. It's been so long," he groaned. "I want this to be good for you, but I don't know if I can hold out for long."

"Take your pleasure, Cane," she whispered with a smile.

He did, but not before giving her pleasure. He made love to her, and she soared to the heavens and back with him. Afterwards, all she could think was how she'd die if she lost him. She wouldn't want to continue living without him. They dressed after making love.

Later, Cane wakened to the smell of fire. Then he remembered. They were in the library, door locked. The fire in the fireplace must still be burning low, he decided, closing his eyes again, reveling in the warmth of pretty Annie asleep in his arms.

The smell of fire grew stronger, more pungent, and Cane coughed. His eyes shot open then, closing just as quickly as he'd opened them. He rolled off the divan, eyes burning at the smoke filling the library. He coughed again and stumbled to the door. He touched the brass knob and yanked his hand away. "Shit!" It was hotter than a branding iron.

"Annie? Annie!" Cane shook her shoulder, but she hardly stirred. He checked the pulse in her neck.

Still breathing, thank God!

Shouting to alert the others in the house, he picked Annie up in his arms. He wrapped two woolen blankets around her but laid her back down on the divan again.

Grabbing a poker, he smashed a window until every jagged edge of glass was gone. Returning to Annie, he picked her up, climbed through the window, thankful they had been sleeping on the first floor. Just as he'd maneuvered them outside, something hit him on the head.

≈

*a*nnie gasped in the fresh air, her body shivering where she lay on the snow. She sat up, sobbing when she discovered Cane beside her. "Cane? Wake up, Cane!"

As she crouched over him trying to rouse him, she saw color in her side vision. Looking in that direction, she saw a man's boot just as it disappeared around the corner of the house.

Blood seeped from a cut on the top of Cane's head and one across his forehead. Looking skyward, she saw the house engulfed in flames. She picked up a large piece of wood and knew it was the piece that had felled Cane.

"Annie!"

"Father! Over here, outside the library window! Is Mark with you?"

Her father appeared from the back of the house, his face frantic. "No! I thought he was with you!"

"We've got to find him!" Clutching the blankets wrapped around her, she rose and started to run but her father hauled her back, keeping his grip on her.

"You can't go inside. The house is too far gone."

"But Mark! He has to be upstairs."

"I glanced in his room and most of the others before we left the house, and I didn't see him. I called to him, too, and there was no answer. I thought he was with you, or one of the hands took him out. Where else would he have gone?"

"I don't know, but we have to look for him."

"Not inside," her father said. "He's got to be outside somewhere."

Harvey, one of their hands, appeared. "Come into the barn," he shouted. Glancing at Cane, he said, "I'll get Paul to help me get him inside."

"We've another priority. Mark's missing. I want all hands out searching for him," her father said.

Annie stood in the cold, shivering, tears falling down her cheeks and freezing upon them.

Harvey said. "Come on, Miss Annie. We'll find the boy."

Two more hands arrived and carried Cane into the barn. Annie followed, searching for Mark along the way. The snow had stopped, but the temperature had fallen and the wind still blew. As she pulled the blankets tighter around her, she saw movement behind the barn.

As she rounded the barn, she saw a big man, head uncovered, blonde hair blowing as he mounted his horse.

"Hee-yah!" he shouted and spurred his horse into a gallop.

Chills tore through Annie as she put a name to the man, though she hadn't seen his face clearly. Jed Porter! Something lay in the snow, metal-colored, and she slowly approached it. She peered closely and saw a can of some sort, then reared back at the smell of kerosene. Dear God, Jed had set the fire.

Annie ran around to the front of the barn, looked up at the house, the porch below, and saw a figure at Mark's window. "Mark!" she yelled.

"Annie! Help me!" Mark mouthed.

Scampering as quickly as she could through the snow, her feet near frozen, she heard a roar. Looking up once more, she cried, "No!" as glass rained down from several windows in the house

Annie ran to the front door and opened it. She choked on the smoke that billowed outside. Pulling the wool blanket from her shoulders, she wrapped a tail of it around her head and another across her mouth, keeping her eyes uncovered. Racing around the back, she remembered the old set of stairs, once used by servants in the household. The same stairs she'd scolded Mark for using. Praying the fire hadn't caught there yet, she rushed to the kitchen. She yanked at the old door's handle until it opened on the third try. Looking up the rickety old stairs, she was glad to see just a fine mist of smoke.

Annie called up the stairs, "Mark! Head to the old staircase, down by Pa's room."

She heard him sobbing out her name.

When he didn't appear, she shouted again, "Mark! I'm in the kitchen!" She kept calling him until she heard his footsteps overhead drawing near.

He appeared at the top of stairs, then clattered down them, coughing and sobbing at the same time. He flung himself into her arms. "I was afraid, Annie, so I hid in my closet."

"I know. I'm glad you followed my voice. Come on, we have to get out of here."

They reached the kitchen when an explosion rent the air. Annie screamed as chunks of the roof started falling down on them. Dense smoke poured into the kitchen. Pulling Mark with her, she ran to the kitchen door just as a flash of fire ignited the wallpaper, then flamed around the door, blocking their exit. She groaned, seeing the only escape route was the window high above the stove. Both of them were too short to reach the window, even standing on the stove, but she might be able to hoist Mark onto her shoulders and ease him through it. The danger of the fall he'd be taking to the ground outside made her look for other options.

In the living room, she saw nothing but flames. A hissing sound over her shoulder prompted her to look back in time to see the parlor curtains burn up faster than dried tinder. Then she remembered the kitchen pantry. It might offer them protection if they couldn't get outside—until someone found them. Or it would be their final resting place. If nothing else, at least she could give Mark some peace in his final minutes.

It was their only chance. Dragging Mark along, both of them coughing, they stumbled into the kitchen again. Annie pulled on the pantry door. The cedar-lined room was stacked with food supplies, free of smoke and fire for the moment. She cleared out a corner, closed the door tight and sank to the floor, pulling Mark down with her.

"Annie?"

She looked down, barely making out the glint of his eyes in the darkness.

"Are we gonna die?"

"No, we're not."

Please, God.

The stinging in her eyes subsided and the coughing as well. The pantry door seal at the floor was fairly tight and kept out most of the smoke.

"I'm tired," Mark complained.

"Then close your eyes and lean against me. We'll rest a bit."

As the boy fell asleep, and then her own eyes started closing, she prayed somehow someone would put out the fire, or come for them.

~

"*W*here are they?" Cane shouted.

"We've looked everywhere," Callahan said, sounding defeated.

No! I won't lose my family now that I've finally found them.

He'd been searching for Annie and Mark himself for what seemed like forever, with no success. He paused and stared at the burning house, knowing it was lost. Could Annie have gone back inside to search for Mark? He prayed she hadn't, but knowing Annie's love for the boy exceeded all things, including her safety, he realized he had only one choice but to go inside.

He ran toward the house, whipping around when Callahan called out to him. "Cane! She wouldn't have gone back inside!"

"I have to see for myself," Cane replied. His voice was cold and uncompromising. He wouldn't allow anyone to stop him.

Fire blocked his path through the front door. He ran around to the library window. More fire. He needed something to protect himself, so he returned to the barn. There was a horse trough filled with water that was frozen.

No good, damn!

He paused, feeling the other men's eyes on him, watching him in silence. Snow would work. He tore a blanket down from a peg and ran back outside. He covered it with the heavy snow, waited a minute, then rubbed the moisture into the wool, hoping it was wet enough to afford him the protection he required.

Whipping the wet blanket around him, he ran to the back side of the house, to the kitchen area. He stood there shivering. When he touched the kitchen doorknob, it was hot. Callahan appeared. "Step back, Callahan," he said.

He saw smoke and fire inside through the window, but he had to go in. Bracing himself, he flew against the door, dodging to the left and falling to the snow. The damage the fire had already caused weakened it, and it crashed in while a backdraft explosion of heat and flames rushed out.

Fire spread across the kitchen. He heard whimpering then coughing. Whirling around, he followed the intermittent sounds, shouting, "Mark! Annie!"

No reply, but he heard more coughing and followed it until he stopped outside the pantry door. His hand burned when he touched the doorknob, and he pulled it back. "Shit!"

Grabbing a hank of the blanket, he covered his hand and grabbed the knob once more. He yanked it open and, as he stood in the doorway, his heart filled with joy. Mark and Annie sat slumped on the floor against a wall. Praying they were alive, he squatted and checked their breathing.

They were alive! He reached to take Mark, but Annie suddenly opened her eyes—eyes filled with horror.

"You can't have him! You can't!" she screamed, hugging Mark close.

She appeared to be awake, but Cane believed she was asleep or in the midst of another premonition.

No time to think or reason with her now!

He wrenched Mark from her arms.

She moaned, "No, no! You can't take him."

Not wasting any time with words, Cane backed out of the pantry with Mark. He saw Callahan standing just outside the kitchen door. "Mark, Grandpa's right outside. Go to him."

Mark was groggy and ignored Cane's command, shouting, "Annie! Annie, don't let him…"

Cane smacked Mark's cheek and shook him. "It's me, your Pa, and Grandpa's here, so go on!"

His shouts and slaps startled but alerted Mark to his surroundings. Confusion filled his face as he stared at Cane. "Pa?"

If a heart could break, it would be his. *Damn!* His words had slipped out accidentally, and now Mark needed to be told. He prayed Annie wouldn't be angry, but there was no turning back now.

Urgency prevailed once more. "Get outside now. Grandpa will help you. I'll help Annie."

"I don't have no grampa!" Mark wailed as he tore outside.

Cane returned to the pantry. Annie fought him, screaming in his ear, flailing her arms and wind-milling her legs. "Shh, it's me, darling," he whispered, trying to hold her against him. "Wake up, damn it."

She slumped in his arms and tears poured from her eyes as she stared at him unbelievingly.

With a sob, she latched onto him. "You were the man in my vision, Cane, only you were trying to *save* us. The evil I felt was the fire."

Hauling her into his arms, he strode out of the pantry.

"Later," he said brusquely. He rushed outside. Mark and Callahan stood with worried faces, watching for them to exit. The sizzling he'd heard earlier happened again, and Cane snatched Mark up in his arms and hauled Annie along with him.

"Run!" he called to Callahan.

Callahan came behind and helped Annie. Together, they ran across the yard to the barn, then stopped and saw the house walls crumble and the roof tumble inside, the timber creating more tinder for the fire.

Annie sobbed. "Our house! Oh, Father, what are we going to do? And our possessions—all gone."

Callahan swiped soot from his face. "But we have our lives, every one of us, and that's a blessing."

Annie shivered as tears streamed down her cheeks. Cane stood beside her, his arms around her. "Honey, we have to go into town. Hopefully, Katie can find room for us at her place."

Teeth chattering, Annie nodded. All of them loaded up into two wagons and headed for Bozeman. The road was packed with snow, rough and uneven, but thankfully, the storm had passed. By the time they arrived outside The Palace, they were all frozen. Cane was worried about Annie and Mark since neither of them had any feeling in their fingers and toes.

James rushed out of the saloon and, without a word, hustled them inside. James and Katie made room for all of them. Callahan's hands had their own rooms at The Palace, to which they retired in exhaustion.

When Mark was resting, Cane sat with Annie. "You can cry, honey," he said softly, kissing her thawing fingers.

She sniffed. "I don't want to scare Mark."

"Mark had all of us hovering over him to keep him warm as we could. He's fine."

Annie nodded and allowed a few tears to streak down her cheeks. She closed her eyes and leaned back against the divan in Katie's parlor. Exhaustion unlike any she'd ever felt overwhelmed her. She snuggled into his strong, safe arms, felt herself being lifted but was too tired to respond. Warm blankets covered her, and she fell asleep.

Cane carried her up to one of the Palace's bedrooms and he stood over her, watching her for a while, until he was sure she was sleeping soundly, then left for his own room.

*S*he wakened in the dark of the night, crying out even as another vision came to her. She was staring out the library window in her home, watching in horror as Jed Porter poured liberal streams of kerosene over the ice and snow, then struck a match.

She screamed in time with the first explosion and sat up straight in her bed. Cane was there and pulled her into his arms from where he sat beside her.

James burst into the bedroom and stood in the doorway. "What happened?"

"Annie had a vision, that's all, or maybe a nightmare," Cane replied.

"No!" Annie looked between the two of them. "I have always had the visions *before* an event happened. This time, I experienced it afterwards. Jed Porter set the fire at our house, James. I saw him!"

Frowning, James moved closer to her. "You saw him where? When?"

"In the vision, yes, but I saw him when we were back there, after we got out of the burning house. I saw him escaping on his horse, but I couldn't dwell on it. I had to look for Mark," she said. "In my vision, just a second ago, he set the fire. N-No one actually saw him set the fire, though, so it'll be his word against mine, won't it?"

"Afraid so," James said, "but I believe you and your visions. You may think of it as a curse, but honey, it's a gift. It truly is. Of course, it would help if we can find some evidence or proof since folks don't want to believe in your "gift." Try and get some more sleep."

"I saw a kerosene can by the barn—it wasn't one of ours. Oh, what in the world is wrong with Jed? My God, we've been friends forever! How could he do something so awful? I can't believe how much hatred he has for me," she sobbed.

Cane knelt beside her. "He was in love with you, Annie, and sometimes love can make people do awful things, especially when they realize their love isn't reciprocated. Mostly, though, love is the most wonderful thing that can happen to a person. I know, because I've found love with you, sweetheart."

He took her into his arms then and held her as she cried.

≈

*T*he following morning, Cane, James and his two deputies rode out to retrieve the gas can Annie mentioned, then went to question Jed. Ironically, he had no witnesses to vouch for his whereabouts last evening. Even his ranch hands confessed to not knowing. The gas can matched several others in his barn. James brought him in and locked him up, saying Jed could rot jail until the circuit judge came to town. Arson was a serious crime, and he intended on forcing a confession out of the man.

James conferred with Cane's testimony of having heard Jed's fury and complaints to others in town that Miss Annie hadn't accepted his marriage proposal, instead choosing to marry a criminal. Of course, he'd already had to put Jed in jail once because he couldn't accept that Annie didn't want him.

One of the deputies noticed snow prints in the fresh fallen snow, around the Callahan family's barn and house, prints that matched Jed's boot size perfectly, but then, many men in the area wore the same size boot as Jed. And then, positive evidence was found; a small, silver cigar case with Jed's name engraved on it. A confession wouldn't be needed after all.

That night, Cane, Mark and Annie sat at Katie's dining room table with her family and ate beef stew and cornbread, a moroseness filling the air.

Cane noticed Mark's typically upbeat disposition wasn't so happy. "What's the matter, son?" he asked.

"We don't have no house, no more, no clothes—nothing—but you know what's really bad? The best Christmas tree we ever had is gone."

Katie patted Mark's hand. "Christmas will still happen. Only you'll be celebrating with us, here, if that's all right with you."

Mark nodded and swiped self-consciously at a stray tear.

Callahan took Mark onto his lap as the boy sobbed harder. "James, Katie," Callahan said, "We can't thank you enough for taking us in. But it might be a while longer than you think since the soonest we can start building a house is spring.

Katie laughed. "I'd love the company. So would James. And we will enjoy the merriest of Christmases together."

"Mark," Callahan said, "we need to talk with you about something else."

Katie and James wisely left the dining room to allow them privacy.

Mark's eyes widened on Callahan. "He said you were my grampa! I told him I ain't got no grampa, just you. You're my pa!"

Cane saw the sorrow in Callahan's eyes and stepped in to help. "Mark? You know you were adopted when you were a baby."

"Yup. Pa said my ma died."

"She did. I loved your ma—a lot. I made my way from Texas to Bozeman every year, driving cattle, and met your ma here. When I left for Texas again, I had planned on it being the last time 'cause I asked your ma to marry me. She would have if she hadn't died right after you were born. Then I got into some trouble in Texas and couldn't return— until I came earlier this year. I didn't know anything about you being born for a long time. I had no idea I had a son, but as soon as I did learn, I came right here. I want you to live with me 'cause you're my son. We look a lot alike. You said so, remember?"

Mark started crying. Between the tears, his voice trembled. "But I don't wanna live with you! I wanna live with Pa and Annie."

Annie said, "Mark, you know me and Cane are getting married soon. Cane…your pa…asked Grampa to live with us. We'll build a big house, and we'll all be together. You'll have all of us, all of the time. How does that sound?"

Relief flooded Mark's face. "Real good," he said, wiping the tears on his cheeks with his shirtsleeve.

Cane smiled. "You don't have to call me Pa, at least not until you get used to me. I'm hoping you learn to like me soon, son."

"I do like you, Mr., uh…Pa."

Cane's heart lurched at the shy look on his son's face.

"I love you, Mark. I feel real bad I missed out on so much of your life. I plan on making up for all that lost time."

Annie took his hand and he turned to her. "And, God willing, I hope we have children, brothers and sisters for you, son."

"Holy cow! I always wanted a brother! No sisters, though," Mark said, his eyes pleadingly looking at Annie then Cane.

"But you love Melanie, don't you? She's a girl," Annie said.

"Yeah, she's okay," the boy said grudgingly.

"Sorry, son, only God is in control of that, not us."

*O*n December 20th, Cane and Annie were married in the First Lutheran Church in Bozeman. Katie gave her friend her own wedding gown to wear. To Cane's mind, as Annie walked down the aisle toward him, he believed she'd look every bit as beautiful wearing a potato sack.

A reception was held at Katie's Palace, and the wedding feast was sumptuous. Cane couldn't recall ever having eaten so much and so well.

By nine o'clock that evening, Cane was growing weary of the guests that still lingered.

At ten, James took Cane's silent hint and proceeded to escort folks out of Katie's Palace.

By eleven, Cane finally got to make love to his new bride.

~

*L*ater that evening, Annie lay beside her husband. She sighed, thinking how wonderful love was. She wore only her white silk stockings and frilly garters. Cane had insisted she keep them on, saying how they fired his blood. She grinned into his chest as heat stole through her body. It had fired more than just his blood and hers.

She thought about how handsome he looked, whether in his jeans a simple shirts or in the black suit, brocaded vest, white shirt and string tie and Stetson he wore today for their wedding.

"You are a wonderful husband, Cane, and I can hardly wait for us to build our house together and raise our children there."

Cane's eyes filled with tears. "I love you, Annie Smith. Never forget it."

"I won't," she said and kissed him again, cementing their promises to each other.

"Do you foresee a happy future for us, Mrs. Annie Smith?" he asked with a smile.

She closed her eyes and concentrated, tormenting him just a little. Slowly, she replied, "Yes, I envision the happiest future anyone could have."

"I've found heaven, a reason for living, with you, my son, and any other children God gives us. This Christmas of 1888, I'll remember with perfect clarity for the rest of my life."

"So will I, my love." Giving him an innocent little smile, she said, "I think I'm through talking. For now."

"What about screaming?" he growled softly. "Bet I can make you scream."

"You can't, you won't!" she said on a giggle.

Pressing against his chest, she tried levering herself up off him, but he wouldn't allow it. She relaxed after he gently kissed her neck. "Well, perhaps a little scream or two would be okay."

She heard him chuckle as he rolled them over until she was beneath him—exactly where she wanted to be.

THE END

JANIE AND THE JUDGE

Left homeless and destitute, widow Janie Miller is forced to take the only job she can as a prostitute in a saloon. But before she even beds her first customer, she's arrested for prostitution.

Judge Simon Hopkins oversees Janie's case and sentences her. Upon her release from jail, Simon assists her in finding a job at a reputable saloon. Soon Simon, a confirmed bachelor, begins to fall in love with the calm and gentle woman.

However, Simon has put away plenty of criminals, some of whom have been released and could come gunning for him. He'd like nothing better than to marry Janie, but can he take the chance?

CHAPTER 1

December 1888
Butte, Montana

"Quiet!" Judge Simon Hopkins ordered, pounding his gavel on the hardwood table that served as the bench of law in Butte and Bozeman, Montana. Simon was the only circuit judge to appear in Bozeman one month, then in Butte, the next. Having given his one warning, loud voices dropped to murmurs.

He hated the atmosphere today—eagerness mixed with anticipation —for folks in Butte knew everyone appearing today had been arrested for prostitution.

"Baliff, first one?" Simon said, directing his gaze at his assistant, Jordan Peterson.

Mrs. Janie Miller, rise," Peterson announced.

When Simon had first read the sheriff's report of the crime, he'd found it difficult to believe a married woman would prostitute herself, but then he saw that her husband was deceased, which meant she'd likely been left destitute.

Simon shoved his spectacles higher on his nose and looked up to see a tall woman in her mid-twenties standing before him. Her black hair she'd pulled back severely from her face and she wore widow's weeds. Looking closer, Simon saw wisps of curls framing her face. The bit of fluff softened her features. Her lips were closed tight, her small chin pointy and slightly defiant.

Good. The woman was a fighter. She'd need to be.

"Mrs. Miller, have you legal representation?"

She gaped at him and he felt more than a bit foolish. He guessed she didn't have a lawyer because she couldn't afford one—yet it was a standard question he asked everyone before sentencing.

"Yes, she has, your honor," a loud voice from the back of the courtroom called.

Simon saw a stocky man, slightly receding hairline, forty or so. He was dressed well, in a fine brown summer weight suit and he used an ebony cane as ornamentation rather than need. He was also sweating profusely. Simon caught the heated look in the man's eyes as he looked at Mrs. Miller and knew the man possessed unsavory thoughts about her.

"No!" Mrs. Miller declared. "He's not my lawyer but my husband's brother who only wants—"

She didn't finish her response but looked away, that chin held high once more.

Simon met her hazel-colored eyes that begged him to understand why she didn't finish speaking. Beneath her deceivingly plain appearance was a beauty, one who'd fallen on hard times. "He wants what?"

After a long while, when she didn't reply, he prompted, "Mrs. Miller?"

"Me," she whispered, looking down at her hands which she kept twisting in front of her.

Simon nodded at his bailiff.

Peterson looked at the man standing in the back of the courtroom. "Proceed to the bench, sir."

The man walked swiftly to the front, stopping beside Mrs. Miller, who seemingly cringed away from him.

"Your name?" Simon demanded.

"Clive Miller. Mrs. Miller was married to my brother, Robert."

"Has Mrs. Miller hired your services? Are you a solicitor?"

"I am an attorney, your honor, but alas, Mrs. Miller has too much pride to take up my offer. My poor sister-in-law has been distraught since my brother's demise, and not thinking clearly."

"That's not true," she said in a trembling voice.

"It seems the lady has a difference of opinion. She has obviously refused your offer, so that's that. You may sit down."

"But your honor—"

Simon's eyes riveted on the man. "You heard me, now sit down, or leave."

The man stalked out of the courtroom, murmurings following in his wake.

"Order!" Simon slammed his gavel down on the desk.

The voices subsided. Looking over the top of his spectacles, Simon asked, "Are you pleading not guilty, Mrs. Miller?" Poking his finger at the report in front of him, he added, "It seems there's more than one witness to your crime at the White Pearl Saloon. Do you deny that? If so, then we go to trial. If not, then I will proceed with sentencing."

"I am guilty," she whispered, "but not of the act itself."

"Finish, please," Simon demanded, though he kept his voice soft and gentle. He knew precisely what she meant, but he had to hear her say the words, though they wouldn't clear her. Even if she hadn't bedded a man she'd been caught with intent to do so.

"We hadn't fornicated yet."

～

*L*ouder murmuring filled the courtroom then and Janie saw the condemnation in the women's eyes, and lewd looks from several of the men. Her cheeks burned. She glared at the judge and knew he'd known what she meant before she'd confessed the words aloud, furious he'd made her say them.

"Yet you were there, in Farley Hanson's room at the Pearl to do exactly that, correct?"

Bowing her head, she looked down at her folded hands and nodded.

"I'm afraid you'll have to speak up, Mrs. Miller."

"Yes, I was." She kept her focus on her hands, which she'd kept clasped together to control their shaking.

"Why?"

She looked at him, raising her brow as humiliation flooded her body. "Ex...excuse me?" How much more explanation did he want?

"Allow me to rephrase that. What were the circumstances that would drive you to do such a thing?"

"Why...I...oh dear," she whispered as tears welled in her eyes.

Murmurings started again and she squeezed her eyes shut, hearing whispers of 'whore' among the crowd.

"Quiet!"

She caught the agitated expression on the judge's face as he pounded the gavel again and rose. Looking at his bailiff, he said, "I want a moment of privacy with Mrs. Miller." He strode out of the courtroom, his robes flying away from his long, lean body with each long stride.

A deputy opened the door for the judge and he sailed through it. Janie stood there, quivering, and wondering what to do. Should she just follow him? Then she saw the bailiff headed toward her and she cringed when he grasped her arm and led her the same way the judge had gone.

"No need to worry, ma'am," the big, burly man whispered. "Judge is a fair man."

In the judge's dark-paneled chambers, Janie stood before his desk, in silence. She watched him look through several pieces of paper before setting them down, settling back in his chair and fixing a disconcerted look on her.

Janie clutched her hands and met his irritated gaze.

"Stop doing that," he said. "I'm not going to eat you for my supper."

Janie wondered about that but relaxed her hands, observing the man who would decide her fate. He was perhaps only a few inches taller than her, whipcord lean with straight black hair sprinkled with a tiny bit of gray.

His piercing dark eyes unsettled her. She caught a light shadowy color along his jaw-line, telling her he was one of those men who grew a beard an hour after shaving. He appeared to have an innate strength in him. The man made her nervous—very much so. But then, he would be the one handing down her sentence.

Heaving a deep sigh, he dropped the papers, came around the desk, pausing beside a chair. "Have a seat, Mrs. Miller."

She slid into the hardwood chair and kept her gaze lowered to her lap.

"Good."

She looked up and saw he'd folded his arms across his chest and was leaning against the desk. "Explain to me how you came to be at the White Pearl last evening, and why. What purpose did you have for going there?"

"I already said, I needed money." Her reply was terse but she didn't regret it. Men had been bullying her all her life and she'd had enough of that treatment.

"And prostituting yourself was the only way to go about earning your way?"

"I'd applied all over town for work but no one would hire me. I recently learned someone had been a step ahead of me and was sabotaging my chances at securing a position."

"Your deceased husband left you with nothing? No home to possibly mortgage? Was he a rancher?"

"A farmer. Shortly after his death, I discovered he'd lost our home and the little livestock we had in a card game."

"To whom?"

"I have no idea," she lied. "The day following his death some men I didn't know arrived at our place—eighteen miles south of here—to say they owned the property now and I had forty-eight hours to vacate the premises. Believe me, I questioned them thoroughly. They told me how Robert had lost our homestead gambling."

"Yet you don't know who these men were?"

Janie started to shake her head but stopped when she saw him staring at her hard, obviously weighing her words for the truth. But she also saw something in his expression she hadn't seen from any other man in her life—kindness—and decided to tell him the truth.

"The same man who won the property was the same man who claimed to be my attorney."

Simon's eyes widened. "You mean to tell me your brother-in-law took your home from you? Because the gambling debt was between him and his brother?"

She nodded and swiped at tears running down her cheeks. "I'm fairly certain he's also the person standing in the way of my securing any work in Butte."

"Why?"

"My husband has always had a weakness for gambling, of which I had no idea when we married. My brother-in-law has always...well, he's always coveted me."

~

*Y*es, Simon could see why a man would want Mrs. Janie Miller. She was pretty, seemingly intelligent, softly spoken, feminine, everything a man could want—even Simon—that is, if he were looking for marriage. He was like most men, wanting certain things in life; a comfortable home, bed, a decent job to make a living, wife and children. But he was also a pragmatic man and knew that in his chosen work he'd made plenty of enemies. He refused to marry and have children, which could jeopardize their safety—their lives. He'd remain a bachelor all his days, not that he hadn't been involved with any women—he had—but not in a long while.

Simon cleared his throat. "All right. You've admitted your guilt, that you had every intention of fornicating with Farley Hansen. Correct?"

She nodded.

"You understand that I'll be sentencing you to spend the next month, incarcerated in the Bozeman jail, don't you?"

Her eyes widened and she shook her head. "No, why, the thought never crossed my mind."

"How did you think you'd pay for your crime? You've no money to pay the fine, I assume."

"No," she whispered.

His heart clenched at the tears streaming down her cheeks. "I'll order the sheriff to place you in a cell by yourself for the thirty days. You'll be well protected. Then, once you've served your time, I'll be back, with a job offer for you."

What a mixed blessing, Janie thought; a thirty-day prison sentence and the possibility of a job at the same time. Yet, doubts surfaced. Much of her life had been spent in servitude—first to an abusive father, then husband. Why should she even think to have hope in what this man had to offer? Narrowing her eyes, she asked, suspiciously, "What sort of job?"

"Help in managing a place called Katie's Palace."

"A saloon?" Dread filled her heart.

"It's a lodging, restaurant and saloon in one." She opened her mouth to tell him under no circumstances would she work in a saloon again, in any capacity when he held his hand up, stopping her.

"The place is legal and the owner, Katie Freeman, has recently had a baby and wants to spend most of her time at home caring for her baby and her little girl. Her husband is James Freeman, Bozeman's sheriff. She's looking for someone to manage her business. She needs a trustworthy replacement, and I've been told throughout my life I'm an excellent judge of character. You'd be the perfect person for the job."

She sputtered, "But I know nothing about managing a saloon!"

"Like I said, it's a lodging house and restaurant and you've managed a home before seeing as you'd been married, so I assume you'll manage this place just fine. Of course, you'd have to move to Bozeman."

Biting her lip, she thought about his offer. Since Clive had sabotaged her chances at getting a respectable job in Butte, and she had to survive, she decided this offer was a good one. What were the chances that a judge could be as evil as Clive, after all? She just didn't think it possible. She met his gaze. "I have nothing here in Butte to hold me. Have you mentioned me to Mrs. Freeman?"

"I will when I return to Bozeman this week."

She rose to her feet and stuck out her hand. "I accept your very generous offer, Judge Hopkins. Thank you. I'm just hoping Mrs. Freeman will hire me."

"She will. She trusts my judgment in people." He took her hand. "Don't thank me too soon, though. The Palace is a popular place and busy most of its open hours. You'll work hard for your money, believe me."

"Hard work never bothered me."

He squeezed her hand, then released it. She caught a glimmer of admiration in his eyes before he concealed it and took her arm.

"Come. I hate to do this but the law's the law. He escorted her to the door and back into the courtroom where a full crowd still waited. People were talking loud and babies were crying. Good grief, Janie thought, how could a person bring a baby to something like this?

The judge left her at her seat and she stood, facing him as he sat behind his desk once more. He smashed his gavel down again and the room quieted. "After private conversation with Mrs. Miller, she's admitted her guilt. The city of Butte remands Mrs. Miller to a sentence of thirty days in jail, in Bozeman. Next case!"

As the Bailiff led Janie out of the courtroom she glanced back at Judge Hopkins who'd already moved on to hearing testimony of one of the prostitutes she'd met at the White Pearl Saloon. The woman had legal representation and she wondered if this would help keep her from jail.

Later, Janie learned it hadn't helped a bit for that same prostitute was housed for the next month in the cell next to hers. Over the next thirty days the woman kept to herself even though Janie would try and talk to her from her cell, especially when the woman's caterwauling kept Janie awake at night.

Janie's month in jail dragged, until Christmas. For the first time in years, Janie celebrated Christmas and enjoyed herself, even if she was behind bars. Judge Hopkins had arrived with a picnic basket luncheon he'd had a local eatery pack for them. In three days, she'd be leaving her cell and the judge would escort her to The Palace.

Janie was nervous and excited at the same time about starting a new life for herself. She didn't know how she'd ever be able to repay this kind man for coming to her aid. She'd find a way, though, because she refused to be beholdin' to anyone.

∾

Simon sat with Sheriff James Freeman and his wife, Katie, as he told them about Janie Miller, keeping his fingers crossed that they'd trust his judgment.

"So, the woman sounds like she's had her share of suffering in life, that's for sure," James Freeman said.

"Yes, she's been dealt a raw hand," Simon said. "I promise that she'll work out fine for the job."

"Simon? We believe you, and trust your judgment in people. Always have," Katie added with a smile. She pecked Simon's cheek then rose to her feet. "If you gentlemen will excuse me, I've a baby to feed."

Simon stood up and watched Katie leave the parlor and head upstairs to feed her baby. He glanced down at James when he heard him laugh.

"That boy possesses the most voracious appetite. It seems Katie is hardly finished feedin' him when he wants to eat all over again."

Where's your older kids today?"

"Luke and Hannah are out at the Lawson farm. Madeline Lawson was having a birthday party for her two." He chuckled. "Haven't had this much peace and quiet since the two of them were born."

"You're a blessed man, James."

James came to his feet. "I am." Tilting his head to one side, he added, "You should try marriage, Simon."

"You know how I feel about that. I've plenty of enemies and refuse to put a family in harm's way."

"A body can't live like that forever, and you know it. There are plenty of judges and lawmen who've married and have had no problems."

"Yes. And there are just as many who have. Have you any idea how many men I've put behind bars, and how many of them are now free and possibly looking for revenge?"

"No idea, but like I said, you can't live looking over your shoulder your entire life."

"What you say makes sense, but I haven't changed my mind on the topic."

"Maybe because you haven't met the right woman, yet. I was a lot like you, my friend, before meeting Katie. It's like lightning striking and your life changes. For the better, I might add."

"You could be right," Simon said, thinking about Janie Miller.

CHAPTER 2

January 1891
Bozeman, Montana

"Mrs. Miller? There's no need for thanks and there's nothing I can think that you can do to repay me. Simply put, you needed work and I knew of a position."

Janie nodded and didn't say another word.

Simon slapped the reins against his horse' back as he sped down the snow-packed road in his wagon toward Bozeman. Having made the trip several times over the years, he knew they'd be there within minutes. He was tired and cold and annoyed at Janie Miller telling him how much she appreciated his help, for the tenth time this trip. Damn! Hadn't anyone ever done anything kind for her?

Holding the reins in one hand he managed to button the top button of his coat. He hated Montana's winters and longed for summer's warmth. Glancing down he caught her wringing her glove-clad hands again. "Please, stop doing that."

She frowned. "Doing what?"

Simon met her worried look. "That squashing, wringing thing you do with your hands. There's nothing to worry about you know. You'll love the Freemans and they'll love you."

"I...well...I was thinking over the job duties. I don't know much about book keeping, but that's the only part of the job I've never done."

"No problem. Mrs. Freeman said if you didn't have any bookkeeping experience she'd do her own books at home. She requires someone to watch over the general operation of Katie's Palace." He smiled and added, "Stop it now, you'll do just fine."

She gave him a shy smile and his heart lurched. Good grief, this sad, worried, downtrodden woman was doing things to him no woman had ever done before. Yes, she was pretty, but she lacked confidence in herself. Of course, if he'd been treated so shabbily he supposed he would behave much the same way. But then, he was a man, and men were the stronger breed of mankind, therefore a man should treat a woman with the utmost gentleness and kindness. He was curious to hear her story for he had a feeling her husband had been far from kind to her. He'd seen abused animals and women before, and she fit that perfectly.

"Tell me about yourself, Mrs. Miller. How long were you married?"

"Please. I'm Janie." There was that shy smile again. "You are one of few I can call a friend." I had been married to Robert for fifteen years."

"Fifteen!" At her nod he said, "Good grief, you don't appear old enough to have been married that long. You must have been a child bride."

She laughed. "If you can call sixteen a child, I suppose I was."

"We're you happy with him?" She didn't reply and when he looked down at her he saw her cheeks had turned pink. He ineffectually patted her hand and said, "I'm sorry. I've no right to ask such a personal question."

"No," she said, her voice cracking, "I was not happily married. Robert could never control himself and spent most of the years we were married at the gambling tables, which is why I'm in the current sad state that I'm in."

Simon frowned. "Why didn't you leave the man?"

"You mean divorce him?" At his nod, she continued, "Because I would have found myself in the same sad state earlier, for one. And, I'm a Christian woman who believes in marriage, not divorce."

"Didn't you have any family to call on for help? No men-kin that could have talked some sense into your husband and make him accountable for his behavior?"

"I was an only child and both of my parents are dead. I have an aunt and uncle and a few cousins but they live in New York City. I've never met them. Once a month I'd have about a week reprieve. Then I'd squirrel away money from the sale of eggs from my laying chickens, and milk from the few cows we had left, to pay the mortgage and feed myself. I'd also taken in mending and sewing."

Simon raised his brows. "Reprieve?"

"Yes. Robert would get into a drunken brawl with someone at the tables so the sheriff would toss him in jail for a week to dry out."

"I see." Simon had seen so much of this type of behavior during his years as a judge, which sickened him. And the poor woman had had no one to come to her rescue. If he'd known her and her situation, he certainly would have intervened. Apparently, her husband must not have committed any crimes for he'd never come before Simon in a courtroom for sentencing. He wished he had.

"No," I don't think you do. Someday, I'll tell you, perhaps, but not now. I took care of myself as best I could, working our homestead." She sniffed. "I loved our home and now it's all gone."

"To your brother-in-law who coveted you."

She nodded. "He's a hateful, awful person, and would do anything—legal or otherwise—to have me." Her eyes widened. "Heavens! I wouldn't put it past him to come here and retrieve me."

"We'll keep a watchful eye out for him," Simon promised. Reaching down, he grasped her hand and squeezed it. "I'm sorry your life has been so miserable, but think of this as a fresh new start, hopefully a happy, satisfying one."

"You are so wise, Judge Hopkins," Janie said. Her small smile grew larger the longer she gazed upon him.

"If I'm calling you Janie, then use my name, Simon."

"Simon. I like it."

His pulse sped up at her sweet, dazzling smile. Looking away, he cleared his throat. "We're here. Take a look at your new home."

~

To Janie, Butte resembled Bozeman as she looked up and down both sides of the street, though Bozeman had decorated their town for the holidays with pine branches tied with velvety red ribbons. And several stores still had holiday decorations in the front windows.

They pulled up in front of a two-story gray clapboard sided building and she read the sign, "Katie's Palace."

"This is the place," Simon said. Then she heard him heave a deep sigh. He seemed satisfied to be here which made her wonder if he was more at home in Bozeman than Butte.

He jumped down from the wagon just as a tall, handsome man stepped out of the establishment. Her eyes narrowed on his coat, opened down the front, caught the flashing tin of a badge on his woolen shirt. The local law enforcement had come to greet them? She wasn't sure if this was a good or a bad thing.

The man reached out his hand to Simon. "Glad you're here, Judge. You missed the holiday party, though. And we missed you."

Simon shook James Freeman's hand. "Glad to be home, at least for a month or so. Sorry, got tied up over the holidays and couldn't get here."

Tied up? Janie felt heat seep into her cheeks as she thought about how Simon had spent Christmas with her—in a jail cell.

Janie slid her gaze from Simon to the tall, dark-haired man, who had leveled his eyes on her. Again, heat slid over her face and up her spine.

After a long moment, the man said, "And this must be, Mrs. Miller."

"Sorry," Simon said, "Yes, this is Janie Miller. She's ready, able, and willing to start work whenever you're ready to have her. Janie, this is James Freeman, our local lawman."

James tipped his Stetson to her. "Glad to have you here with us, Mrs. Miller. My wife will be happy you've arrived."

"Thank you for giving me the position," Janie replied, realizing this lawman was the husband of the owner of Katie's Palace.

Just then a baby's high screams filtered from inside the saloon.

"Sounds like my wife needs some help with our youngest. Come on in, then, time to meet Katie."

Simon took her elbow and guided her inside, following the sheriff. Swinging doors led into a kitchen and Janie found herself smiling at the beautiful red-haired woman perhaps a bit younger than herself, stirring something in a big kettle on a stove while holding what appeared to be a newborn in the other arm.

She looked up when they entered the kitchen. "It's about time you returned. Here." She settled the baby in the sheriff's arms. "It's past his naptime. See if you can get him to sleep. He just won't settle down for me." Giving a quick glance at Simon and Janie, she added, "Janie Miller?"

"Yes, ma'am," Janie replied.

"I'm Katie, and please, call me that. Ma'am makes me feel old."

Right then and there, as Janie considered Katie Freeman's twinkling eyes, she knew she'd found a friend in the woman. "I can't thank you enough for this position."

Katie shook her head. "No thanks needed. You'll be doing me a favor. I've tried for weeks to find someone already here in town to take the job but no one was available to help. I've three children who need me at home, the last born just two weeks ago. Excuse me while I finish this batch of beans." She grinned at Simon. "Good seeing you, stranger. You missed Christmas with us."

"Sorry."

"Don't let it happen again," she groused.

"No, ma'am." Simon just smiled at her reproachful expression. Then she turned back to the pot on the stove.

James looked wistfully down at his son. "Isn't he something?"

He was, for certain, Janie decided. The baby was gorgeous. Janie saw the deep brown hair on the baby's head and soft, creamy complexion. The little boy had his eyes open and they appeared a bit crossed as they focused on James. Yes, definitely a newborn, Janie decided, and a decided 'ringer' in appearance to his father. 'Daddy' was smitten.

Simon stroked the baby's cheek. "He sure is a keeper." He shook his head and lifted one eyebrow. "Never thought I'd see you father of one child let alone three."

"Me neither, but being a father and a husband to Katie, is the best thing that's ever happened to me." James looked over at Katie. "I'd be nothing without them. Lost, you know?"

Simon nodded. "Yeah, you would, for sure."

"Later," James said, then left the saloon.

"Let's have a seat while Katie finishes in the kitchen. I'll fetch us some coffee."

After Simon, left Janie looked around. The boarding house was big, beautiful and bountiful, no other way to describe Katie's Palace. Wood paneled walls gleamed from a recent varnishing. Copper clad decorations, including a huge clock on one wall graced the place. Warmth exuded from every corner, from the checkered tablecloths to the polished wooden chairs. Janie had noticed right off the modern kitchen and looked forward to preparing food there. A deep warmth of contentment settled inside her; she had a feeling she'd be very content here. Maybe even happy.

She settled down at one of the tables and removed her thread-worn coat, glad they'd arrived, apparently, between lunch and supper. Being new in town, not knowing anyone, gave her a sense of ease. Since her reputation was now in tatters in Butte, she was glad she'd left. Besides, too many sad memories… She watched Simon head back to her, a steaming cup of coffee in each hand. He sank into a chair and slid the coffee across the table.

"Thank you," she said, winding her hands around the cup, the heat warming her. She looked around then met the gentle look in his eyes. "I'm nervous. Sorry."

"No need to be sorry, or nervous for that matter. You'll get along well with Katie. She's a wonderful woman, and a good friend. So is James. They're good people. The type of folks you perhaps haven't had much contact with in your life."

"No, guess I haven't. I can't thank—"

He banged his cup down on the table, and she caught the glint of steel in his eyes. "Thought we'd established no more thanks were required."

She jerked away from him and looked around nervously.

"What's wrong?" he asked.

"You sound angry."

"I'm not. Just exasperated with you, that's all. I didn't mean to startle you."

"You didn't, all right, you did, but that's okay. I'm just not used to people being nice…"

"He hurt you, didn't he?"

Tears filled her eyes. "Fifteen years I'd been married to Robert. Fifteen years that seemed to last a lifetime," she choked. "Yes, he hurt me, nearly every day."

"Why'd you marry him? You weren't…"

"No. I wasn't pregnant. The Lord above never did bless us with children, but it was for the best. I married him to escape my home life."

"Was that so bad?"

"I can't talk about it. I just can't," she whispered. She couldn't tell a virtual stranger about her abusive father, the reason she'd married Robert at such a young age. She also couldn't tell him how Robert had abused her as well for he'd think her a fool.

Katie arrived, wiping her hands on her apron. She sat down beside Janie. "Sorry, but my main server, Annie, can't come in today."

"Hope everything's okay with her," Simon said.

"Nothing that seven more months can't cure, I suspect, though she should be feeling much better sooner than that.

Simon spewed his last sip of coffee, then apologized, "Sorry about that but are you saying she's having another baby?"

Katie nodded and smiled.

"But that's three babies in three years!"

"It sure is, and Cane and Annie can't be any happier."

"I worry about her, that's all. She had a rough time of it having the first two."

"Let me tell you something, judge; birthing babies isn't easy for most women, no matter if it's the first or last baby. She'll be fine. She's been experiencing a queasy stomach lately. It's wonderful Janie has arrived."

"So, I'll be cooking and serving by myself?" Janie was worried about handling all of the job on her own.

"Heavens, no! I've got two other servers and a full-time cook besides. You'll be overseeing the three of them, filling in though if one of them can't come to work."

Janie nodded. "I can do that."

"Good." Katie slapped her hands on the table. "You'll take your lodgings here, of course."

"Yes, if that's all right with you."

"Yes, I insist. I like having the person who'll be managing my place staying here. Come upstairs and I'll show you to your room so you may freshen up before I explain more about the job." She looked at Simon. "I imagine her bags are in your wagon?"

"Yes. I'll get them." He left the saloon and Katie led Janie up the stairs.

Katie paused outside a door at the end of the hallway and opened it. "Come on in. Tell me what you think."

Janie gasped, "It's lovely! Oh, and it's so large."

Katie grinned and hustled to an armoire, beside it another door. She opened it with a flourish and Janie drew closer.

"Your very own bathing room, too. It's the only bedroom that has its own, everyone else has to share."

"Oh, but I couldn't take this room, Katie. Why, you must keep this for paying guests."

"Nonsense. My paying guests stay but a day or two at a time. You'll be staying for quite a while, at least, I hope you will."

"Of course I'll be staying, as long as you need me...Katie."

"Wonderful."

Just then Simon arrived. They'd left the bedroom door open and he leaned down and set Janie's two bags down inside the doorway.

"Oh! Look at this room," Janie said. "Isn't it the loveliest?"

~

Simon had eyes only for Janie, though he flicked an inquisitive glance at Katie first. "It's the best room Katie's Palace has to offer," he said. "Better than my room, that's for certain."

Janie raised her brow. "You live here?"

He nodded. "I do, when I hold court here, which is about every other month. I alternate between Butte and Bozeman and a couple of other towns as well. Interesting that my room is right next to yours, isn't it?"

Katie gave him an innocent little smile before sauntering past him. "I've work to do. When you're finished unpacking, Janie, meet me in the kitchen."

Simon followed Katie with narrowed eyes. The woman looked entirely too happy for his taste. It was obvious she'd set Janie beside him, to tempt him. She was playing the matchmaker again. Since marrying James, Katie believed everyone should be so content and happy and went out of her way to try and match folks up. She'd been successful half of the time.

It made perfect sense that Katie would give Janie the best room in the palace, since she'd be staying indefinitely—living here on a full-time basis.

"Well, then, I'll unpack. Thank you, Simon."

Simon turned to find Janie standing in her doorway, the door half shut, an apologetic expression on her face. "Yes, you do that, though you don't seem to have much by way of possessions."

"I have enough," she replied.

He'd heard the cool tone in her voice and decided the woman had more than her share of pride. Somehow, he knew, that pride would sustain her and help her make a new life for herself.

"If you need anything at all, don't hesitate to ask me. I'm here for the next twenty days or so." He didn't wait for her reply but turned away, opened the door to his own room and entered.

In his room, he shrugged out of his coat and walked to the window overlooking Main Street. There were few folks out since it was close to evening, and winter had arrived with a wicked cold fury.

He sighed as he sank to his bed, his eyes cutting to articles of his own few personal possessions. As he lay back on the bed and folded his arms beneath his head, the thought struck him; is this all he'd have in life; this tiny room in a boarding house with his few possessions? Is this all? And if it was, why did that thought seem so depressing to him when it hadn't bothered him before?

Simon knew the answer; he hadn't known Janie Miller until now.

~

April 1889
Bozeman, Montana

The man scowled from his position on the second floor of Tate's Boarding House. "Damn!" he spat. "Won't the bastard ever leave town?"

"You talkin' to yerself again, boss?"

Clive Miller looked at, in his opinion, his useless piece of crap foreman and spat a wad of chewing tobacco from his mouth, which landed on his foreman's jacket front.

"Why you gotta do that?" Bart Swenson whined as he looked down at the wad soaking into his jacket.

"Cause you never shut up, that's why," Clive snarled. "Now get the hell out of here. I don't need you hanging over my shoulder, watching me do the job you're supposed to be doing."

The older man snatched his hat off the bed and stalked from the room, slamming the door in his wake.

Taking up his daily vigil as he'd done for the past week—Clive Miller watched the doorway to Katie's Palace for any sign of movement. He'd learned the judge's pattern well and knew he rose early and headed for the jailhouse every morning.

He shouldn't have waited almost three months to come after Janie, but his deceased brother's property had consumed his attention. He also hadn't counted on another man snatching her up, either. Unfortunately, Simon Hopkins clung to Janie like a feather to tar paper, never leaving her alone for a moment when she was out in public. In fact, he hadn't had an opportunity to confront her because she was never alone.

Once he got her alone, he'd have no problem using threats to convince her to marry him, especially now that the judge was interested in her. Pretty Janie. Sweet Janie. The only woman he'd ever loved, yet his damned brother had gotten a hold of her first. He'd hated Robert after that, but had maintained a familial relationship with him only to see Janie. His older brother had taken the only woman Clive would ever love. With Robert's passing though, Clive had been given a second chance. He wouldn't let it slip away—wouldn't let Janie slip away. She belonged with him.

Clive would give her what his brother hadn't been able to—children. He recalled how, after Robert and Janie had been married a year, how Robert had come to him with an unusual, shocking request; to try and see if he could father a child for him and his wife. Clive had refused, unable to believe his brother was that desperate, but he had been. In hindsight, he should have taken his brother up on his offer because now Janie would be bound to him—with their child.

He wouldn't squander a second chance.

CHAPTER 3

*C*ontentment speared through Janie. She had a home, surrounded by people who were friendly and liked her.

Katie Freeman was the nicest person she'd ever met. Her husband was a gem, though somewhat taciturn at times. Janie and Simon, Katie and James, frequently met for supper at Katie's Palace after the supper time crowd dwindled. While she didn't participate in conversation much, Janie listened and enjoyed the friendly bantering between the other three. Oh, to be so comfortable with even one person would be wonderful! To be so in love with one man, to share her hopes and dreams with him, even if they were never fulfilled, would be so satisfying.

After fifteen years suffering abuse and neglect from Robert, Janie had never felt so appreciated and protected. In hindsight, she realized she should have left Robert years ago, but she had been bound to him. She could have returned home to her parents' home when Robert had first showed his true self, but she'd endured a lifetime of abusive treatment from her father. It made no difference; there was no choice. She'd made the same wrong choice as her mother. Now she would live only for herself, though she sighed at what she saw between Katie and James; such devoted love for each other.

Stabbing pain shot through her body then as she thought about Robert's hurtful words and his hands attacking her body; it was her fault they hadn't been able to have any children he'd said. Whose fault it was she had no idea, and neither had the doctors she'd visited in hopes of finding some simple cure. While her heart longed for a child, she knew the Lord had been looking after her; knew Robert would not make a good father so he'd denied them that joy.

But now, as she thought about Simon, she wondered... He'd make a wonderful father, no question in her mind. The man had more patience than ten people and a soft-spoken manner, unless someone infuriated him in his court room, then his deep voice would boom through the space. Yes, he would have made a wonderful father, but she guessed he was several years older than her thirty-two years and, being a bachelor, set in his ways. Getting married and becoming a father were, she guessed, the furthest things from his mind.

Now the four of them sat in the dining room of the palace, eating a late supper when James asked, "Well, Janie, tell me, after three months of working here at Katie's Palace, do you plan on staying put for a while?"

Janie smiled and briefly touched on each of her new friends' faces. "Yes, I feel like this place could be a permanent home for me. You've all been so wonderful. I don't know how to thank you for your kindness."

"There she goes again," Simon exclaimed, throwing up his arms.

They laughed at his remark, and Janie reminded herself to stop thanking them. She was leading a blessed life now, and had these three people to thank for it.

"I love staying home with my brood," Katie said, "and, thanks to you, I can do that now and not feel guilty or anxious about the running of this place. So, the feeling's mutual, Janie. Have you thought at all about your future plans?"

"Now, Katie," James warned.

"What?" Katie gave her husband an innocent look. "I'm just wondering how long she's thinking about staying, that's all."

"Right now," Janie said, "I think I could spend the rest of my life here."

Katie grinned. "Oh! You won't hear me object!"

Simon smiled. "I'd like that." He lifted her hand to his lips and kissed it, releasing it before she could even think about pulling it away.

Janie was disconcerted to find she wanted him to kiss her hand again, and again. Then she caught the smiles on Katie's and James's faces and, flustered, her cheeks feeling hot, she rose from the table. "Excuse me but I'm exhausted and must retire for the night."

"Of course you are," Katie said. You were on your feet making pies all day. You need a good night's rest. Why don't you come in tomorrow at ten instead of six? I'm afraid I'm overworking you so I'll cover the early morning hours, with Annie."

"Oh, I couldn't do that, Katie! You stay home with the children. And I forgot to mention to you that Annie won't be here tomorrow, and Eileen is ill. I'll be down at six as usual."

Annie Smith and her husband, Cane, had had a baby girl they named Eileen, nine months ago, born a month early. The couple had prayed for a miracle and the babe had survived, though she was frail and small and prone to picking up illnesses. And now Annie was pregnant again already. Janie couldn't help but feel melancholy at the thought of having a baby and thought how lucky Annie was to have her children. And Katie, too.

"Sick?" Katie said. She looked at James. "Have you heard about this?"

"Nope, but you know how kids catch everything that comes along, honey," James said, trying to reassure Katie.

"Baby Eileen cannot afford to get sick. I think I'll stop by her place tomorrow morning." Katie rose from the table and, with a chagrinned expression at Janie, said, "Sorry, but you'll have to start at your six o'clock time after all. I'm worried about Annie and her baby. She needs help, being sick herself in the first place with another pregnancy."

Janie patted Katie's shoulder. "If there's anything I can do let me know."

"Thank you."

"Well, goodnight, then," Janie said.

The trio replied in kind and Janie went up the stairs, deciding Katie was the kindest person she'd ever known. Janie was being paid well to manage Katie's Palace, and she would do her job the best she knew how. Then she thought of poor Annie Smith and her baby, praying the babe would gain health soon.

~

*T*he next morning, Janie left her room, closed, and locked the door and bumped into Simon leaving his room.

Grasping her shoulders to steady her, he said, "Sorry. Didn't mean to run into you like that."

Janie had frozen at his touch and her heart sped up as she stood before him, unable to formulate a sentence.

"Are you all right?"

He looked at her, concern in his eyes as Janie thought, no, she wasn't all right. From the moment he'd grasped her shoulders. Her mind had a way of wandering, thinking how easy it would be to fall in love with a man like Simon Hopkins. He was everything her young, girlish heart dreamed of years ago, but then she shook herself out of her reveries. Looking down in embarrassment at her plain black sensible woolen gown and white apron, she decided the bloom of youth had long ago withered away.

"I'm fine." He released her shoulders and she took a step back. "You're up early this morning." She started down the stairs and felt Simon following her.

"I'm holding court today beginning at nine but wanted to head out to the old Rawlings place first. He died a few months back and his family from out east has put his farm up for sale. I thought I'd take a look at it."

"I had no idea you knew anything about farming." She paused outside the kitchen door.

"I don't. I grew up in the heart of New York City. But I'm thinking of trying my hand at it a bit, nothing real serious though."

"If you need any help, don't hesitate to ask."

"You know about farm life?"

She nodded. "My parents were farmers and my husband, too. Yes, I know farm life well."

He grinned. "I may take you up on that offer."

"So, you'll be hanging up your judge hat?" She couldn't imagine him being a farmer, but stranger things in life happened.

"No, but I am thinking of hanging up a shingle with 'barrister' on it. Haven't practiced law for years, but Bozeman could use another attorney seeing as it's just Bob Jensen and Perry O'Connor here. Besides, I'm getting tired of not having any permanent place to hang my hat, though I have to admit I just started having that feeling."

Janie's face burned when she saw the significant look he gave her, and wondered what he meant. Why did he suddenly want permanency? It was none of her business. For all she knew he had a fiancée tucked away somewhere. She knew very little about Simon, except that he was kind, gentle and smart. She bit her lip, unable to think of any more small talk.

"Well, I've got to get to work." Before she could turn away he took her elbow and held her in place.

"There's a barn raising and dance in two weeks out at Annie and Cane's place. Would you go with me?"

Just then Annie came hustling out of the kitchen.

"I didn't expect you here!" Janie exclaimed. "How's the baby?"

Annie, pretty, tiny and blonde with blue eyes swiped a strand of hair off her forehead. "She's doing much better. Fever's gone and she's got a slight cough is all. Cane's caring for her." She smiled and added, "Did I just hear you two talking about our barn raising?"

Simon nodded. "Sure did. I'm waitin' on Janie's reply."

"We'd love for you to come," Annie said.

"Well, let me think…"

"Then that's settled," Simon said. With a tip of his hat, he murmured, "Ladies, until later."

Janie scowled as she watched Simon leave. "Darn it. I hate men making up my mind for me."

Annie gave her a puzzled look. "I don't blame you. Cane has long ago given up on telling me what to do. But Simon doing it is very unusual."

"What do you mean?"

"Being demanding. He's generally not like that, except when he's in his courtroom."

"What does it take to get a cup of coffee around here?"

Janie saw James Freeman sitting at a table near a window and smiled. "You're in here early, Sheriff."

"Early? The sun's been up half an hour already," he groused. "I'll have you know I passed up my wife's coffee to come here for yours, Janie."

She laughed. "Hmm, now that's interesting seeing as your wife's the one who taught me how to make a good cup of coffee."

They all laughed, then James' smile faded as he looked at Annie. "How's Eileen?"

"She's with Cane for the morning and doing much better."

James nodded. "Good." He glanced at his pocket watch. "Got to get to the jailhouse soon, to relieve Harvey earlier than usual. He's got harvesting to do."

"Of course. Coffee comin' right up," Annie said. "And how about some hash and eggs?"

"You twisted my arms."

Both women turned into the kitchen. Janie was surprised that Ethel

Haroldson wasn't in place behind the stove. In fact, the stove was stone cold.

"Ethel's ill this morning," Annie said. "I was just going to start up the stove when you came down. Do you want to cook or serve today?"

"I'll cook," Janie said. Usually, with Ethel here, the both of them cooked and managed to easily keep up with the typical brisk morning crowd on a week day morning, but today she'd be busy alone, which was fine with her. Busy kept her mind off things she had no business thinking.

All morning, as she cooked eggs, bacon and hash and kettles of oatmeal for her hungry customers, she thought about Simon's offer to attend the barn raising and dance. She'd attended plenty of them when she was a young girl, but since marrying at sixteen she hadn't been to one in years.

She thought about Simon, trusting him to be the gentleman he'd thus far proved to be. He would pose no threat to her of a physical nature, but recognized the fact he could do irreparable harm to her poor heart, though, if she let him.

~

*T*wo weeks later, on the day of the barn dance, Katie closed the Palace down early. Most everyone in Bozeman would be out at the Cane place erecting the barn walls that had been built over the past two weeks.

Excitement strummed through Janie, plucking away at the strings of her heart. She recalled the barn raisings she'd attended in her youth and decided they were some of the happiest times in her life. Then dread settled inside her at the thought of dancing. She hadn't in years, and was embarrassed at the thought of making a fool of herself, still, she knew she wouldn't be able to resist an invitation.

Annie had arrived to help her dress in one of Katie's dresses since she hadn't purchased nor found the time to sew herself an appropriate one. Now she looked at herself in the mirror and, twisting side to side, she saw a woman she didn't recognize; one with hope in her eyes. Then memories returned and she saw the woman she'd been the day she married Robert; young, pretty, hopeful…

The dress was peacock blue which enhanced her blue eyes and contrasted well with her dark hair.

Annie pressed down on Janie's shoulders, encouraging her to sit on the edge of the bed.

"Just a bit of color in your cheeks and you'll be the prettiest woman at the dance," she enthused.

Janie pulled back from Annie when she saw she held a small glass jar of rose colored paint in her hand. "Only women of less fortunate circumstances would stoop to wearing face paint, Annie!"

Annie laughed and dug her finger into the jar. "Nonsense! You're a beautiful woman in her prime. And the good Lord would not find fault with you enhancing yourself."

"Maybe you're right," Janie said, hearing the hesitancy in her own voice, "but just a very tiny bit. I don't want people thinking I'm… thinking I'm something I'm not."

"They won't. They wouldn't dare since you'll be with Simon. He'd never allow anyone to say a word against you." She grinned. "Simon has a hankerin' for you, don't you know?"

"He most certainly does not," Janie said stiffly.

Annie just laughed. "He does. And I guarantee he won't be able to take his eyes off you today."

Janie wasn't certain she liked that idea at all. Annie left then to return to her home to finish food preparations for the event. She'd dressed Janie's hair into a braided coronet atop her head, wisps of dark tendrils she'd coerced into curls on either side of her face. With a sigh, she rose and headed for the door to check to make sure she hadn't missed closing down anything in the kitchen before heading out, snatching up her old woolen gray cloak since evenings were cool.

She met up with Simon in the hallway. He wore a chambray shirt. Dungarees and a black leather vest and string tie.

He swept Janie a long, intent look that left her feeling breathless.

"You look beautiful," he murmured, taking her cloak from her hands.

"You do too," she said and smiled at how handsome he appeared, even in the simplest of clothes. Yet, she wondered why he was dressed so casually when Katie and Annie had instructed her to wear party attire. Then she remembered; he'd be doing hard labor lifting walls. She saw the satchel he carried and knew he'd probably packed a good set of clothes as well to change into afterwards.

"Thank you," he said, setting the satchel down on the floor. "Turn about."

"Excuse me?"

He flung the cloak over his shoulder and drew a small, tight circle with one finger in the air. "Turn for me."

"Simon, really...."

"Please. I want to get a look at the entire pretty picture before we head out for the dance. I've a feeling once we get there I'll be lucky to secure even one dance with you."

Janie couldn't help it. She laughed and self-consciously turned in a full circle, her hands holding out the skirt of her gown.

"Like I said—beautiful," he whispered, drawing nearer once she stopped turning.

She stiffened when she felt his hand slide around her waist, then relaxed. *This is Simon, not Robert or Clive!*

He draped her cloak around her shoulders, picked up the satchel and said, "Come along, lovely lady."

She allowed Simon to lead her out of Katie's Palace.

Standing on the boardwalk, Janie exclaimed, "Why, Simon! What a beautiful carriage."

"I rented it for the evening." He looked up at the carriage owner, Harley Fuller, who was grinning down at them. "To the Smith place, Harley."

"Yes, sirree, Judge. I plan on stayin' the night for the party, too, so you just let me know when you're ready to return home."

"Will do," Simon said.

"It's not all that far to the Smith place. We could have walked, or taken your wagon."

"We could have, but I wanted this first time stepping out together to be special."

He assisted her into the carriage and settled down beside her, setting his bag on the opposite seat. She thought about what he'd said and murmured, "We are not stepping out, Simon."

"We're not?" Simon raised his brow.

She sniffed. "No, we're simply sharing a conveyance to a dance we happen to both be attending."

He scoffed, "Call it what you will, but that's not how folks will see things."

"What!"

"Haven't you heard how people have been talking about us for the past few months?"

"Absurd, absolutely absurd," she snapped. "There's nothing to talk about."

"Suit yourself, but I can't believe you haven't heard any rumblings from Katie or Annie, at the least."

Oh, she'd heard all right. Plenty of times. She just couldn't face the possibility that Simon might be interested in her in any way but as a friend. She said, "You've been a good friend."

Taking her hand in his he leaned over and kissed her cheek. Janie was stunned and she sat frozen.

"I aim to change that."

"You...you don't want to be my friend anymore?" Janie heard the trembling in her voice and damned herself for being such an open book.

"Sure, but I'm beginning to think just being friends isn't enough."

"Simon? Don't say something you'll regret later. Please," she begged.

"I won't regret it. It's high time I allowed myself to have some happiness in life before I get too old."

"Oh, Simon, you are not old."

"Forty in June. Life is passing me by and I want a piece of the pie before I leave this earth."

Janie's spine stiffened. "So, now I'm a piece of pie?"

Simon groaned. "That's not what I meant. I haven't been with any one particular woman for long, until you came along. And now I find I want more of you, but I must be careful, for your sake."

"Well!" she huffed, "If you think you'll get a piece of *this* pie..."

"I don't want a simple piece of pie, I want the whole thing; I want it for a lifetime. But we can't always have what we want."

"I still don't understand."

"I've been a judge for several years. Consequently, I've made enemies; lots of them. I've never married because of that."

"Because you believe an enemy would harm your family."

He nodded. "That's right.

"Oh, Simon, don't you know people have to take chances in life?"

Leaning near he looked deep into her eyes. "Not with you I can't. I won't. But we can enjoy ourselves tonight, can't we?"

Janie saw the sincerity in his face and nodded. "Yes, I believe we can."

His smile lit up his face and he leaned toward her. Janie closed her eyes as she felt his lips gently press against hers in the lightest of kisses. He released her then and sank back against the seat with a smile.

"Save me a dance?"

"Of course!"

They arrived at the Smith's place and Janie was surprised by the crowd. It seemed everyone in Bozeman was at the barn-raising. Excitement strummed through her at the thought of a party and she could barely wait for Simon to assist her from the carriage. She managed to stay in her seat until he came around and opened the door for her. Placing his hands around her waist he swung her to the ground, tucked her arm in his and walked around the Smith's house to the back yard.

Several red and white checkered oilskin cloths covered tables had been set up outside, beneath a canvas awning offering protection from the sun. The crowd of Bozeman folk roamed the yard, visiting and laughing, the women and children drinking punch and the men a dark ale. Most of the able-bodied men were dressed for the hard work of raising barn walls.

Katie rushed over to Janie and Simon, a child clinging to each hand, James followed with baby Rory cradled in his arms. James and Katie's eldest, Luke, was a tall, sturdy, handsome boy at three and a half, the image of his father while the little girl—Hannah—shyly clung to Katie's hand.

"Oh, you've finally made it. Let me tell you the plan; while the ladies make food preparations the men pull up the walls and secure them."

"Sounds just like the barn raising's I attended as a child back home."

"Good. Then you know what to expect."

"Honey, you'll have to take Rory now."

"Can I help?" Janie asked. She couldn't help envying the couple with their three adorable children. She especially wanted to hold the baby.

James plopped the baby in Janie's arms. Immediately, Rory started crying. Instinctively, Janie started rocking back and forth and he quieted.

"Hey, you've got the touch," James said. "Doesn't she Simon?"

Janie caught the grin on Simon's face when he sauntered up beside them.

"Seems she does, doesn't it?" Simon drawled.

Heat seeped into Janie's cheeks when Simon turned his gaze on her.

He swept her body a long, intimate look before saying, "Don't forget you're saving me a dance or two."

"I won't forget," she promised.

He shrugged out of his vest and looked around, obviously seeking a place to set it while he worked.

"Here, I'll take it. Look for our table," she said.

"Thanks." "Make it a table close to the food. I'm going to be hungry after all this work."

James laughed and slapped Simon's back. "You, old man, aren't used to physical work so you're probably right." As the men sauntered away, James tossed a smile at his wife over his shoulder. "Let's join them at their table, darlin'."

Katie laughed. "You got it, sheriff."

They found a table. Janie sat and held the baby until he started squalling. Obviously, it was meal time again. Katie went inside with her children to feed her baby while Janie watched the men raise the barn walls.

Her eyes focused on Simon's tall, lean frame as he bent, grabbed hold of one edge of a wall with several other men and pushed it up into position with the help of a crew of men using a rope, pulley-fashion opposite them. She knew how heavy those walls were so it always amazed her how easy the men made the task appear.

Within an amazingly short time, the men finished and the roar of applause made Janie laugh. She focused on Simon striding toward her table. When he reached her, he sank down on the bench beside her, leaned over with a twinkle in his eyes and bussed her cheek.

"You look so calm, cool and beautiful sitting here. I feel guilty being all hot and sweaty in your presence."

"You've nothing to feel guilty about. Let me get you a cool drink. What would you like? Water, lemonade or ale?"

"You don't have to wait on me," he said as he started to rise.

"I'm not. It's the least I can do since you've worked so hard. Now, what would you like?"

"An ale would be appreciated."

With a nod, she lifted her skirts and made her way to the refreshment table. After pouring Simon a tall glass of ale from a pitcher she started back but stopped abruptly when a man blocked her way.

"Clive!" she gasped.

CHAPTER 4

*C*live Miller clicked his tongue. "Surprised you, didn't I?"

Janie looked around for help but everyone was busy socializing. Though she had no doubt any one of her new friends would come running if she screamed for help.

"Thought I'd stop by and let you know, you'll be returning to Boise with me—tomorrow. Meet me around four, before dawn, on the northern edge of town. Oh, and don't let your beau know, that is if you want him to live. And you know I mean every word. You belong to me, no one else."

She noticed Simon heading her way and she whispered, "No, I won't say a word." She had to go with him for she couldn't let anything happen to Simon.

Clive saw Simon then turned away with a curse and walked swiftly around the back of the Smith's house. Just as Simon reached her he took her arms and held her gently, concern on his face. "Are you all right? Wasn't that your brother-in-law?"

"Yes! Here." She handed him his beer and grabbed his free hand. "Let's return to the party."

They took just a few steps when Janie heard the thundering of a horse's hooves nearby. Simon grasped her arms and she dropped the glass of ale. He pulled her out of the path of the horse, to the ground and rolled them out of the way of the oncoming animal. The pounding sound of Clive's horse dwindled into the distance as Simon scrambled to his feet and pulled Janie up.

"You okay, sweetheart?" he asked, brushing off her gown, his hands sliding up and down her body.

Embarrassment flooded Janie as she pushed his hands off her behind, gulping down her anxiety just as James arrived.

"Who in the hell was that fool? He just about ran over the two of you!"

Simon snarled, "Janie's brother-in-law. Seems he's not too happy about her starting over a new life here in Bozeman." He looked at Janie. "What did he say?"

"Like you said, he's not happy I'm here."

"What else?"

Janie bit her lip and her eyes filled with tears. She couldn't tell him. She just knew that she would have to leave with Clive in the morning, scolding herself for having let down her guard; believing Clive had given up on her.

"Janie?"

"Nothing." She shook her head. "Nothing more than that."

$\sim$

*S*imon didn't like how she wouldn't meet his eyes. Something had happened—Clive had frightened her. "I'll ask once more, what did he say?" He managed to keep his voice calm, but fury tore through him. Something the bastard said had upset her.

"Little, very little."

"Then why is he here? What purpose does he have in Bozeman?" When she didn't reply but stubbornly lifted her chin and looked away, he turned to James.

"We have to go after him. You know that, don't you?"

James nodded. "In the morning. I'll round up a few other men and we'll head over to Butte."

"No." Janie grasped Simon's arm. "Just leave him be, I beg you."

Simon saw how all color had drained from Janie's face. "Janie. You can't live the rest of your life with the threat of Clive Miller hovering over you."

"But what can we do?" she whispered. "He's committed no crime —yet."

"She's got a point," James said dryly, "Much as I hate to admit it. We have to wait for something to happen."

"You mean wait until the bastard harms her? No," Simon growled.

"Please, Simon. I'm safe at Katie's Palace."

Finally, much as Simon hated caving, he nodded. "All right. But you go nowhere alone. Understand?"

Janie nodded. "You'll get no argument from me on that."

Breathing a little easier, Simon took Janie's arm and they joined the other guests.

As Simon guessed, Janie was never without a partner. While he wanted to keep her to himself, he couldn't. But by the end of the dance he was burning with jealousy toward the steady stream of men who kept Janie dancing all night, though he kept his feelings hidden. He'd also come to a decision; Janie would be safe if she married him. Ironically, the very reason he'd chosen not to marry—was the exact reason he decided he must marry her—to protect her.

When the last dance was announced, Simon turned to Janie. "One more?"

With a smile, she took his hand and followed him out to the dance floor, and he took her into his arms. Simon pulled her closer, tucked the top of her head beneath his chin as the music filled the barn and they danced. Most of the lanterns had been extinguished, affording couples some privacy.

A protective streak unlike any before settled inside Simon and he knew he couldn't let this woman out of his arms—out of his life. With the last notes from the musicians Simon stopped moving.

"Thank you. I had a lovely time this evening," she whispered.

"Me too." A kiss from her was what he needed to seal his silent commitment to her which he'd soon reveal. He drew near to her lips. Initially, he felt Janie's arms braced against his shoulders, maintaining her distance. He sighed when he realized she was trying to push him away from her. But just when he started releasing her she pulled on his string tie, keeping him close, her lips meeting his with sweet excitement.

Simon breathed deeply as surprise, then determination tore through him and he deepened the kiss. Tightening his arms around her waist he lifted her clear from the floor. Her womanly curves built a fire inside him, and all he could think about was taking her to his bed. He felt her kiss change, from one of a young girl's to aroused womanly desire—until the lights in the barn unexpectedly brightened. It was only then, as they broke away from each other, staring with confusion around them, that they noticed the music had ended.

Janie's cheeks turned pink. Simon looked around in chagrin when he caught the grins on folks' faces watching them.

Lifting her skirts, she wouldn't meet his eyes and murmured, "Excuse me," and fled the barn.

Surprised, he stood a minute, trying to decide what to do before following her outside. He found her leaning against a fence surrounding one of several corrals, arms folded protectively over her chest. She must have sensed his coming for she said, "I want to go home, Simon."

"You must be exhausted from all that dancing. Of course we'll leave now."

"I mean, I want to return to Butte."

Coldness settled in Simon as he cautiously formulated a reply, "Bozeman's your home now."

"It never truly was, not really."

"You told me you felt it was." Simon couldn't hide his exasperation.

"I had thought...had hoped." She laughed mirthlessly. "Suffice it to say I've been wrong several times in my life. Bozeman can't ever be my home."

"But—"

"Simon, don't ask me any questions. Please! Just take me back to Katie's Palace."

"Did I frighten you with my kiss? Is that it?"

She whirled to face him and with the moon shining down on her face he caught the tears sliding down her cheeks as she shook her head. "No."

He smiled. "So, what's wrong?"

Janie frowned and shook her head. "I don't want to like you too much. Especially since you've made it clear you'll never take a wife."

Looking up he saw the brilliant stars, felt he could reach right up and pull one down from the sky, just for her. Yes, she had been right; he had told her exactly that. But he'd changed his mind. Now he geared himself up to propose marriage for the first time—ever.

"That was a foolish thing for me to say. Life is always changing, including my feelings. Plain and simple, cause I'm too old to romance you with pretty words, I'm in love with you. I want you for my wife."

"Simon! You can't mean it."

"I do." He frowned when he saw how distressed she looked. "Maybe you don't love me but I know you've got some feelings for me. I'm not blind."

Her hand slowly came up, stroked his face. He covered her hand, held it there. "Oh, if I only could—marry you. But I can't. I just can't."

His body went cold with her words. "Ever?"

She nodded, pulled at her hand until he released it. "Not ever. Take me home now, please. Know that you did nothing wrong; it's me. I need to work some things out in my life before I can truly begin living it the way I want to."

Before he could press her further, Janie picked up her skirts and rushed toward the waiting carriage. Simon stood there, looking down at the ground unseeingly. What in the hell happened? He felt as if he'd been pole-axed. There was no accounting for women and their temperaments, he mused, as anger filled his heart and soul. He swiveled on his heel and raced after her.

He settled inside beside her. She hugged one side of the carriage and he snapped, "Stop cringing away from me, for Christ's sake."

She gasped and bit her lip worriedly. "You're very angry with me."

"I'm stunned." He sighed in exasperation. "I don't understand. And yes, I'm furious at this situation, but not at you."

"Perhaps, someday, I'll be able to explain things. But I can't—not now. Suffice it to say I do love you but it wouldn't work out between us right now."

Leaning toward her he reached out and cupped her chin, forcing her to meet his eyes. "You owe me an explanation—now—not at some later date—since this is our future happiness at stake here. In the morning, I want a full explanation. I want you to spill your guts to me, Janie Miller. Because I want you to become Mrs. Simon Hopkins soon. Whatever the problem, we'll work it out. I believe that nothing can stand in the way of us marrying. Nothing."

Strange how his words brought a chill to her for those had been nearly the same words Clive had spoken to her.

~

*J*anie opened her bedroom door a crack and peered into the hall. One lantern against a wall burned with a low, yellow light and illuminated Simon's face. She gasped, surprised to see him asleep in a chair directly across from her room. Darn it, apparently, he didn't trust her. Dressed in the same clothes he'd worn at the dance she knew he hadn't sought his bed last night. She opened the door wider—thankfully, it didn't squeak. He didn't budge. Observing him, she saw his hat tipped low over his forehead and his arms folded across his chest. She waited. His light snoring told her he was sound asleep.

She opened the door wide enough to take her bag out with her as she stepped into the hallway on silent feet. Her skirts rustled as she headed for the stairs, pausing to look at Simon again. He hadn't heard her and he slept on. Taking the steps quietly she reached the bottom and breathed a relieved sigh.

As she stepped outside, darkness met her eyes. It was four o'clock in the morning and the town was quiet, not a soul stirring. She stepped down from the boardwalk into the street, looked up and down at the shops darkened windows and swiped at a tear sliding down her cheek as she headed toward the end of town to meet her fate. She knew she would be several hours ahead of Simon for she had no doubts he'd track her down. But then she'd be married to Clive. It would be too late.

Clive had arrived early, thank God. He slid out of his carriage and assisted her inside without a word. Janie couldn't see his features well, but she thought she caught a satisfied look in his eyes, heard the quiet tone in his voice when he said, "We'll be marrying tomorrow. I've made all of the arrangements."

She had no idea what to say, until he said, "Well, have you no words for your soon to be husband?"

"No, not a word."

Janie gasped when suddenly he lurched up and sank onto the seat beside her. He took her face in one hand, squeezed her cheeks hard. "That's what I like, sweet Janie. No words. Just use those lips in the only way I want you to—kiss me."

She pulled away from him, shaking her head from side to side. "I hate you, Clive. Things didn't have to be like this between us."

Clive sank back against the seat and folded his arms. "No, they didn't have to be—but it was your choice that made things turn out this way.

I've…you know I've loved you, even before Robert staked his claim to you."

"You've no idea what loves means," she whispered, thinking about Simon. She'd left him a note, begging him not to come after her, for his own protection. She didn't explain any more than that, but she also left a note for James Freeman, asking him to restrain Simon from following her. In her note, she'd explained how Clive was a powerful, dangerous man and would kill Simon if he came after her.

~

Simon sat in a wooden chair in James's office, spiking his fingers through his hair.

"My God, man, I didn't think it was possible but your hair's turned grayer overnight."

"That's what worry will do to you," Simon snarled as he crossed one leg over the other knee. When are we leaving for Butte?"

James sat in his chair behind his desk and stretched his arms above his head. "As soon as Harry and Roger get here. Listen, Cane wanted to come, too, but with the baby being sick and Annie not doing so well, he can't leave them."

"Tell him when you see him not to worry. His family needs him," Simon said.

James continued, "I've wired ahead to Chase Borgstrom, the sheriff in Butte, explaining the situation. He said he'd go out to the Miller homestead and check things out. But if Janie appears willing and isn't being held against her will, there's not much he can do, he said."

Simon nodded. "I know. But he is holding her against her will, though she won't fight him and likely won't say so, either."

"I know. She doesn't want you to die."

"But I'm dying inside at the thought of living my life without her," Simon groaned.

"Yeah, well, if we don't bring her back with us Katie threatened not to let me through the doors of The Palace," James grumbled.

At that comment Simon raised his brows. "That sounds…dire."

"You know Katie."

"Sure do. You've got nothing to worry about any way this turns out. You can do no wrong in Katie's eyes."

"And that's the way I feel about her. Thanks for the encouragement."

The two deputies arrived. Then the four men set out on horseback for Butte. Along the way, a thought struck Simon. He guessed Clive wanted to make an honest woman out of Janie and prayed they wouldn't be too late.

As Simon rode beside James, he said, "I've got a plan."

James grinned. "I figured as much since you've been quiet for a while. Let's hear it."

Once Simon explained, James said, "Did I ever tell you you're a damned smart man, my friend?"

Simon raised his brow. "On several occasions."

Laughing, they whipped their horses into a swifter gait.

❧

"*I*'m not wearing a wedding dress, Clive."

"Well you sure as hell aren't wearing widow's weeds!" He snatched up the slightly yellowed gown she'd worn when she and Robert married and tossed it at her. "Put the damned thing on or so help me God I'll put you in it myself."

Janie sat on a bed—her old bed in the home she'd shared with Robert, feeling light-headed. He suddenly squatted down in front of her. As she looked at his angry face she wondered how they could have been friends as children. He took her hands in his, startling her. When she went to pull them away he gripped them tighter.

"Why can't you love me, Janie?"

Stunned, she looked down at his bowed head as he kissed her knuckles. "I've loved you forever it seems," he said with a sigh.

"I don't love you, Clive. In fact, I hate you. Is that what you want in a wife?"

"No, but at this point, I'll take what I can get from you." Arrogantly, he added, "Someday you will love me."

"No, never, love, Clive. We were friends, before I married Robert. But everything changed after that. You've ruined my life by taking my home and my husband from me. Did you think I'd be grateful?" she scoffed.

"Yes, Robert beat you so often I'm amazed there are no scars." He rose to his feet and scowled down at her. "You will appreciate what I did for you...one day." Turning on his heel he strode to the door, pausing there to give her a warning. "Get dressed. Ceremony's in an hour." He left, slammed the door behind him and she flinched.

Her old homestead was only ten minutes by buggy from town so she had a few minutes to collect her thoughts—thoughts that included more thinking on how to get herself out of this situation. But then she thought of Simon again and knew there was no way out; she loved him and wouldn't have his death on her conscience for the rest of her days.

She heard a wagon's wheel in the drive and moved to the window overlooking the yard. One of Clive's hands drove the wagon and Clive waited for her leaning against it, smoking a cheroot. Clive looked polished and shiny, and appeared in control of the situation. That control unnerved her. Never had she realized how tenacious Clive could be; never had she realized what an awful judge of character she was.

Just then Clive looked up at her window. She saw a wicked smile slide across his face and she shook her head, dismayed. He shouted, "Finish up, Janie. We're leaving in five minutes, whether you're ready or not."

She turned away, picked up her reticule and left the bedroom. She opened the door leading outside and paused at Clive's words.

"I asked you to change your clothes."

Lifting her chin, she said, "And I chose not to."

He grimaced and watched her come down the steps. Once she reached his side he fairly tossed her up onto the wagon's seat. Oh, she knew he was not happy for his grimace deepened and his hold on her waist had been painful. What she'd done—leaving Bozeman for Simon's safety—she didn't regret because Clive was ruthless and mean enough to kill Simon.

Clive tried several times engaging her in conversation but she turned her back on him and stared out the window, tears filling her eyes. The thought of being held hostage for the rest of her life was awful, but to save Simon's life, she had no choice. Eventually he cursed and gave up.

They arrived at the town hall. Clive had wanted her to marry him in the First Presbyterian Church but she'd refused. A legal ceremony was all he'd get from her.

A deputy strolled into the hall shortly after they arrived. "Judge's on his way over. Just a couple more minutes, folks."

"Not more than that," Clive snarled as he pulled Janie over to a bench and sat down beside her. He picked up her hand and held it on his knee. She struggled for ownership of it but he wouldn't release it.

The deputy frowned. "Something wrong, folks?"

Clive squeezed her hand hard in warning. "Oh, nothing but a bit of a quarrel," that's all," he said. "When did you say that judge is getting here?"

"He's here now," a low, firm voice said.

"Oh, no," Janie whispered. She knew the owner of that wonderful voice.

~

"*W*hat in the hell…" Clive began then yanked her to her feet and wound an arm around her waist.

Simon strolled in and stopped in front of Clive. His clothes were dusty from his travels. He tore off his hat and slapped it against his thigh which set Clive coughing. Janie covered her mouth with her hand and she cast a pleading look at Simon.

"Where's the judge?" Clive demanded.

"That's me," Simon said, keeping a jocular tone though he wanted to pound the man.

"The other one!"

"Sorry, he couldn't make it. Which is rather unfortunate for you," Simon said, keeping his voice calm though it was damned difficult. Simon narrowed his eyes and added, "Because there's no chance in hell I'm marrying the two of you, especially since Janie wants no part of it. I'm only going to say this once; let go of her and stay out of her life. She's returning to Bozeman with me and we're getting married."

Clive immediately released her, then yanked up his pants and puffed out his chest. "She's consented to be *my* wife. She came of her own accord." He nudged Janie's shoulder. "Tell him it's so."

"It's true." She looked at Simon, her eyes begging him to understand.

Simon shook his head, took her hand and pulled her toward him.

Clive protested, "She said she's marrying me!"

"She did but I don't believe her. I know a threat when I see one, and she's only going along with you to protect me." Simon looked into Janie's eyes and added, "But she doesn't have to do that." Then he turned to Clive again. "Now get the hell out of here."

"Says who?"

"Says me and four other deputies from Bozeman."

James Freeman and his deputies stood just inside the door, hands resting on their guns, ready if necessary to defend Simon and Janie.

"Got some trouble brewing, boys?"

Simon saw Sheriff Chase Borgstrom standing behind James and his men.

"Not anymore," James said as he moved aside to allow Borgstrom into city hall.

Borgstrom looked at Clive. "Appears you ain't getting' married after all, don't it?"

Clive's face turned red, then purple in his rage as he headed out the door. From outside he shouted, "You ain't heard the last of me yet!"

Simon looked at Janie, saw tears sliding down her cheeks and she hastily brushed them aside. Simon took her in his arms and held her tight against him. Knowing they required privacy, the others filed outside and closed the door. Simon walked backwards until he felt a desk at his legs. He sank down on it and pulled Janie between his thighs.

"What in the hell were you trying to do?" he asked, concerned.

"You know!" Her voice wavered as she wound her arms around his neck and leaned against him.

"Clive threatened to kill me, didn't he?" At her nod, he added, "I figured it had to be something like that."

He sighed, loving the feel of her in his arms, unable to even think what could have happened if he'd arrived too late. She sobbed against him until she'd thoroughly drenched the front of his jacket. Then she stepped away from him but Simon pulled her back into his arms.

"Don't ever run away from me again," Simon warned, his smile slipping away. "I make my own decisions. I take care of myself and what belongs to me."

She pressed on his shoulders until he released her. "You've no business telling me what I can and can't do, Simon Hopkins. I'm a woman full grown."

"Who behaved rather childishly...and completely unselfishly." He smiled again. "Like I said, don't ever do that again."

"You don't know how tenacious Clive is, Simon. You don't. My husband died because of him."

"Has he killed men in the past?"

"I have no idea, but it wouldn't surprise me if he has. At any rate, he hasn't been arrested for any crimes. But like I told you before, he's wanted me since before I married Robert. He won't forget this happened, and that worries me."

"I'll do the worrying. In fact, speaking of worrying, according to James, you're turning my hair gray"

"It's already gray—just a bit."

"It sure is but it doesn't need to get any grayer—for a while."

CHAPTER 5

On an early spring day in May, Simon saved Janie from marrying Clive Miller. He married her himself, in the First Lutheran Church in Bozeman. It appeared the whole town turned out for the ceremony, even though Janie hadn't wanted a big fuss. But then, lots of folks had come to know and like Janie, and everyone had known Simon for years. She couldn't invite one without inviting them all.

Simon thought Janie the most beautiful woman in the world as she walked down the aisle toward him. She wore white silk and carried a bouquet of yellow roses. As a judge, Simon had married plenty of couples but never had he viewed a more stunning bride than Janie.

She reached his side at the altar and he took her hand then turned to face Reverend Anderson. Simon heard Janie sniffling beside him and wondered if she wasn't coming down with a cold. But when he looked at her he saw love shining in her eyes and knew her emotions were running wild. His were too, but he kept them confined.

It came time to pledge their troth to each other and she replied to the reverend with the words, "I do," in a trembling voice.

Finally, the reverend took them each by an elbow and turned them to face the congregation. "I present to you now, with much joy, Mr. and Mrs. Simon Hopkins."

The congregation applauded and cheered as Simon kissed his bride.

"I love you," he whispered, unable to believe he'd been so lucky in finding Janie.

"And I love you, always," she whispered against his lips.

Solicitously taking her arm, he guided her swiftly down the aisle while the organist played a final song. Janie's cheeks were pink and she gave Simon a dazzling smile. She exited the church with Simon close behind holding her hand as they made their way to the carriage. Everyone was eager to be on their way to Katie's Palace, where they would imbibe in a fine meal and beverages.

A shot rang out. The crowd exiting behind them were laughing and talking loudly and didn't seem to notice the shot, but Simon had. He didn't take the time to look but pulled Janie down to the ground. Folks behind them dropped to the ground as well at the sound of another shot. Women were screaming, men shouting, children crying as the rapid fire from several guns rang out.

It was only after he and Janie had hit the ground that Simon saw the blood on his hands. He looked at Janie with horror and his voice rang out a tormented, "No!" Her eyes were closed and her face was devoid of all color as he held her close. He saw her lips move and he leaned close.

She opened her eyes and whispered, "I'll be okay, Simon. It's Clive, I know it. Please, don't leave me." She closed her eyes then and Simon caught the sob in his throat.

"Lay still, sweetheart. I love you and I'm not going anywhere."

Janie opened her eyes a moment and smiled. "And I love you, too, forever and always."

He saw the tears in her eyes just before she shut them again. His heart clenched and his body shook in horror as he cursed Clive to hell.

Thank God, she was still breathing.

He half sat up, looked around and saw people lying huddled on the ground in front of the church right behind he and Janie. He noticed their carriage a short distance away, straight ahead. A movement at the side of the church made him tense up until he saw it was James, head sticking out and motioning to Simon to head for the carriage. Simon started to rise, bent to pick up Janie when another volley of shots came. He sank to the ground again and covered her body, trying not to hurt her any more than she already was. If she died, his life would be meaningless. And Clive will have written his own death warrant.

He cursed himself for having believed they could be happily married; cursed himself for not having protected her; and cursed himself too for having married her and bringing this danger upon her.

A thud on the ground beside Simon made him look up and into the stark dark eyes of his friend, Cane Smith. He'd helped Cane from spending his life in jail for a robbery he hadn't committed.

"I owe you," Cane said, laying low beside him.

Simon knew Cane had always wanted to pay him back for his help. It seemed now he'd have his chance.

"Here's the plan," Cane said. "There are four of them—only four. On our side, there's you, me, James and two other deputies. Other than you and me the other two are in position alongside either side of the church. The shots are coming from beyond your carriage, in the brush along the road. So that you can get your wife into the carriage, I'm going to cover you, understand?"

"Cane, you can't leave yourself open to that!" Simon protested.

With a grin, Cane half rose and said, "You can't stop me so start moving, Judge."

Cane crouched then ran across the church yard, shots ringing through the air. Simon swore when he saw Cane duck just as a bullet tore through his Stetson.

Simon knew he'd wasted precious time so he lifted Janie into his arms and ran for the carriage. Luckily the horses wore blinders for while they danced to the tune of the ringing shots they hadn't lurched away. Just before Simon reached the carriage, pain tore through his shoulder. He nearly dropped his precious cargo but hung on and yanked open the carriage door. Simon laid Janie gently on the floor, slammed the door shut and crouched at the side of the vehicle.

He lay flat on the ground now and peered under the carriage. He was in direct line of three pairs of boots, running toward him. He started to stand, ready to jump up onto the carriage seat to drive away but paused when more shots fired and shouts came, then all was quiet, except for the sobs of women and children. Looking beneath the wagon again he saw three sets of boots lined up in a row, soles up. It appeared James and Cane and his deputies had taken control of the situation.

Simon slowly rose, pulled a handkerchief from his pocket and pressed it against his bleeding shoulder. He saw it was only a flesh wound, but he groaned when he thought about Janie's wound he hadn't had time to tend. He yanked open the door and found her laying on the floor still, her eyes closed. The wound had stopped bleeding but she was so still. He'd lost her.

Tears started sliding down his cheeks until he saw her chest rise and fall. A prayer of thanks resonated in his head. He had to get Doctor Wiseman, likely with the others near the church.

He stood up and looked behind at the crowd of people rising cautiously to their feet and spotted the doctor.

"Doc! Doctor Wiseman!" he called.

"Here, judge!"

Simon looked toward the church and saw Wiseman headed for him."

"My…my wife's been shot." He heard the trembling in his voice. *God in heaven, I can't lose her!*

Wiseman arrived and leaning inside the carriage checked Janie quickly. "She's got a bullet in her," he said. "Thank God it's above her heart, still it needs to come out immediately."

Annie and Katie arrived and saw Janie lying prone on the floor with her eyes shut. Katie whispered, "Let's get her over to your office, doctor."

"Yes," Simon agreed.

"No. I've got to get that bullet out right now—right here. With the jostling of the carriage the bullet could shift position, which could be worse for her."

Simon cursed and swept his hair back from his forehead. A crowd had formed around the carriage. He saw worry on people's faces, mirroring his own. Annie stepped up beside him.

"Don't worry. Doc has the steadiest of hands. I know. Besides, I've had no bad premonitions, but several dreams of happiness for you two."

Simon smiled. "Thank you, Annie. I needed that."

Annie was known for having premonitions—usually before something awful happened. Why she hadn't experienced any regarding this awful event taking place, though, Simon had no idea—unless she had and didn't want to tell him.

"You've been shot!" she exclaimed.

"I'd forgotten I had." Simon looked at his shoulder. "Just nicked me is all."

"I'll tend to you after your wife, judge. I've got my medical bag with me. Simon, fetch it from my rig, please."

James stepped through the crowd. "I've got it here, doc," and handed over the big black satchel. James turned to the waiting crowd, their faces filled with worry. "Everyone? Head on over to Katie's Palace. We'll be along shortly. There's plenty to eat and drink."

"James? Cane? We'll take your children on over there," said the pastor, his wife at his side.

Both men nodded, as did Annie and Katie before the two women turned back to Janie and the doc, ready to lend assistance.

Slowly, the crowd dispersed with varying expressions of sadness as they left.

"What needs to be done, doc?" Simon asked.

"I want you to go sit on the church steps until I'm done. That's the best thing for you to do, Judge."

"No way in hell am I leaving my wife's side!"

James grabbed one of Simon's arms, and Cane the other as they dragged him over to the step. "He's right, Simon. Katie and Annie have helped the doc before so let them do their work."

"She might need me."

"Of course she will, after the doc's done with her."

It took all of Simon's willpower to stay put on the steps, and when Janie screamed from inside the carriage, Simon wilted on the church step and shuddered. Then all was quiet. A long time passed before Annie returned to their side.

"Doc says she'll be fine. He got the bullet out, thank heavens. It wasn't in all that deep." She smiled at Simon. "She's awake and asking for you."

Simon crossed the yard and stopped in the doorway of the carriage. Leaning over his wife he saw her white complexion and tear-filled, anguished eyes. "Simon?"

"Yes, darling," he choked out.

"I love you. And I don't want you to blame yourself for what happened."

He leaned down and kissed her forehead, taking her hand in his. "We'll talk later."

With assistance from Cane, Simon lifted his wife carefully from the floor of the carriage and into his arms as they rode back to Katie's Palace in the carriage.

Cane went to Clive Miller and his gang, now lying on the ground, sprawled in death. Bending down, Cane placed his fingers against Clive's neck, then shouted, "James! Miller's alive!"

James and the doctor came over and stood beside Miller. "Damn, this does not make things easier, does it?"

Just then the man's eyes opened and James saw blazing hatred in them. "What?" he whispered, "Not happy I haven't met my maker yet? That's too bad, isn't it?"

Between gritted teeth, James said, "For you it is. You'll be spending a lot of time in jail, Miller, while Simon and Janie have many years of happiness together."

"One day, I'll be out—I'll be back…" Clive closed his eyes again, unable to finish his sentence.

Cane met James's eyes. "We have to tell Simon he's still alive."

"I know."

"You know how he's going to react to all of this, don't you?"

James sighed. "Yeah. I'll probably have to lock Simon up until after Clive goes to trial and is sentenced and sent to prison."

Doc kneeled down to Clive while James and Cane stood guard over him.

~

*A*s soon as Janie and Simon returned to Katie's Palace, Simon helped Janie into her nightgown and put her to bed. Simon's heart wrenched at the sight of all the bandaging across her chest and swore if Clive hadn't died he'd kill him.

Janie didn't argue about being put to bed. As she sat, back against the headboard, she scowled at the doctor.

"What did you give me, doc? I can hardly keep my eyes open."

"Just a bit of laudanum. It's a relaxant and you'll sleep like a newborn all night long."

"But this is my wedding party! I can't miss it."

"We'll have another party, honey, when you're well," Simon promised. Leaning down he kissed her forehead.

She gave him a wan smile. "Okay. I'm holding you to that promise, dear husband." She sniffed and wiped at the tears streaming from her eyes. "It's just not fair. Give folks my apologies and tell them to have a good time without me. There's enough food for two wedding parties."

"Don't cry," Simon whispered.

She did, more so now that he'd mentioned it.

"I'll be back tomorrow, Mrs. Hopkins, to check on you."

"Thank you, doctor." She looked at Simon. "Now go join the party while I sleep."

"I'm staying here with you." He held up his hand when she opened her mouth to protest. "James, Katie, Cane and Annie are entertaining our guests. Like I said, in about a month you'll be good as new and we'll have another party."

"Oh!" Janie gasped.

"What is it?"

"I'd hired Jerald Hagstrom from the apothecary who promised to take our wedding portrait!"

"He's coming back when you're well enough. Katie's going to try and clean up your gown. If it's irreparable then we'll purchase you a new one. You'll get your picture."

Janie reached out and pressed her hands against the sides of Simon's face, pulling him closer. She kissed him gently on the lips and his heart beat rapidly. How he wanted to return her kiss with all the pent up passion he felt for her but he restrained himself. She wasn't well, and he had a lot to think about—including releasing her from their wedding vows.

He sat with her and held her hand until she fell asleep, which was only a few minutes, then he rearranged her covers and left her, quietly closing the door behind him. Downstairs, the crowd had thinned. Once people ate and socialized a bit, without the bride and groom, the party ended early. He found Cane and James at a back table, seemingly deep in conversation. When he arrived at their table they straightened up in their chairs, noticing him with matching wide grins.

Simon grew suspicious as he took a seat. "What's with you two grinning like a couple of hyenas?"

"Just welcoming back the groom, that's all," James said.

"How's Janie?" Cane asked.

"Do you believe she wanted to come down to the party?"

"Can't say as I blame her. Don't think I had much of a chance to congratulate the two of you." Cane looked down. "You might want to go and change into another jacket. You've got blood on that one."

"I don't feel like changing clothes. Besides, everyone was witness to what happened. It doesn't matter," he grumbled. "And don't worry about the well wishes." Glancing between the two men, he saw the confused looks on their faces. "I'm not consummating the marriage. As a matter of fact, once Janie's well, I'm filing for an annulment."

"What in the hell!" James said. "Why would you do such a thing? That woman loves you."

"And I love her. But I made a mistake by marrying her."

Cane stretched his legs out beneath the table. "Little late to decide that, isn't it?"

Simon sighed. "You two don't understand."

"Then explain." Cane added, "We're listening."

"Janie was shot because of her being important to me."

Cane and James exchanged confused looks. "We don't understand," James said.

"It means exactly what I said; I'm the one to blame for Janie nearly getting killed."

Cane shook his head. "No, you aren't. If anything, Janie's the responsible party. It was her brother-in-law, after all. Hell, you'd never even met the guy until he showed up in your courtroom."

"True, but he wanted vengeance. He wanted Janie which was why she went along with him that night back to Butte. She went willingly because she was afraid Miller would kill me."

"And today proves your little woman has damned good insight." James frowned and looked at Cane. "Why do you suppose Annie hadn't had any premonitions about all of this happening?"

Cane looked uncomfortable and he pulled at the button at the neck of his shirt. "Uh, when she's expecting a baby, she seems to lose a lot of her abilities. We've both noticed it. She thinks it's a blessing."

James grinned. "We all know how Annie hates having those premonitions. Do you suppose that's why she'd been so quick to have another baby?"

"Damn it. You are too perceptive. That's exactly the reason." Cane sighed. "Enough about me and my family." He looked at Simon. "You can't annul your marriage. You'll break Janie's heart and you'll be unhappy."

"I need her every bit as much as she needs me, but by association with me she'll always be exposed to danger. I refuse having her live her life constantly looking over her shoulder, and I refuse to be always guarding her back and worrying. It's not fair to either one of us."

James said, "You knew all of this before you proposed marriage to her. Why in the hell did you?"

Simon groaned, "After Clive convinced Janie to return to Butte with him, I knew she was protecting me. It wasn't right. And I knew, with Janie gone from my life just that one day, I couldn't live my life without her."

"So, what's changed?" Cane asked. "You were able to put your fears aside then."

"This time Janie's been harmed—could have been killed. That's the difference." He rose from his chair and added, "I'm turning in."

Simon took the steps quietly and entered Janie's bedroom—their bedroom now—and sank into the chair for a nightly vigil. She was sleeping soundly he saw and while the bed looked inviting, he couldn't chance harming her in the night, not to mention the fact if they didn't consummate the marriage, an annulment could easily be obtained.

He'd sleep in the chair. Then, in the morning, he'd need to pretend everything was fine between them. He'd tell her, eventually, about an annulment, but not until she'd healed. Meanwhile, he'd have to find the fortitude to keep his hands off his beautiful wife.

~

One week was about all the time Janie could stand being abed. One week of seeing the guilt and sadness in Simon's face was enough. They had to talk about what happened to her, but he avoided her, or managed to change the topic each time she mentioned the incident. She knew he believed it was his fault she'd been shot, which wasn't true. It was due to her past with Clive and had nothing to do with Simon. Yet, she imagined his old fears had risen to the surface, but she had had plenty of time in bed planning how she'd make him forget everything that had happened.

Janie sat on the side of her bed and dressed in clothes, for the first time in a week, she smiled. While she'd never played the coquette before, she found the thought exciting, and it would be an easy thing to do— seducing her husband. She loved him and she knew he loved her but was fighting his feelings for her now. She'd have to work hard to change his mind, and the only way she could think to do that, if talking didn't work, was to seduce him.

Once they consummated their marriage, she hoped his doubts would diminish.

She looked up, startled when the door opened. Simon strode in with a scowl on his face. He whipped off his hat and glared down at her. "What in the hell do you think you're doing?"

Janie stood up and glared right back. "Getting dressed."

Simon pointed at the bed. "Get back in there right now. Doc said—"

"Doc said I'm fine to get up and start moving around. Ask him yourself." She took a step forward, drawing closer with a smile. "Besides, I am past the point of being coddled and need to start living my life as Mrs. Simon Hopkins, beginning now."

Janie put her arms around Simon's neck and urged him down to her. She kissed him full on the lips and eased her body right up against his, ignoring the dull ache in her chest from her injury, which was easy to do since Simon was returning her kiss with an urgency that boiled her own blood. She heard a thud and smiled against his lips; he'd dropped his hat and now his arms were around her waist, holding her against his long, lean body.

After a few moments he released her, settled his hands on her arms and stepped back, putting distance between them. "Now, now, none of that. You're still very ill."

"No, I'm not," Janie insisted. "Stop treating me like I'm a china bowl in a shop"

"If you insist on being up and about, come down stairs and have some breakfast."

Moving close again Janie drank in the lovely sight of her husband, from his straight dark hair to his piercing eyes to his rangy body clad in a light weight jacket. She met his gaze, briefly, until he broke the connection between them. Janie felt a coldness sweep through her body, a disturbing atmosphere in the room made her frown. He was keeping his distance from her.

"Simon? We need to have a little talk about us—our marriage."

He blew out a deep sigh. "Figured we'd have to get around to that sooner or later."

"Do you love me?"

"You know I do."

"Then why are you behaving as though I'll break apart into a million pieces if you touch me?"

"Getting shot has a lot to do with it," he said dryly. "You're still healing."

"I'm *fine!* You feel guilty, don't you?" she whispered, even as tears filled her eyes.

"Don't you see that my worst nightmare has become reality?"

"Clive shooting me wasn't your fault."

"But it was because you married me."

"Yes, it was, but he's in jail now and, according to James, likely to be there for a long, long time. As I said when you first came in, I want to get on with our lives. I want to be your wife in every way."

"Oh, sweetheart," he groaned, "I don't think that's a good idea."

Janie narrowed her eyes. "What are you saying?"

He swept his hair back from his forehead and paced the floor, ending up at the window that overlooked Main Street.

"Simon?" God, she hated how her voice quivered, but she knew what he was going to say.

Simon gave her a sad smile as he slowly turned to face her. "I've started the paperwork to have our marriage annulled."

"You can't do that!"

"I can. I did. It's for the best." He walked to her, took her face in his hands and kissed her with sweet tenderness. Releasing her he bent and picked up his hat and set it on his head. "As soon as the paperwork's ready to be signed I'll let you know."

"You would tear us apart because of yours fears, then? "Why? Clive's locked up good and tight now. And there were so many witnesses to his crime and I can't see, once he goes to trial, being released. Can you?"

"No doubt he'll be found guilty. But there'll always be another 'Clive' around the corner, waiting. I don't want to do this, sweetheart, but it's just not safe for...for me to be married to you."

With irony in her voice, she replied, "You mean it's not safe for me being married to you, don't you?"

"I suppose it does work both ways, doesn't it?"

Tilting up her chin, she whispered, "Never would I have believed you to be a coward, Simon Hopkins. Never. Don't you see I'd rather have a week, a day, a single hour of happiness with you then without?"

CHAPTER 6

S imon gulped. He felt the same way, but he couldn't take the chance.

Closing his eyes against the pain on Janie's face he thought about how she'd called him a coward and he couldn't deny it. It would make it easier for her to agree to the annulment if she thought of him that way.

"A coward," he said flatly then shrugged. "Guess I am. Have to admit no one's ever called me one to my face, though." He headed toward the door. After he opened it he paused, his back to her, when she spoke.

He heard sadness, tinged with some anger when she said, "If you change your mind…"

He stopped himself from racing back to her and taking her in his arms. "I won't." And then he left, closing the door gently behind him. At the foot of the stairs he halted, just in time from running into Katie.

"Where are you off to in such a hurry?"

"Butte. I've got court for the next two weeks."

Katie moved to a table a short distance away and served her customers, slamming the plates down on the table a bit hard, causing the two older men to flinch.

Simon took the opportunity to head for the door.

"Simon, stop! I'm talking to you," Katie snapped.

James came in the door, blocking Simon's way. He looked at Simon then at his wife.

"Something wrong?" he asked.

"He's leaving for Butte and will be gone for two weeks, James. Leaving Janie behind, right after getting married. You could have taken some time off, couldn't you?"

Simon sighed at the accusatory expression on her face then looked at James and saw understanding. For once he was glad he'd confided in James and Cane already about his plans.

"Listen, I'll be around all the time since I'll be hanging up my solicitor's shingle soon, and I purchased the Rawlings farm besides. You explain to her, James. I've got to head out."

After he left, Katie ran to James's side then tried going around him but he grabbed her around the waist. "Now hold on a minute, sweetheart. We've got to have a little talk."

"You have to stop him! Why, he hasn't been married but a week and he's leaving his wife behind. You know what I'd do if you did that to me, don't you?"

A big grin stole across James's face. "I sure do, and that's why I've never left you, never would."

She sniffed and gave him a sidelong look. "All right, Marshal, talk to me."

"Over a cup of coffee, and maybe some breakfast?"

Katie gave him a dimpled grin. "I think I can manage that."

Within moments Katie carried a plate filled heaping high with eggs, bacon, and toasted bread with jam. Then left and returned with two cups of coffee."

Once he explained Simon's feelings about Janie her anger returned full force. "That is so unfair of him! I know Simon is in love with her. How fair is it for him to make that sort of decision for both of them?"

His hunger appeased, James stuck his legs straight out beneath the table and slouched in his seat. "Well, now, the way I figure it, there's a way around this."

"What way? How? Oh, you mean we might be able to change his mind about annulling his marriage?"

"Hell, no. We would have no success. I know Simon and he'd just dig his heels in deeper. Nope, I'm saying it takes two of them signing those papers and I say we just tell Janie not to sign them."

Katie's eyes widened and she whooped and hopped out of her chair, landing on James' lap. James heard applause from the few customers in the restaurant and grinned at his wife.

With her arms around his neck, she whispered against his lips, "Now I know why I'm so crazy in love with you."

~

*J*anie's body healed over the next few weeks even though her heart was broken. She went back to cooking and serving at the Palace. Now, as she served breakfast one fine spring morning, her attention was caught by the sunlight shining on her gold wedding band, which she refused to remove. She'd heard not a word from Simon—no one had.

She took a short break with a biscuit and coffee in the kitchen during the lull before the lunch crowd arrived, chatting with the other palace cook, Ethel. She finished and heard the front door open and shut several times and she heard voices. Folks were arriving for lunch and she would be serving meals since Annie was sick again. This pregnancy was hard on her, but Janie didn't mind serving. Talking with folks kept her mind off Simon. After tying on her apron, she headed out the door with a pad and pencil in hand to take orders.

An hour later the crowd had dwindled and several tables were still full with folks eating when a silence suddenly came over the dining room. She was standing by the buffet, drying forks and knives and placing them in the drawer when the dining room quieted. Looking up she followed people's gazes. Simon stood in the doorway, looking straight at her. Janie nodded and breathed a relieved sigh when he nodded a greeting in return then walked to the end of the dining room and sat down at a vacant table next to a window.

Standing frozen in place she had no idea what to do. Should she approach him? Take his order? Her heart cried out for him. How she wanted him to take her in his arms and kiss her the way he used to, but then she thought about the annulment papers that had arrived a few days ago and anger rose to the surface, ready to boil over.

Ethel came out of the kitchen, untying her apron but paused when Janie said, "Please, Ethel, would you take Simon's order? He just arrived."

The older woman said in a kindly fashion, "Of course. You go put up your feet for a bit."

Janie scurried into the kitchen and stirred several pots of boiling food on the stove. Ethel returned with Simon's order of beef stew and cornbread.

Slopping beef stew into a bowl her anger rose as she thought about those darn papers sitting on her bureau in her room—papers she'd refused to sign. She handed the bowl and a plate of sliced cornbread to Ethel and watched her leave the kitchen. As soon as Ethel returned she decided she'd call it a night and go upstairs. Now, after all the pining for Simon she was full of pride and too angry to talk with him. It hurt so much to see him. She had to admit, from the sad expression on his face, that he wasn't happy about this situation between them, either.

The kitchen door swung open and she looked up, stunned to see Simon, looking heartbreakingly handsome and somber. She drank him in, dressed in his typical 'judge' suit of black, brocaded vest, white shirt and string tie.

"Janie? The papers Do you have them?"

Fury flared through her at his first words to her in two weeks. Heavens, couldn't the man have said he'd missed her? Couldn't he say he ached for her as she did him? No, he had to remind her of the papers. She knew her cheeks were red for she felt fierce heat sear them. Casually she turned away from him and started stirring the stew. "I've no idea what you're talking about, Simon."

"Darn it, Janie!"

Her skin prickled at his impatient tone but she refused to give in to him.

Slamming the spoon down on the stove she whirled around to face him. "All right. You must know I received the papers, after all they were hand delivered to me, by James himself."

"Uh, if you want to just hand them over I'll take them and file them in Butte."

"I've no idea where I put them." She leaned back against the counter and put her finger to her temple. "Hmm, let me think on this. I had thought about throwing them in the fireplace, but didn't. I thought about using them to wrap up potato peels, but didn't, and then using them to pack away fish guts and burying them—but didn't. But, for the life of me, I just can't recall what I did with them."

"Okay, so I never knew you had such a funny bone," he said dryly. "Go get them."

She frowned. "Like I said, I've no idea where they've gone to."

Simon sighed. "This won't change a thing, Janie. Not a darned thing and you know it. Be reasonable."

"Reasonable?" she shrieked. She sauntered over to him and flipped the string tie around his neck. "I'd say I'm the only reasonable one of the two of us. Seeing as you're the judge, not me, that's not saying much."

"Fine, be that way. I'll look for them."

He strode out of the kitchen and she heard him clomping up the steps. Whipping off her apron she followed him. In her room, he'd paused at the bureau and had the annulment papers in his hands. "Now, if you haven't read any of it that's okay. Trust me, I've filed several of these for other folks, and basically it's just dissolution of…"

"I don't care what it says!" Janie exploded. "Like I said before, you're a coward."

His eyes turned cool as he looked down and flipped through the pages one by one. When he got to the last page he said, "You didn't sign it."

"That's right, I didn't." She lifted her chin, her hands still on her hips. "And there's not a darned thing you can do about it." She sank down on the bed and leaned back on her elbows, giving him a mirthless smile.

"Damn it all," he began but she stopped him.

"Tut, tut, is that any way to talk to a lady?"

He cursed beneath his breath and proceeded to pace the floor, back and forth. He stopped then and said, "James and Katie put you up to this, didn't they?"

"In fact, James mentioned not signing it until we had one more discussion, just to see if either one of us changed our minds."

"Which I haven't," he snapped.

"Me neither, which means we've got a problem." Janie sat up and felt tears filling her eyes. "Nothing I can say will make a difference to you, will it?" Her voice trembled and she hated it, but she couldn't control her hurt and sadness any longer.

The bed dipped when he sat beside her. The familiar scent of his tobacco and soap filled her senses and she had to do everything in her power not to throw herself into his arms.

"I don't want to hurt you, but it could happen—again—if we stay married. If something happened to you because of me, well, I'd have to live with it my entire life. And if we were married and you died, I don't think I could live without you."

"Something already has happened," she said softly, glancing up at him as he sat with his hands folded between his legs. "And I'm fine. Don't you see that us being married is worth taking a chance, especially since we'll both be miserable apart?"

"No, it's not—not to my mind. Sign the papers." He set them in her lap and pulled a pen out of his jacket's breast pocket. "Please, just do it."

She shook her head and tears fell freely then, blotting the papers on her lap. "I can't."

"Let me help you," he encouraged, shoving the pen into her hand. He wound his hand around her fingers to hold the pen and smoothed the papers on her knee.

Through her tears she saw the line on which to sign, felt his hand moving hers into position. She jerked her hand, ready to pull away, but he held her hand tightly.

"Sign it, for me. If there's just one thing you can do for me, it's this, if you love me at all."

Looking up, she met his sad expression but she also saw his love for her in that look. And she knew that no piece of paper would ever make a difference between them so she signed the document. When she finished he released her hand.

Janie stared down at her name, saw how she'd pressed down with the pen too hard and had made a hole at the end of her signature, through the paper. Tears fell more quickly now and she threw herself down on the bed and sobbed into her pillow.

∼

Simon felt like crying himself. She'd done it, signed the papers, yet it hadn't relieved him a bit. And now her sobbing was breaking his heart, and all his resolve to keep his hands from her. Leaning over he gently stroked her back and murmured, "It'll be all right. We can still see each other. I bought the Rawlings place for…" All right, he'd bought it for the two of them and now it seemed silly owning a homestead when it would just be him living there. "Anyway, I'll be living nearby and I'd like to see you from time to time and…"

Like a whirling dervish she sat up and lurched to her feet. She looked so beautiful, even angry. "Damn you!" she exploded. "Crumbs? You're offering me crumbs? I've had enough of men taking advantage of me. I've lived a life of abuse, and I certainly don't need to take anything you have to offer. I'm living my own life now, the way I want to. And I'll tell you now that doesn't include allowing you into my life in any way. You made your decision and forced my hand and me to accept it."

She'd been jabbing her finger into his chest with her last words, and before she moved her hand away, he grasped it. "You've made your point." He gave her a wry smile. "The problem is Bozeman isn't all that big."

"You're right. This town isn't big enough for both of us." Lifting her chin, she said, "One of us will have to leave. And it won't be me."

He scowled as he rose to his feet and towered over her. "And it sure as hell isn't going to be me. Like I said, I just bought the Rawlings place."

"Then sell it! Now, get out of my room. I don't want to see or talk to you again—ever."

She whirled around and stomped to the window overlooking the street. He stood there, quietly watching her. His anger matched hers; she was being unreasonable; she was behaving like a child who couldn't have what she wanted. Swiping his fingers through his hair he saw her shoulders shaking and he knew she was crying again.

His heart broke a little more and through his own gathering tears he glanced down at the papers in his hand. She could be right in her evaluation of them; she could be right that it was better being together, even for just a short while, than to live a life of sadness apart. But then he thought about Clive sitting in jail, may he rot there, he mused, and knew he couldn't change his mind. Janie's safety was paramount to everything. He knew, if something happened to her, if one of the men he'd locked up came looking for him upon release and he had Janie in his life, she'd be directly in harm's way. Cursing inside for having believed he could ever have such happiness like Janie in his life, he stalked from the room.

CHAPTER 7

The month of June in Bozeman was idyllic weather, in Janie's opinion. The sun shone brightly, birds chirped happily, the brooks and streams ran merrily and the flowers were in pretty bloom, but Janie's heart was heavy.

She had started packing, but each time she placed an article of clothing in her satchel, Katie pulled it out and tossed it across Janie's bedroom.

"But Janie, you can't leave me high and dry like this!" Katie protested.

Janie looked at her friend sitting on the bed beside the open satchel. "I don't want to leave Bozeman, and you and my new friends and my job, either. But what can I do? I can't stand the thought of running into Simon again! It hurts too much. Now that he's practicing law again and has the new homestead he's staying put. Good grief. And now his office is directly across the street? It's too hard for me! And he refuses to leave. I can't say as I blame him. I see all of the wonderful things in Bozeman and understand perfectly why he won't."

"I told you, you shouldn't have signed those papers. Now we have to move on to a new plan."

Janie saw the calculating look on Katie's face and sat beside her, "Uh, what are you talking about?"

Janie kept her eyes on Katie, thinking how Katie appeared much younger than her thirty plus years. Never had she seen such a pretty, proper woman, yet upon occasion, like now, possessed a mischievous gleam in her eye.

"Simon's in love with you."

"No, he's—

"Uh-uh, no interrupting. It's true and you know he is or he wouldn't have asked to marry you in the first place."

"Then he has a mighty strange way of showing love, doesn't he? The strings were hardly tied before he changed his mind," Janie said dryly.

"Simon's full of fears. If you could have seen the worry on his face while you were recovering from your gunshot wound, you'd understand. And you know how, all the time you were abed, he kept a vigil until he knew you were going to get better. Let me think a minute."

While Katie chewed her lips, deep in thought, Janie rose and started packing her suitcase again. Before she could pack two clothing items Katie shouted, "I've got it!"

Janie narrowed her eyes. "What are you planning?"

"You have to make Simon jealous."

Janie rolled her eyes and sighed. "Now how am I supposed to do that? You know I've only been courted by Simon."

"Yes, well I know of several men in town who'd asked me about you upon your arrival, but kept their interests to themselves when they saw Simon had claimed you. But there's no reason why you can't allow any of these men to court you now, is there?" She slapped her knee and stood up, proceeding to pace the room. "We've all been invited to the Anderson's annual summer picnic and to a dance down at city hall so those two events will afford you an opportunity to meet someone else. The Anderson's party is tomorrow afternoon, after church services."

"But I don't want to be with someone else," Janie protested.

"Of course you don't, but you must do this. You simply must." A slow grin spread across her face. "I can just see Simon's reaction while you dance with another man. He'll seethe with jealousy. I don't think it'll take him long to realize he make a mistake letting you go."

Janie thought, why not? Maybe Katie was right; maybe Simon would regret the annulment and ask her to marry him again. Nodding, Janie said, "I think you're onto something, my friend." She laughed then and gave Katie a hug. "Who shall be my first victim?"

Katie's laughter rang out as she hugged Janie. "Now you're talking!"

The first man Katie suggested Janie flirt with was Horace Manley, a blacksmith in Bozeman, because he'd asked Katie more about Janie than any other man. So, early the following morning, Horace arrived for breakfast. Janie approached his table. Stopping beside him she smiled and softly said, "Well, hello Horace. What can I get you?"

Horace hardly looked at her, but she saw his face go red. Of course, it just happened that Horace had been blessed with carrot-colored hair and a fair complexion so most of the time his face looked flushed.

"Well," he drawled, "think I'll have the steak and eggs, Mrs. Hopkins."

"It's Mrs. Miller," Mr. Manley. "Simon and I have parted ways."

His head jerked up at that and his face glowed even redder as he looked into her eyes. "Oh, yeah. I heard about that. Real sorry, ma'am."

She nodded. "Yes, it was unfortunate."

Janie braced herself as he gave her a long, intent sweep of her body, a grin forming on his full lips. Somehow, she couldn't imagine those lips kissing her yet she straightened her resolve and smiled at him. Then she saw movement at the palace entrance and saw Simon walk in.

"I see." Horace rose to his feet and saw they were eye level with each other, though his frame was big and bulky. Taking her hand, he raised it to those full lips, kissed it and said, "Then do me the honor of allowing me to escort you to the Anderson's picnic next Sunday?"

"Why, Horace!" Janie said with a sweetness in her voice that made her want to spit, "I'd be honored to attend the picnic with you." She caught the stunned look on Simon's face, saw how he turned around on his heel and strode outside.

Horace grinned. "Thank you, ma'am."

He stood staring at her for a while before she replied, "I'd better get your order in. I'm sure you've work to do."

"Sure do, ma'am." He sank into his chair with a smile still lingering on his lips.

In the kitchen, Janie held a plate while Annie dished up the breakfast. She hadn't realized she had a scowl on her face until Annie commented on it.

"What's wrong?"

Janie sighed. "Horace Manley asked me to the Anderson picnic just as Simon walked in."

Annie smiled. "Well, that's a good thing, isn't it? You're trying to make him jealous."

"Jealous, yes, but what did the darned man do but turn on his heel and leave, without a word."

"Then he's really jealous, and he might be mad, too," Annie replied. "As I said, that's a good thing. I guarantee it won't be long before he's knocking on your door again."

$\sim$

A month later, Janie decided it best to inform the besotted Horace Manley that she didn't want to see him again since their courtship had made no outward difference to Simon.

She'd arrived at a few dances on Horace's arm only to find Simon with the town's librarian, Miss Mary Hunnicut, who was younger than Janie. Let him take up with the younger woman, Janie thought, it made no difference; she knew it was all a sham, just as her courtship with Horace had been. Simon could deny his feelings for as long as he wanted, but she knew he loved her, yet his fear for her safety kept him away from her. And she'd just received a letter stating hers and Simon's annulment had been finalized. Her heart broke at the thought they were no longer married.

Now Horace stood before her in the doorway to Katie's Palace kitchen, hat in hand, sad look on his face.

"I'm sorry," Janie apologized. "We're just too different. I can't see that our seeing each other more would draw us any closer, Horace. You're a fine man, but we're not meant to be together. *Because Simon's the only man meant for me!*

"Well, Miz Miller, if you ever change your mind..."

"I won't," she inserted. "Thank you, though. Now, if you'll excuse me?"

He stared at her for the longest time, then shook his head, as though clearing his brain.

"Oh! Of course. I'm taking you from your work"

She nodded. "Good day, Horace."

In the kitchen, she slammed an iron skillet on the stove and started frying eggs. She looked up with a scowl at Katie who ambled into the kitchen.

"What's wrong?" she asked.

Janie sighed, then turned off the oven burner and sank into a chair.

Swiping at the tears in her eyes, she murmured, "This farce to make Simon jealous isn't working. He's seeing other women."

Katie scoffed, "Yes, James and I noticed and Simon's miserable, believe me. What happened between you and Horace?"

"I told him we aren't meant for each other."

"I suppose that was for the best. I could see you were having difficulty being convincing about your feelings for him and I suppose it wasn't right to lead him to believe there could ever be something between the two of you."

"I beg your pardon?" Janie exploded.

With a laugh, Katie said, "You are not an actress, Janie. If you want to convince Simon to have a change of heart you must be convincing. You weren't, at least not with Horace." Tapping her chin thoughtfully, she said, "We have to find a handsome, virile man you can take up with to convince Simon that you've found someone new.

Janie rose to her feet and turned the burner back on. "No. I'll be a spinster or the rest of my life—unless Simon changes his mind."

"So, you mean to tell me you'll carry a torch for him for the rest of your life?" At Janie's nod, Katie snapped, "Over my dead body."

Glaring at Katie, Janie said, "Why are you so intent on me making Simon jealous? It hasn't worked!"

Katie sighed. "I know. Simon is the most stubborn man I've ever met —second to James, of course."

Janie chuckled. "You are so lucky to have James, and you know it."

"True, I am the luckiest of women. And you could be too. Let's just give things a rest for a while and see if things happen on their own. Maybe Simon will change his mind without our intervention."

"That's the most sensible thing you've said of late, Katie," Janie remarked.

～

*S*imon scowled at his reflection in the hallway mirror as he wound a tie around his neck. His thought was centered on the same person they'd been on a month ago...two months ago. Janie. After all was said and done he still missed her, still wanted her for his wife, but what could he do now? He'd ruined everything between them—had lost her trust and likely her love.

Snatching up his hat in the hallway he left this new monstrosity called 'home' and headed to the barn. Quickly, he saddled his horse, swung into the saddle and concluded that he'd made a mistake and he'd admit it, to Janie, the one and only woman he'd ever be satisfied with in life.

He'd made a mistake annulling their marriage and he'd find her, this day, after he was done with court, and ask her to marry him again. She'd been right all along; she said she'd rather have as much time happily married to him than not have him in her life at all. Finally, he knew what she meant—knew she'd been right. He'd been miserable without her.

Deciding to take the rode that meandered along the river to Bozeman instead of the direct route he usually took, a pretty picture of Janie settled in his mind. They'd spent many delightful moments sitting along the river bank kissing and talking, though he'd never made love to her. Janie had suffered enough injustices in life that she deserved nothing less than marriage before he took her to his bed. Truth be told, she was always in his mind and until he married her again, his life would be meaningless.

A gunshot resounded in the quiet of the morning. He came to an abrupt halt and narrowed his eyes, ducking low in the saddle, scanning his surroundings. A loud pounding from behind him came and he whipped around to see two men heading his way on horseback. Wondering for just a second where they'd come from he whipped his horse into a gallop. Any man he didn't recognize shooting at him meant trouble. That shot had been meant for him but had fallen short due to the distance separating them.

Town was only five miles away. Damn! He realized he'd left his gun behind.

∼

James strode into the kitchen with a deep scowl on his face. "Have you seen Simon about lately?"

Janie's eyebrows lifted. "Why, no, not since last night when he stopped for supper. Janie bit her lower lip then asked, "Is something wrong?"

"We've got a full courtroom of cases to be heard and he hasn't shown yet. Think I'll ride out to his place."

"He's running late is all," Katie said reassuringly. "You'll probably meet up with him along the road."

Janie frowned. "But Simon's always punctual."

"Yeah, I thought the same thing," James said.

James started to leave but paused when Janie said, "Is Clive still locked up?"

"No. He got himself a clever lawyer and is now out on bond as of a week ago."

Chills crawled up Janie's spine and she gasped. "I don't like the sound of that. I've a feeling Clive is up to no good." She tore off her apron. "I'll be back later." She followed James outside.

"Wait! Janie, you can't do anything," Katie protested, rushing after her. Pausing outside the saloon she added, "Let James take care of this."

"If it were James, would you sit still and do nothing?"

Katie scowled. "Of course not, but...all right...I get it. You can't sit by, can you?"

"No. Simon saved my life once, now maybe, it's my turn." Tears filled her eyes and she added, "Though I pray nothing's happened to him."

James rode all the way to Simon's and found no sign of the judge. On the way back to Bozeman he froze in his saddle and slowed down when he saw Janie riding full tilt toward him, stunned, because Janie did not ride horses. She was barely in the saddle and nearly passed him by when he reached out and grasped her horse's reins, forcing her horse to stop.

"What do you think you're doing?" James snapped.

"Trying to help you find Simon."

James sighed. "Get back to the saloon. Simon wouldn't want you looking for him—hell, I don't want you to, either."

"You can't stop me." She cast him a cool-eyed look, her gaze never wavering from his.

James swore under his breath, then snapped, "Fine. Have it your way. But do me a favor before you do any more looking."

"What's that?"

"Look for him on foot or in a buggie. I don't want to be responsible for you if you fall off that damned horse and break your neck."

"He's not home, is he?" Her heart stalled at James's expression.

He shook his head. "No." Looking far down the road, he had a pensive look on his face. Finally, he looked at her and asked, "Did you two used to go somewhere—well—private?"

Janie felt heat seep into her cheeks. "Yes, we have a few."

"Where? He could very well be sitting under a tree somewhere calm and peaceful, dreaming of you, for all we know."

"Not Simon, but I'll tell you where. You know the old apple orchard past his place?" At James nod, she added, "That's one place. And then there's a huge old oak tree along the river, close to the west side of his property line."

James nodded. "I know exactly where that is. I'll take the river and—"

"No, I'll go to the river. But first, can you take me the rest of the way to Simon's place? I'll use his buggie."

"That's a sensible plan." James told her. "Hold on to the pummel while I lead you down the road to his house."

Now that James had arrived, Janie felt much safer and more optimistic about finding Simon. He tugged her horse along behind him while she held on tight. At the farm, James hitched a horse to Simon's buckboard instead of the buggie, knowing the road to the river was rugged. They parted ways with James admonishing Janie, "Be watchful and don't be afraid to use that gun."

She glared at him. "Now, what makes you think I've a gun with me?"

He grinned. "'Cause you are so much like my Katie, and I can't imagine her looking for me without one."

Janie laughed and saluted him. "I'll meet you back in town."

As Janie drove the wagon along the road that led to the river she was watchful. She brought the horse to a slower pace when she thought she saw movement in the brush up ahead alongside the road. Then she came to a complete stop when a horse tore out of the woods and galloped down the road away from her—Simon's horse!

She just started to raise the reins to snap them against the horse's back to search for Simon, thinking his horse had thrown him but stopped when a man stepped out of the woods and onto the road. He had his arm around Simon's neck. Another man stepped out as well and faced Simon. He waved his arms around then poked Simon's chest a few times.

Janie had a perfect view of the three men since they were facing sideways. She gasped when the man who'd been poking Simon's chest pulled a gun out of his holster. Neither of these men was Clive, though she had a suspicion that Clive had put these men up to the dastardly deed.

Her gasp caught the men's attention. She was too close. They'd heard her. The one who'd been poking Simon swore and started running down the road toward her, pointing his gun.

"Get out of here!" Simon shouted.

She ducked down but managed to slap the reins against the horse's back and started to turn the horse and wagon around to head back the way she'd come. Once she'd completed the turn she slapped the reins again, squatting in front of the seat, keeping low when she heard gunshots whizzing past her. Keeping her eyes on the road she was relieved to see James barreling toward her and she pulled the horse to a stop.

"No, James," Simon warned. "Get Janie out of here."

Filled with relief, Janie watched with wide eyes as James kept coming. She knew he wasn't going to stop. *Thank you, James!* Once he tore past her, she whirled around, kept low, eyeing the frightening scene between the slats of the back of the old wooden seat. James, riding faster than she'd ever seen a man ride a horse, also ducked low. He rode, one hand on the reins, guiding his horse, the other holding his gun straight out and pointed at the man still running toward him. The man had to be a fool! Then she knew he was for he came to an abrupt stop in the middle of the road, dropped to his knee and pointed his gun at James.

James made a maneuver that prompted a gasp of surprise from Janie. He launched himself off his horse, did a roll into the brush alongside the road, then popped up and shot the man. Two hits and the man was down. He didn't move and James slowly rose to his feet, his gun still out of its holster.

Janie had been occupied by James and the man attacking them she hadn't looked toward Simon. Horror filled her heart when she saw the man facing them now, his arm still wound around Simon's neck, a gun to his head.

"Shit! Come any closer, Sheriff, and he's a dead man," the man cursed.

James started walking toward them. "Gordon? Is that you? I thought Simon put you away for life."

The man snickered, "Nothin' can keep me imprisoned, no walls, no men, no guns—nothin'!"

Janie noted the wild-eyed look on his face and his voice trembled when he spoke again.

"Ain't no one gonna lock me up again. No one!"

Amazingly, his words didn't give James pause; he just kept on walking. His voice was calm, almost soothing Janie thought.

"Gordon, you're just making it worse for yourself. By the way, how did you escape the prison in Texas, anyway?"

"A desperate man finds a way," he said illusively. "Damn it all, Sheriff, I said stop right there." He cocked the gun.

One of the men Simon had put away had escaped and come for retribution, Janie realized. Isn't this exactly what Simon had warned her about? Gasping then, she shouted, "Wait, James!" He's going to shoot Simon."

James stopped but kept looking straight ahead. "Janie, I said stay down."

"Listen to him, honey," Simon begged.

She jumped down from the wagon, pulled up the buggie seat and yanked out the gun she'd brought with her. Then she started moving forward until she was nearly eye to eye with the horse.

"Janie," Simon warned, "Don't come any closer."

Gordon's eyes honed in on Janie. "My, my, ain't she just a purty little thing."

Janie gulped and stayed glued against the horse, trying to remember the last time anyone called her little. Fury started boiling inside her then. This scum of the earth would not kill Simon, or James or her. She kept her gun hidden in the folds of her skirts as she walked toward them.

"That's right, sweet thing, you come right on over here." Gordon pressed the nose of the gun harder against Simon's head. "She yer girlfriend, Judge?"

Janie saw the spittle on Gordon's face but managed to keep her expression calm, hiding her revulsion. She drew closer still and in a soft, alluring tone, she said, "I'm no one's girlfriend. Listen, Gordon, is it? I work over at Katie's Palace in town. Why don't you stop by tonight? We'll have a few drinks, share a dance or two..." She shrugged. "Then we'll see where the rest of the night takes us."

"Janie! What in the hell are you saying?" Simon stormed.

She didn't reply but drew up alongside James and stopped. Glancing at him she thought she saw his shoulders shaking. Then, the longer she looked at him, she knew they were. His lips were pressed together tightly, and he met her eyes for just a quick moment. Humor blazed in them and she huffed to herself and thought, the man thinks I'm hilarious, doesn't think I can play the part of a siren. Why, I'll show him! She took a step, passed him by. He snapped the gun into his left hand and reached out with his right. She side-stepped him and kept heading toward Simon and his attacker.

"Janie, no," Simon begged.

Her gaze narrowed on him. "Remember, Simon?" she murmured, "you didn't want me. You spurned me, after taking what you wanted from me, you bastard."

A barking laugh tore from Gordon. "So, the old Judge don't know how to treat a whore, does he? Come on, sweetheart, once I get rid of Old Judge Hopkins here, I'll take you up on your offer of a night on the town together."

Her lips widened into a brilliant smile and she heard Simon cursing beneath his breath as she swung her hips and moved closer still. She was between James and Simon and his attacker. Consciously, she kept her eyes on Gordon, who thankfully seemed to only have eyes for her. Then she slid her hand up over her hip, past her waist, the sides of her breasts, then around to the front where she started to unbutton her gown.

A quick glance at the gun in Gordon's hand told Janie he was relaxing and not holding it quite so tightly. *Excellent.* Finally, she stopped directly in front of Simon. She forced a livid expression on her face, her eyes filled with hatred. A quick glance behind Simon and she saw Gordon lowering the gun, though he kept his arm around his prey. Had he loosened his grip? She prayed he had. Hating what she was about to do, in order to keep up the act, she had no choice. Raising her left hand, she hauled back and slapped him across one cheek.

Tears filled her eyes when she saw the painful, sad expression in his eyes, still she said, "You lost your chance with me, Judge, a long time ago. Gordon, on the other hand, looks like he knows how to treat a lady," she purred.

Gordon laughed hysterically. "You ain't no lady, but I don't care. Whores are plenty good enough for me."

Janie felt moisture seep under her arms and sliding down her neck as she continued unbuttoning her gown until her corset was exposed. Gladness filled her soul when she saw she'd caught Gordon's complete attention. He licked his lips as he stared at her breasts above the top of the corset.

"How about we just leave the judge and sheriff alone and head back into town?" she said sultrily. Her hips swung more as she moved around Simon, brushing against Gordon's muscular arm. The man was built like he did hard work for a living, broad with bulging muscles in his arms. She had to keep his attention on her, she knew, to give James the opportunity he needed.

A quick glance and she saw Gordon's arm loosen from around Simon's neck. Her eyes were riveted on Gordon's but she felt Simon tense beside her. Oh, God! He was going to make a move.

The thought had barely entered her mind when he did. Quicker than a rattler attack, his arm shot up and he gripped Gordon's wrist that held the gun. With the other hand Simon shoved her out of the way, so hard she fell to the ground. Scrambling to her feet she watched in horror as the two men grappled for the gun.

"Janie! Get the hell out of the way!" James shouted as he ran toward them.

Gordon's arm was down now, still clutching the gun even though Simon had his hand wrapped around his wrist. Gordon's other hand came down, slamming Simon's wrist repeatedly, but Simon wouldn't release him. Then he did and Gordon stumbled back a few steps and whipped the gun up, straight at Simon's head.

Janie didn't think, just reacted. She snapped her gun up and pulled the trigger.

"Shit!" Gordon shouted and dropped the gun, clutching his stomach. Hatred blazed in his eyes as he glared at her. "You shot me, you bitch!"

Her eyes widened as he sank to his knees, teetered a moment before collapsing, face down. She slumped to the ground, her world tilting as she realized she'd just killed a man.

~

*J*anie wakened to near darkness. As she started to sit up, hands pressed down on her shoulders.

"Lie still, sweetheart. You fainted dead away, and I want to be sure you're okay before you start moving again."

Simon hovered over her and she whimpered and raised her arms, pulling him down to her. "You're all right, then? He didn't shoot you?"

He kissed her lips, then her neck, murmuring, "I'm just fine. He didn't have a chance in hell of shooting me with you gunning him down."

Janie widened her eyes on him when she heard his humorous tone. "I just shot and killed a man! How can you make light of that?"

Simon grinned, his white teeth flashing. "You shot him, in about the worst place a man could be shot—in the gut. But you didn't kill him. He'll be suffering a lot though as he heals, and he deserves every minute of that pain. I had no idea you knew how to shoot a gun."

"I don't."

She heard James laughing and she looked to the opposite side of the buggie. They'd loaded her onto the floor and were standing on either side of it. She struggled to sit up and Simon took her hands and pulled her up and out of the wagon and into his arms.

Janie wound her arms tight around his waist and hugged him, raising her lips to accept his kiss. Oh, the feel of his firm, intent kiss nearly made her swoon again. Gladness filled her heart then sadness filled it again; he was being so loving only because he'd been frightened for her. Nothing had changed between them.

But then he made her own thoughts a lie when he murmured against her neck, "Marry me again, sweetheart. You were right all along."

She grabbed his arms and looked up into his face, her heart pounding. He was serious, she saw, knowing Simon would never joke about something so important. As tears flooded her eyes again she said, "I was always married to you, darling, in my heart, soul and mind—always."

He gulped. "Then forgive me for being an utter fool."

Janie flicked a quick glance at James and saw he'd moved away from them. Then she grinned. "I'm fairly certain I'll make a fool of myself one time or another during our marriage so there's really nothing to forgive."

"I treated you horribly, and you know it," he said.

"Yes, you did," she said slowly, "but I think all along I knew, in my heart, you'd return to me."

"We're getting married as soon as we get to town. I'll find the preacher."

"You'll get no argument from me. But you know, Simon, you were right. There will always be someone at your back, wanting retribution."

His entire façade seemed to sink. "I know," he said softly. "I'm still trying to deal with the idea of living in fear for your life for the rest of our lives together."

"Don't, Simon. For as long as you're looking out for my safety, I'll be looking out for yours. If we always do that, no one can harm us."

"You are one smart lady, do you know that?"

She laughed. "True. And a smart lady knows only a smart Judge is good enough for her."

"You two about done here with all the compliments?"

They looked over at James standing there, looking red-faced and uncomfortable.

Simon said, "Sorry, James, but everyone in town is going to have to come to grips with the fact that I'm in love with this woman and plan on proving it every day of our lives together. To make it official—again—will you marry me, Janie?"

She sobbed and said, "Yes! But this better well be the last time you propose to me, Simon Hopkins!"

"It will be. I promise it will be."

Simon met her lips and thanked God above for this woman who would forever change his life.

For good.

THE END

LAURA AND THE RAILROAD BARON

Laura Elizabeth Woodbury, heir to a Montana cattle ranch, has just lost her father. A year ago, he bestowed upon her the nickname, "princess Sapphire" when he discovered sapphires in a mine where, sixteen years earlier, he'd found gold. The independent Laura is astonished to learn her father has hired a fancily-dressed stranger to assist her in finding a suitable husband, and to help run the ranch.

Matt Black is the right hand man of a Minnesota railroad baron who'd been a friend of Laura's father. Matt's been hired to head up a team of railroad workers replacing damaged railroad tacks across Montana and to find a decent man to marry Laura. Matt is completely unprepared for the headstrong, willful blond and soon finds himself in love with her. Laura feels the same way about Matt—until she learns his secret that will change her life completely.

CHAPTER 1

July 1886
South Central Montana
The Woodbury Ranch

"*N*ineteen-year-old women do not have guardians," Laura Elizabeth Woodbury huffed.

No wonder the ranch hands referred to her as 'Princess Sapphire', thought Matt Black, stretched out in the side chair across from her. If it hadn't been for the curve of her breasts, she could have been a child sitting behind the desk. He guessed her booted feet didn't quite touch the floor. Bright red spots of color appeared on her fair cheeks, her complexion delicate as a porcelain doll. But the steel beneath that refined surface showed in her ramrod straight spine.

"I am sorry, Miss Woodbury," the solicitor, Samuel Simpson, replied. "You *do* need a guardian. Your father was quite adamant that you wouldn't be able to run this ranch on your own. And Mr. Black is a capable man. Give him a chance, won't you?"

"But I had a perfectly capable foreman until Mr. Black decided to relieve him of his position. John Whitman was the best foreman we ever had."

Sitting beside the lawyer, Matt Black decided she was deliberately ignoring him by failing to ask why he had to be present at the reading of her father's will. Though they'd met before, the circumstances were certainly less amiable this time.

"He was…until he showed a little bit too much personal interest in you," Mr. Simpson said uncomfortably.

Matt had found her in the barn, dressed as she was now in buckskin pants and a man's shirt. More specifically, he'd found her in the clutching embrace of her foreman, apparently not struggling to get away. He wondered why a gently born and raised woman would allow a man such liberties.

Laura's father had been a life-long friend of Paul Hill, Matt's uncle. Hill, being too ill himself to perform the duties for his friend upon his recent demise, had relegated the job to his nephew. Matt owed much of his success in life as both a railroad and lumber baron to his uncle, so he'd willingly agreed to attend to Miss Woodbury's future while on business in Montana.

"There's no need to worry," Samuel said. "Mr. Black will be in charge until he finds a new foreman for you. He'll be staying here in one of the guest rooms until he's completed his business."

Laura sputtered, "There was nothing wrong with how John handled the foreman job."

Matt sighed. The man may have been an adequate foreman, but he had no business putting his hands on her. Which was exactly what Matt told him when he tossed the no-good off the ranch.

"Miss Woodbury, this portion of this discussion should be between you and me, not Mr. Simpson."

She turned an ice-blue gaze on Matt, one he guessed likely silenced most men … not him.

His father had passed away when he was but sixteen, leaving him with four younger sisters and his mother to care for. He'd become the 'man' of the house then and, quite frankly, his gentle mother couldn't handle her brood of strong-willed daughters. Soon, he found himself in the unenviable position of being guardian and disciplinarian. A week didn't go by when one of his sisters was planted over his knee for a plain old-fashioned whipping. Initially, he'd hated the chore, but eventually fell naturally into the dominant role, and in due time, the girls listened to him, and the discipline sessions grew farther apart. Now, as they were all married, they were their husbands' responsibility, thank God.

Looking at the cool exterior of Laura Woodbury, he decided she was no different than his sisters and suspected sooner than later she'd be over his knee. He smiled at the thought, thinking how different this would be from spanking his sisters, but he was the man for the job, and would exert his authority over her. Sinking back against the back of his chair he found himself delighting in the prospect.

Trying to reason with her, he said, "Your father only wanted you to be cared for. He wanted you protected. That duty and responsibility has fallen to me." He smiled. "I won't be staying forever, just until you're settled."

Matt had to wonder about the uncertainty crossing her face. She appeared to not believe a single word he said. Her uncertain expression changed to sadness, and he tried recalling what he'd said to make her so melancholy. Recalling his words about how much her father had wanted her cared for must be the reason.

"What do you mean by 'settled'? My father never said a word about any of this to me."

"Settled, Miss Woodbury, as in married." With her long, gold hair and pretty features, Matt had the feeling finding a suitable man to marry her wouldn't be difficult.

She gasped, then started coughing behind her hand, her eyes filling with tears.

"Are you all right?" Matt asked as he went to stand but settled back in his chair at her upraised palm.

She pulled a lace handkerchief from her shirt's breast pocket and wiped her eyes. "You can't be serious!"

"I most certainly am." Matt rose from his chair, stepped forward and planted his hands on the desk. When he leaned toward her, she sank back in her chair, cringing away from him. "You may choose your future husband, but I have final approval."

"What gives you the right to order me about?"

"As Mr. Simpson informed you, I'm your guardian and protector." He straightened up and folded his arms across his chest.

"More like my jailer," she muttered.

"No, you're wrong. Your life won't change a bit, but I have a duty to perform—a job to do. And, remember, this wasn't my idea, but your father's."

Matt returned to his chair. From the high color in her complexion, he knew she was furious with him. He hoped they wouldn't clash too often before he finally married her off, yet somehow, he guessed it would be inevitable. Laura Woodbury needed to learn that she was a woman meant to be cared for by a man. She was young and reminded him of his ex-wife, who'd been little more than a child bride herself when they married.

Women generally followed the natural order in life when led by a strong man with a gentle manner and good intentions. He hadn't risen so far in life due to his sternness, but because of his charm. Treating her with care would make her see the way of things. He frowned and thought, if that didn't work he'd resort to treating her the way he had his sisters when they were ill-behaved—over his knee for a bare-bottomed spanking.

"Uh, could we continue with the reading of your father's will, Miss Woodbury?" Mr. Simpson's voice sounded worried.

She waved a careless hand. "In a moment. I've another question for Mr. Black. How did you know my father? He never spoke of you."

"My uncle, Paul Hill, had been a life-long friend of your father."

Laura smiled. "Yes, I remember Mr. Hill, though it's been several years since I've seen him. How has he been?"

"Not well. Your father appointed him as your guardian. Due to illness, he isn't up to the task. In his stead, he asked me to step in. Since I had railroad business to attend to here in Montana, it was convenient."

"I see." She grimaced. "How nice that my guardianship is so convenient for you."

Damn. *Convenient.* He hadn't meant to put things quite so crassly.

"Is there anything else?" she asked her solicitor, giving Mr. Black the cold shoulder.

"What you've just heard is the extent of it," he replied, obviously trying to mollify her.

As Simpson's low-pitched voice continued, Matt found himself having difficulty concentrating on the conversation. Besides, the rest of the will was standard fair. Miss Woodbury should have no other complaints. She'd been left, as Woodbury's only heir, an exceedingly wealthy woman.

Exhaustion overwhelmed him. His lack of sleep during his journey to Montana over the past week had finally caught up with him. Earlier in the day, he'd glimpsed the bed in the guest room and was looking forward to escaping into blissful slumber.

Laura's soft, melodic voice caught his attention. "That settles things, doesn't it?" She rose from her chair. Matt and Simpson rose as well. She shook Simpson's hand—much as a man would, Matt thought—then strode from the library, without saying a word to him.

He followed her, his gaze riveted to her plump, womanly bottom, her hips swinging alluringly as she left. It hadn't taken Matt long to realize Laura Woodbury had been allowed to wear the pants in her household far too long. That would stop immediately. No more wearing buckskin trousers as she'd worn today. With a bottom as fine as hers, a man could get the wrong impression about her. He sighed. Teaching her how to become a lady would be a major chore, but he guessed he'd be the only one she'd listen to for he'd give her no choice.

Simpson shook Matt's hand. "I warned you that Miss Woodbury was used to being in charge, didn't I?" he said dryly.

"You did. I've never met a woman quite like her," Matt said. Most women of his acquaintance would never want to take up the mantle of responsibility.

Simpson narrowed his eyes. "You admire her, don't you? I hear it in your voice."

"Yes, I do. If she has, in fact, been in charge of this ranch for the past several years, from all appearances she's done well by it."

Simpson picked up his satchel. "You know she'll object vehemently if you interfere with the ranch operations, don't you?"

Matt shoved his hands into his pockets and sighed. "I know. I will only interfere if I believe she's being endangered, or if the work is too difficult. Otherwise, I know little about ranching and will leave it up to her."

"Good luck to you, Black. Call me if you need my services."

"I shall and thank you."

On his way out of the library, Matt caught a glimpse of Laura's well-rounded rear at the top of the stair's landing.

He called out, "Miss Woodbury? Where are you off to?"

She peered down at him. "To change for dinner, of course."

Matt gave an approving nod. "Excellent idea. I'll meet you in the dining room shortly."

Satisfied, he strode down the hall to the dining room, confident Miss Woodbury understood how things would be between them.

~

"*Mary!* Please fetch me my mother's red satin gown. You'll find it at the very back of the closet."

"Your mother wore that gown for a costume party. 'Tis positively…"

"—indecent. I know," Laura said.

"You want to appear a whore in Mr. Black's eyes?" her maid asked, her Irish lilt still evident, though she'd lived in America for ten years.

"You may be the best maid I've ever had, Mary O'Garrity, but you won't be telling me how to dress, thank you very much. I won't appear cheap in the gown, just more grown up."

"No, ye won't, and I won't help ye make a fool of yourself."

Laura narrowed her eyes on Mary, who stood across from her, scowling.

"I'm going to prove a point this evening to my houseguest."

"What point would that be?" Mary said dryly.

"That I'm a full-grown woman and able to take care of myself, including selecting my own husband and making my own decisions."

Mary lifted one eyebrow. "I'd no idea ye were gettin' married."

"I'm not. I just have to convince Mr. Black of the fact that—when and if I do decide to marry—it'll be to a man of my own choosing. Mr. Black *claims* I may choose my own husband, with his final approval, of course, but I don't believe a word he says. Oh, how could my father put that man in charge of me?"

"What in heavens are ye talkin' about?"

"Mr. Black, by proxy, has been appointed my guardian. Father's last will states that a suitable man must be found to marry me."

Mary sighed. "Ye know, your father spoiled ye. Now that he's gone on to meet his Maker, he's left ye in the hands of a man who won't allow ye to have the upper hand. 'Tis the smartest thing he's ever done, in my opinion."

"Mary! How can you even think that?"

"'Tis the truth."

"Haven't I kept this ranch running smoothly?"

"You've done a superior job, Miss Laura, but now 'tis time to take the place the Almighty meant for ye to take."

Oh, she hated when Mary spoke this way; hated how society believed it not normal for a woman to wear pants and to manage her own life. Every Sunday, without fail, Pastor Porter did nothing but lecture about a woman's place in life, looking directly at her the entire time.

She thought about Mary's comment regarding her father spoiling her. He *had* spoiled her—until her brother, Jeremy's death. Then he'd quite simply ignored her. No longer was she his beloved Princess Sapphire. Painful memories of sitting, night after night at the dinner table with him, made her heart clench in agony. Shunned, utterly and completely, he'd removed her from his life, speaking little to her, barely noticing her presence. Frankly, she'd been amazed he'd kept her in his will, but then he'd had no one else.

Mary pulled the gown from the closet and carried it to Laura's bed. As Mary tightened her corset, Laura sighed at her maid's disapproving expression. Once Laura donned the gown, she stared at her reflection in the full-length mirror. The vivid red gown had been fashioned of satin with a plunging rounded neckline, exposing the moon crescent tops of her breasts. The gown was more risqué then she recalled. The waistline was tight over her corset, the skirt slim and fitted, the hem of the skirt billowing into a slight train.

She stumbled, managing to catch herself upon entering the dining room. Mr. Black's initial welcoming smile abruptly disappeared upon her entrance. He scowled as he rose from his seat at the end of the table and strode toward her. His crisp white shirt, black tie, and broad shoulders clad in a fine black, lightweight serge jacket made Laura aware of his male attributes. His raven-colored hair was cut a bit long and reached his collar and contrasted starkly with his steel gray eyes.

Laura decided his dark, brooding masculinity likely appealed to many women, but not her. She much preferred John's fairness and soft spoken, gentlemanly manners. Mr. Black, on the other hand, had been nothing but dictatorial toward her. Though not ungentlemanly, she grudgingly admitted.

Before John had been booted off the ranch, she believed he had been on the verge of asking to court her—his kiss told her so. Perhaps, if he hadn't yet left town, she'd ask him how he felt about her. Oh, she knew most women would play the game for months, or even years, but she didn't have the luxury of time. According to her new guardian, she was on the marriage block, and, though he hadn't said it, she guessed he meant to rid himself of his new responsibility as quickly as possible.

She lost a bit of her confidence when she saw the smoldering look in

Mr. Black's eyes from where he now stood beside her chair. While she had no desire to start a row with the man, she had no intention of changing out of the risqué gown. Smugly, she felt sure Mr. Black would soon understand she was an independent woman. No one told her how to live her life.

He held her chair for her, and she sank into it. Chills ran up over her bosom and down her bare arms, his big body seemingly surrounding her as he solicitously pushed her chair up to the table. She felt superior strength in that push. Unwillingly, she compared John's narrow frame to Black's sturdy build, recalling how weak John's arms had felt around her.

Mr. Black returned to his own seat, and Laura breathed a relieved sigh. Mildred Hanson, the cook, appeared and served them each a bowl of creamy potato soup. The woman's chatter grated on Laura's nerves, but her guest seemed to enjoy it and engaged Mildred in pleasant conversation. After the older woman left, Laura glanced at him. The scowl had reappeared, and he met her eyes.

"I see you've dressed for dinner."

His casual comment on her appearance startled her momentarily, but she murmured, "Father and I have always done so."

Her cheeks felt hot, and Laura knew they were flushed. Lord, why had she done such a silly thing as to wear this gown? Mr. Black appeared ready to ... Well, if she didn't know better, she'd think him ready to throttle her.

He waved his fork toward her, his gaze on her breasts. "I realize this is the hot season, but you may want to cover up a bit next time."

CHAPTER 2

*L*aura had just lifted her spoon to her lips when she set it down. Her voice trembled when she replied, "You can't dictate to me how to dress."

"Someone must, since you've abysmal taste in clothing," he remarked. "I'll examine your wardrobe tomorrow and toss out what I believe are unsuitable garments for a young woman of your age and station."

Rising from her seat, she said, "I beg your pardon?"

One eyebrow lifted. "I see I'll have to call upon a doctor to see about your hearing problem as well."

Lifting her chin, she said coolly, "I won't tolerate you going through my belongings. You'll stay out of my room, and you won't make any decisions regarding my manner of dress." She looked down at her gown, then met his eyes once more. "As you can see, I'm a woman, full-grown. Now, then, if you'll excuse me, I've lost my appetite." She took a step away from the table.

"Sit down, Miss Woodbury," he ordered.

Laura paused when she heard the soft, yet steely tone in his voice. She whirled to face him and met his dark, intent look.

"We haven't finished this conversation. Sit down and eat. After dinner, we'll come to an understanding."

Laura turned away in complete defiance just as Mildred reappeared, platters of food in her hands.

"Oh, you can't be done eating yet, Miss Laura!" she exclaimed. "You haven't even finished your soup."

"As I've just informed Mr. Black, I've no appetite this evening. I'm going for a ride and will return later."

"Absolutely not," Matt declared.

The cook gasped and set down the plates, one at Laura's place, and the other in front of Matt. Lifting her skirt, she scuttled into the kitchen.

Laura jammed her hands on her hips. "I always ride after supper," she informed him.

He rose and tossed down his snowy napkin. "Aside from the fact you've refused to eat, riding alone in the evening is inappropriate for a young woman, not to mention dangerous, be she ever so mature."

When he headed toward her, she started backing away. "I'm going riding, and you will not stop me."

Whirling away from him, she heard him at her heels and knew she wasn't quick enough. His hands grasped her arms from behind. He held her in place and spoke softly in her ear, his breath and words ruffling her hair. "Go to your room."

The contact from his big, warm hands on her arms made her realize his strength once more, though his touch was gentle. Laura pulled out of his grasp and faced him. "How dare you touch me!"

"I haven't begun to touch you in the way you deserve, young lady."

"What!" she gasped. "You mean to ra—"

"Not *that*," he growled. "Young women that behave like spoiled brats require a trip over the knee for a well-deserved spanking."

Laura gasped in outrage, not only at his words, but in the steely look of determination on his face. She felt tears of fury fill her eyes and prayed they wouldn't seep out. While she wanted to defy him, she decided it might be unwise. She knew some men took delight in hurting women to get their way. She'd overheard gossip from one of her maids that John might have been such a man, though he'd never behaved that way with her.

She wouldn't put it past this determined man from doing exactly as he threatened, still, it was difficult to be obedient. No man had ever given her orders—ridiculous ones at that. Not even her father had treated her like a child.

Laura glared at Matt, daring him to do his worst. "I can't believe you'd even try to … discipline me," she spat.

"Oh, I dare, and much more, if you don't behave." He pointed his finger toward the stairs.

She bit her lip so hard she felt the metallic taste of blood. Her plan had, obviously, back-fired on her. Why hadn't she listened to Mary?

With as much decorum as she could muster, she lifted her chin and made her way, nearly running across the hall and up the stairs. She recalled the tingling sensations rushing up and down her spine when he'd touched her, a sensation that had been far from unpleasant. What was wrong with her? She'd stood close to men before—while dancing. She'd been touched before, including being held in John Whitman's arms. But never had she felt this sort of awareness, starting at the top of her head to the very soles of her feet. And, in her center, her heart pounded briskly in acknowledgement of Matt Black's unquestionable masculinity.

As soon as she entered her room, she closed the door and flung herself down on the bed. She felt discouraged and was thoroughly disgusted that she'd obeyed Mr. Black. But then she truly didn't know him, or of what he was capable. A spanking! The nerve of the man, she mused, even as heat rushed through her body, imagining him flinging her over his lap, raising her skirts, and— She cringed and squeezed her eyes shut.

Then she thought of John again. His gentle smile spoke of the possibility of intimacy. She guessed his fair hair and soulful brown eyes would melt any woman's heart. She just knew he would be a tender man. Never would she believe he'd harm her or lay a hand on her.

Tomorrow she'd travel into Bozeman to see if John had left. If he hadn't, she'd hire him back. She knew Mr. Black wouldn't approve of her seeing John, and he definitely wouldn't want her offering him his job back, especially since he'd fired him in the first place. But she'd had her sights set on John since the moment she'd convinced her father to hire him. Thinking of her reasons for hiring John back, though, she admitted retaliation against Mr. Black seemed to be the primary one.

She undressed and pulled on her nightshift. After tossing and turning for several hours, she knew she'd never fall asleep unless she took a ride. The grandfather clock in the downstairs hallway chimed the hour of midnight. She dressed in her shirt and buckskins again, then tugged on her leather boots. She had a feeling John was still in town, likely down at Shorty's Saloon, with his friends.

Reaching up, she pulled her hat from a shelf inside her armoire, left her room, took the iron key from her pocket and locked her door before making her way down the stairs. Just as she approached the library, she saw a light shining from beneath the door. Darn! He hadn't gone to bed yet. Closing her eyes, she took a few deep breaths, deciding it was now or never before slipping past the closed door and out of the house.

~

*M*att trudged up the stairs at half past midnight, having had to meet with the cook before settling down for a long awaited rest. He reached the landing, noted Laura's closed door further down the hall, and was satisfied she'd obeyed him. Just outside his room, he paused. Something gnawed at him—something wasn't right. Laura had been adamant about riding. He wasn't stupid enough to believe she would meekly obey him, so he turned and walked down the hallway, stopping outside her door.

His hand covered the doorknob. He tried turning it but found it locked. No surprise there, seeing as how he knew he hadn't made much of an impression on Miss Laura, except to cow her. He wondered if he'd even managed that. Her father had given her far too many liberties, but then he'd been a tired old man. Maybe he was entitled to spoil his only child, a child he'd raised alone for most of her life. Matt wasn't old at twenty-eight, just tired and skeptical at the moment about his ability to deal with the feisty Miss Laura.

Was she actually behind this locked door? Somehow, he doubted it. He tore down the stairs and out the front door. At the barn, he found Laura's groom sound asleep in a stall. Matt shook the boy's shoulder.

He sat up in confusion, rubbed his eyes, then stumbled over his feet as he tried to stand.

"Where is she?" Matt bit out.

"Went—she went for a ride, sir," the boy stuttered. "Toward town."

"My God!" Matt exploded. "You'd better count on her being safe or you'll pay a heavy price. Next time, you ask permission of *me* first regarding Miss Laura's requests. Understand?"

The frightened boy nodded, then saddled the fastest horse in the stable. Matt leaned over the horse's neck and sped down the road toward town. Why was she headed there? Surely not in search of that bastard foreman. Matt rode faster.

By the time he reached Bozeman, it was after one o'clock and anger surged through him. He required sleep, not storming after this disobedient little wench under his guard.

The town still bustled with activity. He scoured Bozeman but found no sign of Laura. She'd likely just gone for a ride and was now safe and sound asleep in her bed, he decided, wondering how he'd missed not passing her on the road when he heard a man's soft-spoken voice followed by a girl's giggling. Frowning, he moved in that direction. Plastering himself against a building, he leaned forward and peered around the corner.

In the darkness, it was difficult to identify the individuals, but he smelled Laura before he saw her, her lavender scent permeating the air. He stepped away from the wall and managed to make out the small shape of his ward leaning close against a man's body. Then he saw the man take her hand in his. Matt's world turned red as he tore into the alley. He was astonished to see that, beneath the silvery moon's rays, it was John Whitcomb. Apparently, the man hadn't learned his lesson.

He yanked them apart and pulled his arm back.

"Mr. Black, don't!" Laura protested.

Matt smashed a fist into Whitman's gut, then delivered a right uppercut to his jaw. Whitman collapsed to the ground. Matt stared down at the unmoving man, then swiped an errant lock of hair back from his forehead and turned to Laura.

She stood ramrod straight, her hands on her hips. "Just what do you think you're doing?"

Matt heard the trembling fury in her voice.

From inside a saloon, he heard tinny music and a woman singing off-key. No one had heard the scuffle, which infuriated him further. If he hadn't arrived in time, there was no telling what Whitman would have done to her.

"Damn, saving your virtue. Apparently, you didn't want to be saved. Do you know you scared the ever-living hell out of me, leaving the ranch the way you did?" He stepped close and scowled down at her. "Why did you leave? To prove you don't have to follow my orders when you know I'm only doing what your father wanted?"

A mulish expression crossed Laura's face. "I wanted John back. Whatever else might be said about him, he was a more-than-adequate foreman. Even my father approved of him. And I always ride after supper. You've ruined everything. I offered John back his job, but now I'm certain he won't return to the ranch."

"You got that right, Miss Laura," John said.

Matt scowled down at the felled man.

John awkwardly rose and looked at Laura. "I hadn't gotten around to telling you, but I took a job at Stanton Smith's place." He reached down, picked up his hat from the ground and placed it on his head. His fingers touched the brim in salute to her. "Good luck, Miss Laura."

"Darn it," she muttered, scowling at Matt. "Now see what you've done? He's taken another job."

Matt watched the man limp away, damning himself for being so impetuous—something he rarely was, unless it had to do with Laura. This did not sit well with him. But then he thought of her in John's arms in the barn the day he'd arrived and decided he had been right to intervene.

He looked away, grimacing when he noticed for the first time the stench in the alleyway. "Let's get out of here," he muttered, deciding they'd finish the discussion tomorrow.

He gave her a leg up onto her mare. As they rode side by side out of town, they were silent for a long while. Finally, Matt spoke. "What am I going to do with you?"

"I am too old to be spanked."

"Hardly," he scoffed. "Since you're resistant to the idea though, what have you in mind, instead? You deserve punishment."

"Why, I suppose you could banish me to my room or put me on rations of bread and water. But I'll inform you now, I'd not stay put. Besides, Mildred would never let anyone starve."

Matt smiled. Then he tossed his head back and laughed. "That's hardly a practical measure. The one I'll implement will make a deeper impression on you, I believe."

"What would that be?"

He caught the hesitancy in her voice and sighed. He had no desire to hear her complaints but knew she'd badger him all the way home if he didn't explain her fate.

"Tomorrow you'll report to me early in the morning for a list of chores to complete."

"Oh. Is that all?"

"I'm not speaking of outdoor ranch work, which I know you enjoy and wouldn't be a punishment at all. No, you'll stay inside and work along with your maid. You will also give your cook a week off from working in your kitchen, paid, of course, and you'll cook the meals yourself."

She stopped her horse. "Now, just a minute—"

CHAPTER 3

*M*att waited for the tirade to begin.

After a long pause, she said, "I'll handle the cooking. Cook's needed time off for ages."

Good grief. Matt hadn't expected her to be agreeable about his idea, but then he decided time would tell. Her cheery attitude would likely change once she'd put in a day or two of mundane, grueling housework.

He wouldn't allow her to work and dress like a man any longer, especially if he wanted to marry her off quickly. Then he thought, even dressed as a man, she had no trouble garnishing the interest of men. He also grudgingly admitted seeing her dressed in buckskins was enticing and seemed only to accentuate her womanly curves.

The rest of the ride home was accomplished in silence. The young groom ran out of the barn as soon as they arrived, a lantern in each hand. Matt dismounted quickly and hurried to assist Laura out of the saddle, only to find she'd already jumped down.

He came to a decision. "Tomorrow morning, after you've completed the assigned chores, come to the library. I'd like to discuss a few things with you."

She'd taken a lantern from the groom, then started for the house. "Keep up with me if you want to be able to find your way inside," she threw over her shoulder.

Matt's long strides easily followed her until they reached the house.

She opened the front door at the same time he did. His hand landed on top of hers for an instant. Releasing her hand, though he felt strangely reluctant to do so, he said, "Do you always open doors for yourself?"

Laura's brow lifted. "Why, I suppose I do. Is there a reason I shouldn't?"

"It's courteous and customary that a man open doors for a lady. Haven't you ever been courted?"

She bit her lower lip thoughtfully a moment before saying, "If you count the neighboring men folk stopping by for a glass of lemonade after work."

"That's not courting. That's being neighborly. All right, then that will be where we begin. I'll instruct you in what to expect and how to behave when a man comes courting."

She rolled her eyes at him. "If I must."

He found himself holding his breath as he stared down into her eyes. Matt had a feeling this woman had the ability to make a man feel ... well, manly and protective—even dressed as a boy.

"Is there anything else?" she said. "I'm exhausted."

Gruffly, he replied, "Go on to bed. We'll talk in the morning."

"Excellent idea. Good night."

"Yes, good night," he murmured, heat seeping into his face when he found his gaze riveted on her well-rounded rear as she left him. He headed for the library. From a desk drawer, he found a piece of paper and pulled the fountain pen from its stand. He thought about his sisters and their charming ways. What could he teach Laura in regard to the feminine arts?

He started to write, but each idea of what to teach Laura that came from his pen met with him scribbling over it. Finally, he set the pen back in its place. It was useless. Even wearing pants, Laura Woodbury was femininity personified.

She didn't require lessons of any kind, especially from him. Still, he couldn't help but wonder why she favored men's trousers, and why she enjoyed pursuing men's work.

Then an unexpected thought came to mind. Perhaps she needed motherly tasks to bring the femininity he knew that lurked inside her to the surface. And then his son came to mind. He thought, perhaps, he should mention to Laura he had a son, whom he missed immensely, having left him with his parents in Minnesota. Still, he considered the idea of having him come out to Montana to be with him, then set the idea aside, guessing he wouldn't be here long, for Laura was lovely and would likely court and marry in the near future.

He came to his feet. Restlessly, he wandered around the library, pausing before the fireplace. On the mantle were several photographs. He recognized Laura, in varying stages of growth. He smiled, noting her petite size in youth had lingered into adulthood.

His gaze stalled on the next picture grouping, which included several photographs of a young man with hair the same golden color and eyes of blue like Laura's. The resemblance between them was astonishing. For certain they were related, but then he frowned. She was her father's only heir—his only child. Perhaps it hadn't always been that way though.

One of his passions in life was dissembling mysteries. Identifying this boy became important to him. Matt moved along the bookshelves, perusing the titles, searching for something that would give him a clue to his identity. He'd nearly given up when he saw a leather-bound book. Reaching up, he placed the Woodbury family Bible on the desk, sat down and began to look through the pages.

It was nearly two o'clock by the time Matt had what he believed was a clue to Laura's unorthodox behavior. Treading quietly upstairs to his bed, he slipped beneath the covers, exhausted. It felt strange lying down without first having said 'good-night' to his son, Jonathan. They had rarely been separated, and most trips Matt took Jonathan with him. But not this time as Matt had been uncertain about his responsibilities toward Miss Woodbury.

Exhaustion finally overtook him, and he slept.

～

*T*he sun was just beginning to peek above the horizon when Laura wakened the next morning. She'd had difficulty sleeping, waking off and on through the night, until a horse's neighing and voices pulled her from her slumber.

It was only five o'clock, and already her room felt hot and muggy. Still, she shrugged a robe on over her nightgown and moved to the window that overlooked the backyard. Several of her ranch hands had arrived, having traveled from their homes in town. They were ready to head out to various pastures to work. One young man, then another, noticed Laura looking down from her window. Paul, the younger of the two, waved and said, "How do, ma'am!"

Grinning, Laura waved back. "Morning, Peter, Jim. Looks like it'll be a clear day but hotter than Hades, doesn't it?"

"Yes, ma'am," they said in unison.

"Make sure you wear your hats, and take plenty of water," she said. "And finish early so you won't be out scorching in the heat of the day."

The Swede, as he was called, Gary Hanson, sidled up beside the other men. "You comin', Miss Laura?"

"No. Not today." She heard a door slam. Mr. Black appeared, having just exited the house. He tipped his hat to the men with a "Good morning" and moved toward the corral. He hadn't noticed her in the window.

The men left then, their horses kicking up dust as they rode down the road.

Charlie, her groom, was pulling on the lead of one of her new stallions. He'd bridled the horse, for what purpose she had no idea. She'd given strict orders to leave the animal in the pasture to run wild until she was ready to train him.

Mr. Black paused a short distance away from the boy and beast. She couldn't hear his words but saw his lips moving. She also saw how the beast's ears pricked up, his big, rolling eyes riveted on her guardian.

Moving closer, he reached out and took the lead from Charlie. With a gentle tug, the horse followed him into a corral close to the house. Laura leaned down and set her elbows on the ledge, watching him through the wide-open window. *What was the man about, anyway?*

He started leading the horse around the corral's perimeter. At one point, the animal reared up, but Mr. Black turned and faced him, his gentle, unthreatening demeanor immediately calming the horse. She realized then he was no stranger to horses. She liked that. Liked that a lot... which didn't sit well with her. She didn't want to like this controlling man who'd entered her life. *Whatever were you thinking, Father?* But then she remembered Mr. Black's uncle had actually been named her guardian. When he was unable to fulfill the duties required, Mr. Black was obliged to step in.

When the horse reared up again, nearly striking Mr. Black, she gasped and straightened up from her bent position at the window. Donning a pair of dungarees, long-sleeved shirt and boots, Laura tore down the stairs and ran outside. She halted upon reaching the corral.

Mr. Black stood in the center, lead in hand, clicking his tongue, encouraging the horse to pick up his pace as he ran briskly around the corral's perimeter. Laura admired the man's tall muscular body; his long legs he'd spread wide for balance, clad in tapered serge pants. His coat he'd left unbuttoned over a plain but crisp white shirt. Didn't he own any informal clothing?

He saw her and flashed a wide grin. "Good morning."

"'Morning," she murmured, relaxing against the fence, though inside her body her chest felt heavy, her heart doing somersaults. What an incredibly handsome, charming man—dangerously so, she mused. She focused on his tall, strong body, his intent, flinty-eyed look trained on the horse. She tore away from her wayward thoughts of how it might feel to kiss Mr. Black and watched him work the horse. After a while, she said, "I'm going to make some coffee. Want some?"

"Yes, thank you. You'll be preparing it, not your cook," he reminded her.

"Cook's not here, so how could I forget?" Turning on her heel, she walked swiftly to the house. Did he think she'd never done household chores before? Her father had always had a housekeeper, maids and a cook. Nevertheless, he'd insisted she learn to perform household chores, things he believed she would need in her future once she married. He'd always said, 'Unless you walk in the cook's or maid's shoes, you won't know how to supervise them.'

In the kitchen, she poured hot water over the coffee grounds in the pot, then set it on the burner as memories of her twin brother, Jeremy, flooded her. She recalled how jealous of him she'd been the year they turned twelve. He'd been allowed to work outside, alongside their father and the hands, while she'd been stuck inside performing women's work. She knew she wouldn't have minded if her mother had been alive to provide company, but she'd passed away shortly after giving birth to her and Jeremy.

Once the coffee was ready and piping hot, she carried two cups outside, setting one down on a corral post. She took a careful sip and sighed with pleasure at the strong taste of the brew. Looking up, she choked on her coffee when she saw Mr. Black sitting on the horse, bare-backed. She knew better than to make a sound for fear of spooking the animal. She stayed calm and took deep breaths, expecting the horse to toss him to the ground any moment.

He sat there, leaning over the animal's neck, stroking him and talking softly. She couldn't help but wonder at his words. Resentment filled her. She'd tried twice to mount this horse she had yet to name, with no success.

Matt slid from the animal's back, dropped the lead and strode toward her.

Laura picked up the cup she'd set down on the post and handed it to him. His hand brushed hers when he took it. She backed up a step even as quivers of unwanted desire ignited inside her. His touch made her feel all the things a woman felt for a man to whom she was attracted.

"What are your plans for the day?" she asked, deciding it would be good to know the whereabouts of her charming adversary.

One dark eyebrow lifted, and a slow smile tilted up his lips. "I'm walking the line, so I won't be back until after dark."

Laura breathed a deep, relieved sigh. She had plans to join some of her hands to help repair the corral at the west end of the property.

His next words made her think he was a mind reader. "Inside work today, only," he reminded her.

"I know."

She felt too tired to fight him. As a matter of fact, she would enjoy her day indoors—which, unknown to Matt, would be a welcome change. She swept a loose lock of hair back from her forehead, then sipped her coffee. Finally, she looked at him. "You're not a stranger to horseflesh."

Matt laughed. "It wasn't all that long ago my family owned a farm in southern Minnesota. We had lots of animals."

"Hmm, you have the appearance of someone raised in town. I'd assumed you'd have a fine carriage or two pulled by horses and wouldn't think to ride one. You're good with them." Tilting her head to one side, she gave him a faint smile. "Think you'll be able to train this one?"

"No doubt in my mind, and within the next few days. I plan on using him as my main means of transportation while I'm here, if that's all right with you."

"I've no problem with that—if you can get him to mind. He seems to have a strong will of his own."

"Really?" He grinned. "I thought him rather docile."

Laura gave an unladylike snort by way of a reply.

"Have you eaten breakfast yet?" he asked.

"I'm just about to make ham and eggs and biscuits."

"You are?"

Scowling at him, she said, "Contrary to what you believe, I'm no stranger to household work." She took a last sip of her coffee. "What did you mean earlier when you said you'd be walking the line?"

He took her arm with one hand, held his coffee cup with the other and escorted her back to the house. "I'm here to supervise a crew of railroad men who are in the process of fixing broken track in this territory. Walking the line means the railroad track."

"I see. My solicitor said you were here to take care of me and my future."

"That, too," he said.

They entered the house. Laura made her way to the kitchen, aware of him close at her heels. She would have rather prepared the food without his observing her every move, but she knew he wouldn't leave her. An idea for keeping him focused on something other than what she was doing came to mind. "Excuse me a minute," she said.

In the library, she found a newspaper she'd picked up in town last week and carried it into the kitchen. She handed it to him.

He looked at her, raising his eyebrows as he took the paper. "Thank you."

Laura knew he was wondering why she was being so cooperative after her initial negative reaction to him showing up on her doorstep. Wondered why she was cooking and waiting on him. Heavens, if she wasn't careful, he'd expect her to retrieve his slippers for him! And, if she had to, she would, especially if it meant him leaving sooner rather than later.

Truthfully, she enjoyed cooking. Even the dusting didn't bother her. She enjoyed the respite from the back-breaking outdoor work, knowing soon she'd have to return to it. Her ranch hands needed her lead and direction. And she knew she would need to hire a new foreman.

Quickly, efficiently, she whipped up the biscuit batter, rolled and cut out perfectly round biscuits with a jar lid. She set them on the oven stone and slid them into the oven. Then she scrambled the eggs and grilled the ham slices in a pan. She left the food on the back burner, turned to Matt and said, "Do you mind if we eat here in the kitchen instead of the dining room? It'll be simpler."

"Fine with me."

She set the table while she waited for the biscuits to bake.

All the while, Matt sat seemingly engrossed in the paper.

Soon breakfast was ready. They sat across from each other, eating in silence. After his second helping, he looked up and gave her a long, steady look. "You're an excellent cook, Miss Laura."

Heat seeped into Laura's cheeks, not because of his words of appreciation but because of the admiration in his eyes. "Thank you," she murmured as she rose, picked up her plate and silverware and made her way to the sink.

Matt chuckled. She peered at him over her shoulder. "What's so funny?"

He sank back in his chair, his laughter subsiding. She turned hot then cold at his intent gaze sweeping over her body from head to toe, lingering longer on her pants.

"For some strange reason, I believed I could make a woman out of you by taking away your britches. But I realize now the falsehood of my reasoning."

"So, are you saying you'll be leaving me to decide my own future, including choosing my own clothes?"

He frowned. "To some extent, yes. But I also realize you wearing a gown rather than men's britches won't make a bit of difference in changing your state of womanhood. You are woman enough, even wearing britches, for any man, and quite beautiful. Have you an adequate wardrobe of gowns?"

She nodded. She'd worn her mother's gowns whenever she and her father dined together. They were years old. Still, she couldn't see the sense of purchasing new ones when her mother's dresses were serviceable. She knew she'd inherited her father's practical side concerning money, but she also possessed her own 'less is better' mentality regarding possessions. The one place she never scrimped, however, was the necessary equipment for running the ranch.

"Good." He smiled. "It wouldn't do at all for you to wear britches during your courtship, now would it?"

"Perhaps, though most of the men in Bozeman know me and don't seem to care how I dress. I don't think it'll make a bit of difference. Excuse me. I've household chores to do."

"Of course you do." He rose from his chair.

"May I ride the range tomorrow? You see, my hands require my assistance in the mending of fences in several places on my property—before Fall arrives."

"We shall see what tomorrow brings," he replied.

CHAPTER 4

*M*att reluctantly allowed Laura to return to ranch work the following day, on the condition she return home early to prepare their supper. He was puzzled by the fact that she pushed herself to perform men's work, yet she'd easily taken to cooking and cleaning. He recalled how she'd already set the table and had prepared breakfast by the time he came downstairs this morning. He'd expected her to be elated when he told her she could return to her work outdoors, but that she shouldn't tire herself out. That was why she had ranch hands, he'd added. It seemed to take her an inordinate amount of time to make her way out the door this morning.

He thought about the Woodbury family Bible he'd found in the library, and Laura's brother. He'd been told by Laura's solicitor she had been wearing britches since her brother's death, which spoke volumes. Matt believed she was trying to be the boy her father had lost—why, he had no idea. But he planned to find out. He just hadn't found a delicate way to broach the topic.

Matt envisioned how meaningless his life would be without Jonathan and felt sympathy for Laura. It seemed everyone she'd ever loved in life had died.

By mid-afternoon, he'd returned to the ranch, hot and sweaty, in dire need of a long cold drink and a soothing bath. His brown suit and slacks and patterned waistcoat were dusty from the plains where he'd worked, supervising his crew of men. For a fleeting moment, the practicality of dressing in dungarees and a cotton shirt came to mind, but not for long. It had been drilled into him since he was a kid that clothes made the man, even though he sub-consciously rebelled at the idea.

Just as the house came into view, he was greeted by the sight of Laura and a fair-haired man. They sat side by side on her front porch, enjoying tall glasses of lemonade. Matt's mouth fell open at the sight of her. She wore a white dress, full-skirted and sprigged with yellow flowers. But what truly caught his attention was her hair, which she'd left hanging down over her shoulders. All he wanted to do was bury his fingers in the silken tresses. She was a beautiful woman. It wouldn't be long before the entire town of eligible men wanted to court her. He wondered why they hadn't pursued her before now.

Matt left the horse he'd ridden that day with one of the grooms and strode toward the house, eyes narrowed on the man sitting far too close to Laura.

Laura looked away from the man, laughter in her eyes. She sobered when she saw Matt. They rose to their feet, their gaze on him as he climbed the stairs.

"Mr. Black," Laura said, "I'd like you to meet Mr. Andrew Cravens. Andrew? This is my…my guardian, Matt Black."

Matt gave Laura a wry look before turning to shake the man's proffered hand. Sizing him up, Matt determined the man to be years older than his ward and himself.

Releasing Cravens' hand, Matt gave Laura a pointed look. "So, how long have the two of you known each other?"

"Actually, we're the best of friends and have known each other for years, haven't we, Andrew?"

Andrew nodded.

"Old family friends, are you?" Matt inquired.

"Yes. Andrew owns the ranch adjoining ours."

"I see," was all Matt could think to say, disgusted with himself, and his rising jealousy toward a man he didn't know. All he knew was that he didn't like him sitting so close to Laura.

Matt leaned against the railing.

Laura said, "Would you care to join us in a glass of lemonade?"

"Yes, I would. Thank you." Matt folded his arms, staring at Cravens. When Cravens met his gaze straight on without flinching, Matt had to admit to admiring the man. Upon closer inspection, Matt decided

Cravens had an honest look about him, and that he could trust him with Laura.

"So, then," Matt said, breaking the silence, "how is the ranch business?"

Cravens smiled. "We grow the same crops and raise the same kind of steer as Laura does. I'm turning a profit, if that's what you're asking." At Matt's nod, he added, "My place isn't quite as profitable as Laura's, but then I didn't discover a sapphire mine on my property."

"I see." *So that's how Laura came by the name Princess Sapphire!* Matt made a note to himself to ask Laura about it.

By the time Laura returned, Cravens had left. She paused in the doorway and looked around with a frown. "You scared him off, didn't you?"

Matt took the glass of lemonade and sank into a chair. "No, he left of his own accord. He said to convey his apologies, but he had to leave for another engagement."

He took a deep, long swallow before setting the glass down on the railing. Then he reached inside his pocket and pulled out a neatly folded piece of paper. "Here's a list of eligible men I investigated shortly after I arrived."

She stared at him in disbelief. "You had them investigated?"

"Ah, yes, I see I approved your Mr. Cravens. Here is a list of tentatively approved candidates for a husband. You likely know some of them."

Laura set her own glass down, took the paper and unfolded it. She frowned at the first one, scowled at the next, laughed outright at the third. With a sigh, she met his gaze. "I'll agree to an outing with each of them, if that's what you want."

"It is," Matt said, narrowing his eyes on her. "I'm glad to see you can be agreeable."

"I believe my father always thought me quite amiable. I don't think you'll find that I'll give you too much trouble."

Matt cleared his throat. "You know, Miss Woodbury, you and I are closer in age than not. I'd like you to call me Matt."

She smiled. "I agree, and I'm Laura."

"It's amazing," Matt said good-naturedly. "We agree on something."

"Yes, amazing. Now tell me how you plan on 'weeding' out the gold-diggers from the men who are sincere."

"I have my ways. You'll see."

～

September 1886

*W*ith the arrival of autumn, the last hot days of summer had been left behind. And still Laura hadn't found a man worthy to be her husband. Matt's work for the railroad was nearly done and soon he'd be returning home to Minnesota. But he'd recently faced the truth of the matter. He didn't want to go home. This place, with Laura, was beginning to feel like home to him.

The four men on his potential list of suitors hadn't worked out. Would Paul Johnson, the man currently courting Laura—a wealthy widower with a ranch twice the size of the Woodbury Ranch—be the man for her?

As he'd done with each candidate, he started ticking off the good and the not-so-good traits. Ironically, both he and Laura had been in agreement as to the faults of each man. He knew the reason why. Matt was more than a little attracted to her and, venturing a guess, he had a feeling she was equally attracted to him. She was easy to be with—once she'd gotten over the shock of him being declared her guardian.

She was lovely, Matt thought, from where he sat on her front porch. Then he thought about his first love—his wife, Sarah. She'd been the only woman he'd ever loved, until six years ago when she'd left him and their sickly son behind, for a wealthy man. The boy was now a healthy, robust child of seven, and Matt missed him acutely.

After Sarah left him, he'd asked himself if he'd done something wrong to drive her away. He'd never arrived at an answer to his question, which perplexed him. He decided, in the end, that she'd fallen out of love with him and in love with another. He'd been devastated, for he'd loved her. He'd eventually concluded that what she really wanted was a wealthier life than he could ever give her. So he'd sworn off women, refusing to risk his heart again—until now.

There was much to admire about Laura. He appreciated her hard work ethic, her honesty with him and the workers on her ranch. She possessed an enchanting sense of humor and even laughed at her own blunders. On a daily basis, he found himself fighting his strong attraction and ever-growing feelings for her. Yet he knew that, sooner or later, he'd have to open his heart and take a chance on love again. He had no desire to live the rest of his life alone.

So what should he do? Coming to a decision, he nodded. He'd make an offer for her hand. While Laura hadn't been blatantly obvious, he knew she held equal admiration and respect for him. Whether it was his looks, his humor, his sense of duty and justice, he had no idea, but he guessed her feelings for him were based on all those things. But love? No, she probably didn't love him yet. Their attraction for each other would be enough for now. With time, he was convinced they'd fall in love, eventually.

He would assist Laura in managing the ranch and continue his work for the railroad but give up the lumber business, which was waning anyway. There was something about this untamed territory that drew him to it. He loved his home in Minnesota, but he had a feeling he'd experience much more of life staying in Montana. He'd send a wire tomorrow to his parents, instructing them to ready Jonathan for the journey to Montana. They'd been apart long enough.

A horse's pounding hooves caught his attention. He glanced sharply toward the road leading to the ranch. A lone horse galloped toward him. Seeing Laura was the rider, he rose from his chair and ambled down the steps to meet her. Eyeing the horse, he knew it wasn't hers.

"How was your supper with Mr. Johnson?" he asked.

"Fine," she said shortly, swinging down from the horse and meeting him at the foot of the steps.

Raising one eyebrow, he stared down at her. "Then why have you returned so early? It's just half past seven."

There was an unnatural flush to her cheeks. Reaching out, he took her hand and pulled her up the steps and into the house. From the grim look on her face, something was wrong.

In the foyer, he asked, "What happened?"

She swept her hair back from her forehead and tossed her reticule down on a small side table. "Paul Johnson is not the man for me, I'm afraid." She frowned. "Oh, the evening began well enough and, really, we have so much in common, I suppose, because we both own big ranches, but that's about all."

"Did he hurt you?" Matt said, keeping his voice calm when he wanted to shout. "Why didn't he escort you home?"

"This is his horse. He's drunk as a skunk and is currently head-first in a horse trough back in town. I can't marry a man who drinks like that, and in the afternoon of all things! It was only a luncheon we were having, and, he'd taken liberties, I am afraid."

"Damn him."

"Don't get yourself all dandered up. I took good care of him."

Matt could see now she was irritated but hadn't been harmed. He smiled. "Tell me what happened—over a libation would be helpful."

"I think I'd prefer lemonade, if you don't mind," she said wryly.

He escorted her into the library, then left, returning with a glass of lemonade for her and a sherry for himself. Sinking down beside her on the divan, he noticed the sad look on her face. His heart wrenched when she asked, "Why can't I find a decent man to love me, Matt? Am I so unlovable?"

"Of course you're not," he said gruffly, not quite sure how to respond. "Isn't it only because of me that you're looking for a husband anyway?"

Laura smiled. "It is, but not because of you precisely. I've lived my entire life trying to keep my father happy. And, now that I've allowed myself to be courted, I have to admit I enjoy it. I see now that I was spending too much time working and not having any fun." She scowled and added, "Though I wonder if things might have worked out between me and John if you hadn't scared him off."

Matt admitted, "All right, I may have been wrong in running him off as I did, but, according to your father's will, he expected you to marry a man of wealth and position. I don't believe a ranch foreman qualifies."

He thought about her lament about being unlovable. He wanted to tell her he wanted to be the one who'd love her forever—and maybe this time that would be true.

"Of course you were lonely after your father died. But I believe I have a solution," he said. "None of those men was right for you. I've a man in mind, though, one I believe who will be."

Laura's eyes widened. "Truly? Who?"

Matt gauged her expression and said staunchly, "Me."

CHAPTER 5

*T*hough surprised, she didn't laugh because his offer wasn't funny. His suggestion was so unexpected she wasn't quite certain how to respond. Finally, she thought she understood why he'd made it. "Matt, you mustn't sacrifice yourself for me. I'll find someone worthy, as you say, sooner or later."

He scowled and leaned forward, bracing his elbows on his knees. "Sacrifice? What are you talking about? My marrying you is the answer to this dilemma."

She shook her head and heaved a sigh. "No, it would be a sacrifice, because of the duty you feel toward me and to your uncle."

He rose rigidly from his chair and said, "You're rejecting my offer?"

Laura bit her lower lip and nodded. She set down her glass on the table beside her, refusing to meet his eyes.

"Why?"

Tears flooded her eyes. *Because it is duty and not love you feel for me!* "Because I refuse to be the sort of woman you want. Wearing gowns and pretending to be a gentle woman satisfied with household duties. That's not my life. I'm not that sort of woman. Because you deserve to be married to a woman who *does* love you. Because we both deserve to be in love with the people we marry."

Holding her gaze with his, he said, "You could be that woman."

She shook her head and drew away. "No, I gave up that life years ago."

He straightened. "Because that was what you wanted?"

"I had no choice. My father needed me working beside him."

"Why? He had a foreman."

She rose from the divan. Crossing to a window, she looked out into the night. "The foreman always has been second in command—I've been first."

"I see. And where was your father during all of this?"

She faced him. "Managing the books and such."

Moving to her side, he took her hands in his. "But why? He was a healthy man, wasn't he? A hard-working man, I've been told. What caused him to lock himself away in his library all those years ago, leaving you the burden of operating the ranch?"

Laura choked back her tears. "He wasn't well." She pulled at her hands until he released them. "Stop questioning me. It's none of your business."

"But I want you for my wife. That makes it my business, especially since you've turned down my proposal. I deserve to hear the truth. Trust me with your secrets," he murmured, drawing her close once more.

If a heart could break, she knew hers would. Her body began to shake. And when she melted in his arms, he tightened his grip on her. She realized Cupid's arrow had struck her fast and hard. There wasn't a thing she could do about it. Much as she hadn't expected, nor desired to fall in love with anyone—most of all him—she had.

After she'd sobbed against his chest for some time, she pulled away from him and swiped at his lapels with a shaky hand. "Oh! I've wet your coat," she said in distress.

"Doesn't matter. Look at me."

She forced herself to meet his gaze.

Searching her face, he stroked her hair back from her forehead. Comfort flooded her at his tenderness. Then he shocked her out of her shoes by saying, "Tell me about Jeremy."

∼

Oh God, who told him?
    Laura closed her eyes and pressed her forehead against the center of his chest. "Let's go out on the porch. I need some air."

"Of course," he said, escorting her outside. She sank down in one of the wicker chairs. He sat on the railing, leaning against a post as he patiently waited for her to answer him.

She sighed, glad he chose to distance himself a bit from her. The telling of the story would be easier to tell. For once she felt confident that here was a man who could lift her burdens from her shoulders. A man she could trust. One she could love.

As though he sensed she had no idea how or where to begin, he spoke. "I found your family Bible in the library with the notes about Jeremy's birth and death. I also saw the pictures."

She nodded. "Of course you did. He was my brother—my twin, actually—my soul mate and best friend. I miss him still, even though he's been gone for six years."

"Gone for as long as your father had locked himself away, you mean?"

Laura nodded. "I suppose people could look at it that way. But you couldn't blame my father. You see, I'm the one responsible for Jeremy's death."

Matt raised his brow. "How?"

Haltingly, she began, "It happened the summer we turned thirteen. It was a scorching day, I remember, in mid-July. Jeremy had been working with my father and the hands all day, moving from one chore to the next. It was Jeremy's first taste of what it would be like to be in complete command of a ranch. At the end of the day, Jeremy returned before my father did and sat with me on the porch, complaining of the heat. I could see he was sweaty and exhausted—I'd felt the same even though I hadn't been working out in the heat of the day. He suggested we take a dip in the river, even though Father had forbidden us. The river ran a fast current, and I wasn't the best of swimmers. Jeremy, though, was superb.

"I told him we shouldn't. It was dangerous, and father had forbidden it. He ignored my misgivings and convinced me we'd do little more than just sit on the river bank and dunk our feet. Once we arrived, though, Jeremy jumped right into that oasis. I waded in after him, staying in the shallows, while Jeremy swam out deeper. I called to him to come back. I don't know whether he heard me or not, but he kept on going while I crept closer to the bank, afraid for him." She paused, tears filling her eyes. "Suddenly his head went under the water and never came back up. I couldn't see him anywhere. He was just...gone. We...we found him a week later, washed up onto a bank a few miles away." She swiped at her tears. "We figured an undertow had taken him."

Matt pulled her up from the chair to hold her loosely in his arms. "It was an accident."

"One I could have prevented if I had insisted we stay home," she said.

"Your brother chose to go. Do you think he would have stayed home if you'd tried keeping him there?"

Laura shook her head. "No. Still, I let my father down. For years he counted on me to watch over Jeremy." Dryly, she added, "I was always the sensible one—actually more of a mother to Jeremy than a sister—even though we were the same age."

"Still, I can't see how your father could blame you for the accident."

"He never actually said anything accusatory to me, but I saw that look in his eyes. Why wasn't it me and not his son? So, I remade my life, choosing to work alongside my father, until he lost interest in the ranch and shut himself away from everyone. Then I was forced to take charge of it, which wasn't a hardship. I love my home, Matt."

"You were trying to replace your brother."

She nodded, biting her lip. She'd spent years trying to be a good daughter—forsaking her own femininity to be the son taken from her father.

"None of this changes how I feel about you," Matt murmured.

Laura felt the squeeze of his hands at her waist and she managed a smile. "I guessed as much. You are a very persistent man, Mr. Black."

He grinned. "True, but it's always been a help rather than a hindrance."

Her smile disappeared. "Do you love me?"

Laura's heart plummeted at the annoyance and uncertainty that suddenly appeared on his face. He didn't love her, which would make things impossible between them. She'd never marry a man who was unsure of his feelings for her. He either loved her or he didn't.

He released her and turned away. She suppressed the urge to run inside. She knew he wasn't a gold-digger. Shortly after Matt's arrival, she'd spoken with her solicitor about Matt and learned he was a well-to-do man himself.

Matt paced from one end of the porch to the other, seemingly deep in thought. Laura bade her time, waiting for him to reply.

He halted then, hands clasped behind his back, and finally looked directly at her. "I believe I do love you."

"Oh, Matt!" Laura gasped, tears once again filling her eyes.

"Yet I must tell you I've had little success in love."

She frowned. "I don't understand."

"You see—" Matt began, pausing to look off toward the road.

Laura heard it then, the sound of wheels and horse hooves pounding the ground. A carriage appeared, made the bend in the road and headed toward the ranch. Beneath the horseshoe gateway, it came closer. The small cherub face of a child capped by curly blonde hair appeared at the window. A boy shouted, "Papa! Papa!"

Matt bounded off the porch and tore down the drive, meeting the coach. It stopped, and the door opened. Matt swept the child out of the carriage and into his arms. Laura saw the child was male, dressed in a fine blue suit and white shirt that was in dire need of a washing. He also wore a straw hat over his curls, banded in matching blue grosgrain.

Laura was stunned. Matt had a child? Why hadn't he told her before now?

Laura felt frozen in her position on the porch. She wrapped her arms around a post as she watched man and child embracing. A small smile slid across her lips when the boy pounded his father on the back in delight. Matt set the boy down, took his hand and walked toward the house. The boy was tall and older than she'd originally thought, appearing to be of early school age. He climbed the stairs on long, coltish legs with Matt directly behind him. They stopped before her.

"Laura, this is my son," he said with a gentle smile. "Jonathan, this is Miss Laura Woodbury."

"How do you do, ma'am?" Jonathan said. Stepping forward, he held out his hand.

Reaching down, she hesitantly took his hand in hers. "It's nice meeting you, too," she murmured.

They released hands simultaneously. Laura couldn't take her eyes from Jonathan, who was utterly handsome and charming, like his father. But where Matt's hair and coloring was dark, Jonathan was pale and blonde. Must take after his mother, she assumed. Speaking of the boy's mother, she sent a pleading look at Matt.

"I'm not married, if that's what you're thinking," he explained.

"Oh, I'm sorry," she whispered as she sat down. "I didn't know you were a widower."

"I'm not," he said, his gaze moving to his son, then back to her.

Curiosity settled deep inside her. She wanted to hear his story but knew now was not the time, with the boy in hearing distance.

Matt took the chair beside Laura while Jonathan sat on the wood floor.

Laura smiled when one of the new kittens sat down beside him. The boy laughed. Laura's smile widened when the kitten settled down on his lap.

"Jonathan will be seven on Christmas Day. The day he was born was, needless to say, the happiest Christmas for me," Matt said. "He's an easy child to love."

Yes, children—Jeremy. Oh, how she'd missed her brother after he died—still did. The pain had been deep, filling her with remorse at her loss.

The sound of horse's hooves pulled her from her reveries.

Amery Hawkins, one of her hands, stopped at the porch, tipped his hat to her and said, "The south pasture fence is fixed, Miss Laura."

"Good," she replied.

Jonathan stood up, still holding the cat, all his attention on Amery's horse. He glanced at his father. "May I ride a horse, Papa?"

"Another day, son."

Jonathan put down the kitten and walked down the steps toward the horse. Amery dismounted and said, "Okay if I take the boy with me while I rub down Swifty here?"

"Only if Jonathan promises to obey everything you tell him," Matt said.

"Oh yes, Papa! I will, I will!"

As Laura watched the excited boy walk off with Amery and the horse, it occurred to her that Jonathan had to have come here because Matt had sent for him. His arrival so soon after Matt had proposed now began to seem suspicious to her. She waited until Jonathan had moved away before blurting, "So, in all truth, you aren't really looking for a wife, Matt. You're really looking for a mother for your son."

Matt riveted a cold look on her, one she hoped she'd never see again. When he spoke, it was clear she'd made a mistake. "If that were the case, I'd have married years ago. It's you I want. If you look deep inside yourself, you'll see you want me, too. But I've asked, and I won't beg. Think about it. Think about us."

Matt turned from her, took the stairs in two steps and hurried after his son.

～

*T*ension permeated the parlor where Laura and Matt sat on opposite ends—he in one chair—she in her rocker. After she'd prepared a meal for them all, Matt had managed to lull an excited yet exhausted Jonathan to sleep within minutes. Now Matt sat reading the newspaper. She rocked in her chair and darned a pair of stockings she'd pulled from a bushel basket, burning to talk with him. He'd talked only to his son at supper, and since then he'd been silent, seemingly engrossed in his paper.

Laura was sorry she'd blurted out what she had, but it was hard to believe that hadn't crossed Matt's mind. She hadn't meant to upset him, but it did have to be discussed. Because, the truth was, she suspected she was falling in love with him. *Was* in love with him. It'd happened slowly, over the past three months, each time she compared him to one of her suitors. Simply put, there was no comparison.

"I heard some of your hands talking today," Matt said. He folded the newspaper and set it on the table at his elbow. "Why do they call you Princess Sapphire?"

Finally! No more silence. Laura dropped her darning in her lap. "My father discovered gold on our property shortly after he purchased it thirty years ago. Ten years later, in the same mine, he found sapphires—quite a treasure he learned, after sending samples to Tiffany's in New York City. My father hired a crew to work the mine. Men still travel here from afar to see if more of the gems can be found, though it's been dry for five years. It's one of the more difficult jobs our ranch hands perform—keeping the sapphire-seekers off our property. Everyone in these parts knows my father made a fortune from the sapphire discovery. Suddenly, our hands started calling me Princess Sapphire, in jest, but the name stuck. I know it's silly."

"I'd say it's accurate, Laura. You are a precious jewel, whether you realize it or not." He turned away and stared into the fire crackling in the hearth.

"Matt?"

He met her eyes again. She noted his hesitant expression, as though he knew what her next words would be. "What happened between you and your wife?"

"I divorced her when she left me for another man," he said.

Divorced? This was something Laura knew little about. People just didn't get divorces out here. Married folk stayed married until one of them died.

"Jonathan was born early, weighed less than four pounds. We didn't think he was going to make it, but he did." He grinned. "He's a fighter, same as me. Sarah was several years younger than I, much too young to be married to me, or anyone else for that matter.

Our parents were friends and the match was more or less arranged by them. I came to believe that Sarah was actually in love even then, when we married, with the man she later left me for. I didn't understand any of this at the time and, when I began to, it was too late. By then she'd grown tired of being married to a man she didn't love. Adding the burden of being a mother to a sick infant was too much for her. She left with this man, who just happened to be able to give her far more than I could. Anyway, I wasn't the man she wanted to be with."

"I'm sorry," Laura said sincerely as she picked up her darning once more.

"So am I. But it happened years ago. I forgave her, Laura. After all, our courtship and marriage was pre-arranged. And she did bless me with a son."

"Jonathan is wonderful," she said, smiling at the proud look on Matt's face.

He turned to her, sweeping his gaze over her face, and smiled in return. "You'd make Jonathan a wonderful mother, Laura."

Laura's body went icy at the thought. Inside, she heard herself scream, No! Never again would she allow herself to give into her maternal instincts. Everyone she'd ever cared for—Jeremy, her father, and even the mother she'd never known—were gone. She knew if she ever loved a child again and had the responsibility of caring for him, she wouldn't be able to bear the heartache if she lost him.

"Did you hear what I said?" Matt asked.

Laura dropped her darning in her basket and came swiftly to her feet. Snatching up her skirts, she headed toward the doorway, saying, "I can't talk about this, Matt. Not now." *Perhaps not ever.*

Matt scowled as he tossed down his paper and rose to his feet. "Have you even considered my proposal?"

She paused at the door, hand on the knob. "I have. I can't marry you, for one simple reason."

"Why?" he asked.

She heard the hurt and confusion in his voice and nearly blurted out the truth. Instead, she gathered herself to tell a lie. "I don't love you. I refuse to marry any man without love." She gave a raw laugh. "It would be a mistake."

"You don't know that," he said, striding toward her.

Laura held up her hand, palm up. "Stop, Matt, now, before I say something I'll regret—before I say something that will cause you to hate me forever."

He stopped directly in front of her. "I don't understand you. I don't think you understand yourself. But perhaps you're right that we shouldn't marry." He shrugged carelessly. "Perhaps you require more time to mature before taking that step. But I know you love me, Laura. From deep inside my soul, I know it. In two weeks, my work here will be done, and Jonathan and I will be leaving."

Frowning, she said, "Why did you have him travel all this way if your work was near completion?"

"Because, fool that I am, I assumed you'd accept my proposal. I know how much your ranch means to you and I guessed you wouldn't leave with me. There's a position with the railroad currently open right here in Bozeman. I was ready and willing to assist you in the running of the ranch as well." He sighed. "Everything would have been perfect. And now I'll be leaving, filled with guilt." His words held a bitter tinge.

"Why? What would you feel guilty about?"

"I'm leaving you without a husband. I've always fulfilled my duties in life, but I've failed this time. Paul can be no more disappointed in me than I am in myself."

"If it would help, I'll write to Mr. Hill and explain things to him." She blinked back tears, all the while wanting to cry out that she loved him, that she'd marry him and give him more children, but she couldn't. Her father had died, Jeremy, her mother. Everyone she'd ever loved had left her. She couldn't take another chance on loving again. And the responsibility of mothering another child left her feeling cold with fear.

"I appreciate all that you've tried to do for me, Matt. Never doubt that you performed your duty well."

∾

Two weeks later

*A*t the train station in Bozeman, Jonathan sat beside Matt. He scuffed his feet forward, then dragged the toes of his boots back across the floor.

"Stop it now, Jonathan," Matt said, for the tenth time in as many minutes. "It won't make the train arrive any quicker."

"I wanna go back to Miss Laura's house, Papa. I miss her kitty."

Matt slid his arm around his son's shoulders. "I promise that, as soon as we arrive home, I'll find you a kitten. Or perhaps a dog would be better?"

"No, don't want no stupid dog and no other kitty." Tears flooded Jonathan's eyes, and he sobbed, "I want Miss Laura's kitty!"

Matt pulled the boy against his chest, feeling like crying himself. Not over a kitten, but over a woman. A fine woman who drove him mad with desire, mad with anger. Never had he met such a stubborn wench as Princess Sapphire. And poor Jonathan had been whining off and on during their time together at Laura's ranch during the past couple weeks. Matt knew the reason. Jonathan had missed him during his three-month absence and wanted all his attention. Matt vowed never to leave him behind again.

Matt watched a procession of ants crawl across the cement floor, until a pair of black boots appeared in his line of vision. He looked up and into the dry expression on Andrew Craven's face.

"Cravens," Matt said by way of greeting. He glanced at Jonathan, who was settled against his shoulder, relieved to see he'd fallen asleep. He released him and eased him gently down on the bench seat, positioning his jacket beneath his son's head.

"So, you're just leaving her to fend for herself, are you?" Andrew said, his voice laced with sarcasm. "Didn't figure you for a quitter, Black."

Matt rose to his feet, coming toe to toe with the smaller man. "What did you call me?"

"You heard me the first time—quitter."

Matt couldn't get into a fight, not with Jonathan here. Calmly, Matt said, "Look, I'm leaving for home with my son. The territory's clear for you to pounce once more upon Miss Laura. It turns out she's pretty smart about people. Whether or not she gives you a second look is entirely up to her."

Andrew shrugged. "So, you didn't believe her when she said we were nothing but good friends."

"No, I didn't. You seemed too cozy at the time on that porch."

With a sigh, Andrew said, "I suppose she didn't happen to mention I'm engaged to her second cousin, Nadine, either, did she?"

Swiping an errant lock of hair off his forehead, Matt glowered at him. "You aren't lying about this, are you? Because if you are…"

"Nope, it's the truth. Now I hear the town talk—folks are saying you and her would be a good match. What do you think?"

"That might have been true once, but not anymore. She turned down my proposal."

"Go back to her. If you can't shake an honest answer out of her as to why, then talk to her maid, Mary O'Garrity. She knows everything."

"What's to tell? I told you I asked her to marry me and she declined."

"I know you've no reason to trust me but missing this train will be the best thing you could do. Go back and talk to her."

"Why do you care?" Matt said.

Andrew shrugged. "Guess I've got a protective streak in me with regards to Miss Laura. Sure wouldn't want her getting taken advantage by some gold-digger. You know?"

"Yeah," Matt said, a slow grin crossing his lips. "I do."

CHAPTER 6

*M*att returned with Jonathan to Laura's ranch. Now he sat in the parlor taking tea with Mary O'Garrity. Jonathan, of course, was in heaven as he sat on the floor with Laura's kitten once more. Damn, if Andrew Cravens was fooling with him, he'd personally go back and shoot the man. Even worse would be the hell he'd pay pulling Jonathan away from the ranch again.

"It's glad I am to see ye have returned, Master Black."

"Mister Black or even Matt is fine, Mrs. O'Garrity."

"In Ireland it would be Master, mind ye, but Matt it is."

Matt chuckled, catching the twinkle in the older woman's eyes.

"So, it seems ye haven't given up on Miss Laura after all. Good!"

"I had," Matt said candidly, "until I ran into Andrew Cravens at the train station. He encouraged me to come back and talk with you before making a final decision to leave or not. Said you'd know everything."

She sighed. "Yes, I do," she said softly. "Did ye ask Miss Laura to marry ye?"

"I did."

"And she turned ye down, didn't she?"

"Yes. Is she out with the hands now?"

"She is. The funny thing was, I had to drag her out of bed this morning. Since ye came and introduced her to lady-like things—something I've tried doing fer years—she seems to have lost interest in running the ranch. She works too hard, ye know."

"I do know, yes, and I don't like it one bit," he growled. "Explain why you believe she turned down my marriage proposal. She told me she didn't love me."

Mary shrugged. "Now that, I'm telling ye, is a bald-faced lie. Miss Laura's in love with ye, for sure. Never have I seen her look at a man the way she looks at ye."

Matt felt heat seep into his cheeks at her words and had no idea how to reply.

"She's turned down every man who's ever proposed to her. I always attributed it to the fact that she's too fickle, but I've learned the truth of the matter directly from her, mind ye."

Leaning forward, his elbows on his knees, he stared at Mary. "What truth?"

"She blames herself fer Jeremy's death."

Frowning, Matt said, "I knew that. She told me about it."

"Jeremy was young when he died. Did ye notice Miss Laura was, perhaps, a bit more amenable to accepting yer proposal before Jonathan arrived? Before she knew ye had a child?"

Matt thought about how their conversation had progressed just after he'd proposed to Laura. While she hadn't come out and accepted his proposal, he'd felt she would have—if Jonathan hadn't arrived when he had.

All of sudden, everything was clear in his mind. He met Mrs. O'Garrity's gaze. "Her reasons have to do with Jonathan then. He's young—a child—even younger than Jeremy had been when he died." Rising from his chair, he took a step, then stopped. "I need to find Laura. Have you any idea where she's working?"

"Of course, the furthest pasture to the south of the river. Ye understand then. I'm glad. How will ye convince her?"

"I've no idea." He laughed. "Beg her probably. I just won't leave the ranch. She'll have to find someone big enough to boot me off the property."

"Now ye're talking, Master!" Mrs. O'Garrity said gleefully. "I'll keep an eye on Jonathan here."

"Thank you."

~

*L*aura slouched in the saddle upon her finest quarter horse, Charlie. A cool autumn breeze ruffled her hair, which she'd let down moments ago from its pins. She'd been pounding posts into dry ground for several hours. Now searing pain shot through her right arm and shoulder. It might be this particular injury would leave her unable to work alongside the men for a few days. Fine, she needed a rest, mostly to heal her injured heart more than her shoulder.

She sniffled and called out, "I'm leaving for the day, Pete!"

"You go right on home, Miss Laura. We'll be here just a few more hours."

"Thank you." she replied. Turning her horse around, she headed for home, comfortable that Pete was in charge.

For years, Peter Jorgenson had worked as third-in-command for her father and now easily assumed foreman responsibilities. To her, it seemed natural for him to assume the position. She hadn't thought of mentioning this to Matt earlier. There seemed to be so many things she hadn't thought of where Matt was concerned.

She ambled along the river bank, Charlie picking his way carefully along the uneven ground. Soon it would be time to cross the river, which she dreaded. Each time she had to cross, she thought about Jeremy, even though the river had little current in the area where she forded it.

Finally, she reached the small, narrow path leading down to the river bank. As she guided Charlie down it, he pranced and tossed his head. She heard another horse's hooves and looked across to the other side where a horse and rider came into view.

Matt!

Her heart ached and raced simultaneously at the welcome sight of his handsome face, with that brilliant, even-toothed smile she'd never forget. She called out, "What are you doing here?"

He didn't respond, likely because he hadn't heard her with the distance between them.

She stayed riveted in place, watching him as he approached, taking in his broad shoulders, and deep chest covered by his dark suit.

"Are you coming over here?" he called. "If you aren't, then I'm crossing to you."

Gathering her wits, she said, "Yes, I'm coming! Tell me why you've returned."

He paused, slouched in the saddle, one hand resting on the pommel. "To marry you, Princess Sapphire. You don't have to worry though. I'm no gold-digger."

Hadn't the man listened to her? Hadn't he paid attention when she told him in no uncertain terms she didn't love him? Apparently, he hadn't believed her. Oh, how she wanted to marry him. But, like the river between them now, her fears must keep them separated. How could she possibly be responsible for a child when... Her gaze dipped to the water in front of her, anxiety sliding along her nerves.

She stared down into the rippling river, remembering that fateful day six years ago. Remembering how, after Jeremy had disappeared beneath the water, she'd slumped down on the bank, rocking herself, screaming and sobbing her heart out.

Could she be responsible for a child now that she'd grown up? Did she want that responsibility? If she didn't say yes, she'd deny living life and being happy because of her fear of something that had happened when she was a child herself. If she didn't grasp for that happiness now, she knew it would never come her way again. There would never be another Matt.

"Did you hear me, Laura? You know I don't want your money."

"Yes, I know," she called back. "I'm coming over now."

Matt nodded, watching her as she made her way south a bit more, where she knew it was shallow with little current. Laura clicked her tongue, encouraging Charlie to step into the water. Glancing up, she saw movement behind Matt, realizing it was another rider on a horse. As they drew nearer, she gasped at the sight of Jonathan on her old dappled gray pony, Wylie.

"Papa! Papa!" Jonathan called out gleefully. Wylie was at a full out gallop, headed toward his father. "Look at me! I'm riding."

Matt's head whipped around, and he shouted, "Stop, Jonathan! Don't come any nearer. The bank is slippery."

The boy paid no attention, and the pony pounded to the left past Matt, skidding down the river bank, before Matt could grab the animal. The horse's neighing filled the air, along with Jonathan's shriek.

Laura felt as though she'd been hurtled eight years back in time as she watched Wylie slide down the bank sideways, dumping Jonathan, who rolled into the river where he began frantically splashing about, the current carrying him to the middle.

"Don't thrash, son!" Matt, off his mount, called out as he sloshed through the water. "Swim! You know how."

All Laura could think was that she couldn't allow either of them to die. The river water was cold this time of year. They had to get Jonathan out of there—fast. The pony had scrambled to his feet, seeming to stare at the floundering boy. Then she noticed the reins floating in the water. Jonathan must still be holding onto them.

"Wait, Matt! Jonathan's got hold of the reins yet. And Wylie, thank God, hasn't budged. Go on over to Wylie and—"

Matt shouted, "Jonathan! Do not let go of the pony's reins. Understand?"

Laura thought she heard the boy agree, but she wasn't sure. She moved along the bank and guided Charlie into the river, halting him as she neared Jonathan, knowing the river was too deep for the horse to make it any closer, she paused. "You'll be fine, Jonathan," she called to him. "Your father will get you out but keep hold of the reins."

She saw the boy was crying, and her heart lurched. Did he still have hold of the pony's reins? Luckily, Jonathan had fetched up on a sand bar.

She watched Matt guide Wylie up the river bank, while he pulled on the reins with his free hand. She sighed in relief when she saw Jonathan come off the sand bar, drawn by his father. The boy held on. Hand over hand, Matt pulled his son in.

What was she doing here when she could be helping? Laura guided Charlie from the water and cantered to her usual shallow crossing place. Once on the other side, near Matt, who was still hauling the boy in by the reins, she slid down the bank, waded in and grabbed Jonathan. The cold water had rendered him unable to stand, so she tugged him from the river. Matt swept him up into his arms.

Matt held him close, saying, "Now do you understand the rule about never riding by yourself? Whatever possessed you to follow me? And does Mrs. O'Garrity know you left the house?"

Jonathan shook his head. "She fell asleep, and I snuck out. I'm sorry. I won't ever do it again, Papa."

"Let's get you home," Matt said.

～

*D*ark shrouded the ranch house by the time they'd managed to relieve Jonathan's chills by placing him in a warm bath. He grew more animated and talked about his adventurous day in an excited voice. "I wasn't scared," he boasted. "Papa was there and so were you, Miss Woodbury, so I couldn't drown."

Once Jonathan was in bed asleep and the two of them heading for the parlor, Laura started feeling ill at the thought of Matt and Jonathan leaving on the noon train tomorrow. She was sure of her love for Matt, yet uncertain about taking on the responsibility of being a mother to Jonathan. Though she should have shared her doubtful feelings with Matt when he'd first proposed to her, it still wasn't too late. She'd been given a second chance to talk things through with him. This time she wouldn't run like a coward.

She sat on the divan and he joined her, one arm stretched out along the back, his fingers toying with a curl that had come loose from her chignon.

Laura felt his warm gaze on her. She turned to him and lifted her lips to his. Accepting the invitation, Matt kissed her thoroughly, gathering her into his arms. She breathed a relieved sigh, feeling loved and protected, as warmth coursed through her. If only the kiss could last forever! Raising one arm, she wound it around his neck, pressing her breasts against him. His hand wandered up her arm, brushed against the side of one breast until his hand cupped it. He rubbed her nipple with his thumb until she gasped her pleasure.

All too soon he let her go, springing to his feet to pace the floor. His fingers tunneled through his thick hair. Feeling deserted, not knowing why he'd left her so abruptly, she bit her lower lip, watching him, wondering what was wrong.

Finally, he stopped in front of her and said, "I won't take no for an answer—not this time."

She sighed in relief.

He sank down beside her once more. "Why did you turn me down?"

"I owe you an explanation. Perhaps it won't make a bit of sense to you, but it does to me. Remember when I told you I was responsible for my brother's death?"

"Yes, but it's not true."

"For years, I believed it was true. Even now…" She stopped. Maybe she'd feel that way forever, but guilt wouldn't bring back Jeremy. Now was for living. She slipped her hand into his and wound their fingers together. "I love you very much, Matt. When you asked me to marry you, I was so excited. I couldn't believe such happiness could be mine."

"Or mine," he murmured.

"Yet I doubted myself, doubted I could count on myself to be careful, conscientious and responsible for your son. I didn't want the responsibility on my shoulders for fear of losing him."

"The same way you lost your brother."

Laura nodded even as tears slid from her eyes and down her cheeks. After swiping at them, she met his gentle gaze. "Today, when Jonathan landed in the river, I felt like I was living that terrible moment in time all over again. I asked God above how could He be so cruel."

Pressing her to his chest, he murmured in her hair, "That's just it— you *did* come to help, and everything turned out all right. You are everything wise, wonderful and worthy, Laura Woodbury. Don't ever doubt your capabilities. There was no way you could have saved your brother, but you did help me save my son. Look how you've operated this ranch for the past several years. Look how profitable it's become. Look how your ranch hands respect you and your authority. Don't ever doubt yourself again. I won't allow it. And I'm convinced you'll be the best mother to my son, and to any children we will have. Believe in what I say, Princess. Believe in *yourself*."

"I'll try."

"Marry me, my sweet, precious jewel. Now is our time to be together."

She worried her lip a moment before asking, "What if I said I needed more time?"

He smiled. "I'd say that's a better reply than 'no.'" His smile slipped. "*Do* you require more time?"

Laura pressed her palms against his chest. "I was just teasing. I believe we've wasted too much time as it is. Yes, I'll spend the rest of my life with you, Matt Black, loving you, worrying about you and our children."

"Obeying me?" he asked, lifting one eyebrow.

"Perhaps," she said coyly.

"Ah, just what I expected. Stubborn to the end, but I wouldn't have you any other way, Princess Sapphire." His lips took hers. Laura's world narrowed, her heart, love and feelings all for this man.

They sat together on the divan, his arms around her as they enjoyed the silence, and the closeness between them. Laura would always feel responsible for Jeremy's death, but somehow, she now believed, Jeremy was watching them. She imagined seeing his brilliant smile, saluting her, telling her to get on with her life. To be happy.

Matt kissed her again, and she knew his love for her would sustain her for a lifetime. Nothing else mattered.

THE END

~

Don't miss out on your next favorite book!
Join the Satin Romance mailing list www.satinromance.com/mail.html

~

THANK YOU FOR READING

~

Did you enjoy this book?

We invite you to leave a review at your favorite book site, such as Goodreads, Amazon, Barnes & Noble, etc.

DID YOU KNOW THAT LEAVING A REVIEW...

- Helps other readers find books they may enjoy.
- Gives you a chance to let your voice be heard.
- Gives authors recognition for their hard work.
- Doesn't have to be long. A sentence or two about why you liked the book will do.

ABOUT THE AUTHOR

Nancy Schumacher is the owner-publisher of Melange Books, LLC, writing under the pseudonyms, Nancy Pirri and Natasha Perry. Nancy started writing nineteen years ago while raising four children. She is a member of Romance Writers of America. She is also one of the founders of the Minnesota RWA chapter, Northern Lights Writers (NLW).

She has written five full-length novels, and many stories included in anthologies with Melange Books, LLC.

www.nancypirri.com

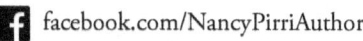 facebook.com/NancyPirriAuthor

ALSO BY NANCY PIRRI

Montana Women
Katie and the Marshal
Annie and the Outlaw
Janie and the Judge
Laura and the Railroad Baron

Contemporary Romance
Bait Shop Blue
All I Ever Wanted
I Wish You Love, a Spicy Romance Anthology
Make Me Behave (An Anthology) with Tara Fox Hall

Historical Romance
The MacAulay Bride
The Duke and the Lady Sleuth

Featured in the following anthologies:
Western Ways
Food and Romance Go Together, Vol. 2

Writing erotica as Natasha Perry
Ruined Hearts
Maid of His Heart

www.ingramcontent.com/pod-product-compliance
Lightning Source LLC
Chambersburg PA
CBHW050726180626
46814CB00002B/626